About the Author

Randy T. Lane writes mystery and thriller books, which, considering that you're reading this book, makes perfect sense. The novel you're about to purchase or have read, depending on where this bio is placed (I can tell you're of high intellect by picking this up, so I know you well), *Blind Perception*, follows my last novel, *Gabrielle*. Those who like suspense and narcissistic characters with all the charm of a boning knife should find this entertaining until the end.

I'm originally from Oxford, Pa. I now reside in Bear, Delaware. Feel free to contact me. I enjoy all positive feedback!

Blind Perception

Randy T Lane

Blind Perception

Olympia Publishers
London

www.olympiapublishers.com
OLYMPIA PAPERBACK EDITION

A CIP catalogue record for this title is available from the British Library.

ISBN: 978-1-78830-626-3

First Published in 2020

Olympia Publishers
Tallis House
2 Tallis Street
London
EC4Y 0AB

Printed in Great Britain

Dedication

To my parents,

No parents are perfect. Mine were not, but they did their best with a brood of eight; no easy task.

My father, Robert Lee Lane, was a member of the greatest generation serving his country in the U.S. Army during WWII.

My mother, Helen J. Lane, picked up the pieces after losing my father to a heart attack at a young age.

They left behind a lot of great memories.

Randy T. Lane

T.B.L. in thoughts.

Chapter One

The town of Wilton, Connecticut, a bastion of wealth with a population of just over 16,000, was small enough to know one's neighbors but big enough that not everyone knew their neighbors' business.

The town, with its brick paved sidewalks and street lanterns on every corner, was listed every year as one of the top five per capita incomes in the US. The local private high school, the Berkshire School, with its yearly tuition of $43,000, had a higher cost than the average four-year college. There was a public high school, Penn Manor, fifteen miles to the south, but that school bus never picked up students in Wilton.

The residential community of Pelican Crest Hills lay at the end of town with its sixteen properties. The two-plus-acre lots were always meticulously maintained, not by the owners of course, but the professional landscapers who worked year-round maintaining the grounds. The tree lined driveways, three-car garages, and in-ground pools were the norm, the latest Mercedes Benz or BMW auto would be seen parked out front of the Estates. Among the owners was Robert Weinstein, better known as Dr. Bob, who resided at 4 Cherry Blossom

Lane along with his wife Marie and son Matt. Dr. Bob, age forty-eight, stood five foot seven and weighed one hundred forty-five pounds. He was trim and athletic with dark hair and hazel eyes was very well thought of throughout Wilton.

A graduate of Harvard Medical, he had lived here since starting his own practice over a decade ago.

Dr. Bob, on this glorious fall afternoon, was hosting some friends, along with his beautiful wife Marie. While Dr. Bob manned the grill, his cohorts Larry and Cal tossed the football around.

Lawrence Sinclair — always Larry to his friends — was a professor of Economics at Western State University. He was medium height, middle-aged, and a little overweight. His wife Susan, with short brown hair, was a devoted jogger and business consultant.

Research chemist Roger Palmer stood over six feet tall with a receding hairline. His stunning wife Lauren was a petite blonde with bright blue eyes, ten years younger than Roger, and an avid cyclist and tennis player. Roger had been told on more than one occasion when he married Lauren that he had outkicked the coverage — a football term used by men when they married someone more attractive than them. Lauren enjoyed material things, but working for them

was never going to be her strong point, as Roger Palmer made a very good living.

Also in attendance were Cal Estrada, forty-eight, a dark-haired, muscular cyclist and outdoors type who was the broker-owner of Briarcliff Realty and Investments, and his wife Diane with long auburn hair, green eyes, and a slender build on her five foot eleven frame. They made a very attractive couple.

The men had more than just a neighborly friendship; they had all become acquainted while in college at Harvard as members of the intermural rowing team and took to calling themselves the Four Oarsmen.

But Dr. Bob's wife Maria would often say, if the truth be told, it probably was more like the four Whorsemen.

The sun was still out, but starting to set, as Bob and the men gathered around the grill with their beers in hand as Bob carefully turned the steaks. The wives sat on the large stone patio and sipped margaritas while discussing who was the best manicurist in town and their men. Marie Weinstein looked at those four.

"It's like they never left college and are still at the frat house."

Indeed, the men were loud and telling raunchy jokes and breaking Dr. Bob's balls over his cooking prowess.

"Damn, Bob, I said I wanted my steak medium-well, not blackened."

"F. U., Roger, like I would take advice from a guy who jumps out of a perfectly running airplane."

"Until you try it, Bob, you have no idea of what you're missing. Parachuting is like sex; the buildup is so intense."

"Cal, would you do that?"

"No way. If I need intense sex, I'll watch porn like every other guy." Everyone laughed.

"Well then, that leaves my good friend, Larry," they all busted up at that one. "Hell, Larry's idea of excitement is watching baboons breed on the Discovery Channel as he downs a bag of chips from his Barcalounger!"

"On a more serious subject, Bob, where is young Matt headed to college next fall?"

"Larry, my friend, why would you even ask that question? Harvard, of course."

All the guys started yelling and giving high fives to Bob.

"Why in the hell didn't you tell us, man? This is big news. The legacy carries on."

"I didn't say anything because, technically, it's not official yet, but I have some very reliable sources that tell me there's nothing to worry about."

"Damn, Bob, you and Marie must be so proud."

"Thanks, Cal, we are. And once we get the official big fat envelope, we'll announce it to everyone."

Cal yelled over to Marie, "I know it's not official yet, but a huge congrats to you and Bob on young Matt carrying on the tradition. I cannot wait for that first fall football game. Damn, this is exciting."

"Thank you, Cal. We're optimistic, but for now, please just keep it amongst us friends."

"Oh, absolutely. That announcement belongs to young Matt to make." The men kept pounding beers and patting Bob on the back. Marie just leaned back in her lounge chair and took a long sip of her margarita.

Susan looked over at her friend Marie. "That is awesome and you never said a word."

"Listen, don't get me wrong, but Matt hasn't received his acceptance letter just yet and I hope and pray he gets in and he better because Bob wouldn't let him apply anywhere else. Who does that? No backup schools? 'Marie,' he says, 'trust me, it's a done deal. Matt will be in Cambridge next fall.' Listen, I want Matt to go there. I'm just trying to be realistic. Let me throw a couple of requirements at you and this is just the basics. A GPA at least 3.95 or higher, the top one percent in class rank, the number of male applicants alone is almost 20,000 and a little over one thousand will be accepted. I didn't even know this; they have a sub-committee that recommends each application to the full committee, who then decide, and they vote — the majority rules, but a degree of support is allowed for certain individuals.

"And then if Matt decides he wants to go onto Harvard Law, the acceptance rate is like six percent out of about six thousand who apply."

"Wow!" Lauren rolled her eyes. "I had no idea it was that hard or that Roger was that smart!" They all busted up laughing. "I mean, look at the guy. I love him to death, but he has geek dot com written all over him," they all laughed again.

Susan piped in, "Crap, look at Larry, professor of economics. It's a good thing because, trust me, he sucks at biology!"

"Hot damn, this discussion is warming up now," cried Diane.

Marie looked at Diane. "Yeah, like you have any complaints. Cal is still in great shape."

Lauren gave her a wicked smile and licked her lips. "Totally."

Diane smiled. "Yeah, for a forty-something, he still has a lot left in the tank."

"Hey, Diane," whispered Lauren. "Mind if I take it out for a test drive sometime?"

"You are so bad," Diane replied.

"Hey, sounds like it's getting pretty rowdy over there."

"Hey, Mister, just fix the steaks."

Bob smiled at his wife. "Guys, I think they're done." He took the steaks off the grill. "All right, men, let's go join the ladies."

As they sat around the large stone patio enjoying their dinner and drinks, the sun started to set, so Bob lit the tiki torches and the fire's glare seemed to dance off the outdoor pool. The banter was light as they discussed everything from football to movies.

"Tell me, Cal, have you sold the Weatherhill Estate yet? I'd like to know who my new neighbors are going to be."

"I'm glad to report, I believe, Bob, you and Marie are going to be getting new neighbors shortly and I think you're going to like them. Gary and Sara Covington have been through twice and have offered full price, 3.8 million for that fixer-upper next to you," everyone laughed. "Wow, full price. Who does that? The Weatherhills moved to Florida. They don't need the money and made it clear to me they weren't taking a dime less than asking price. That scared off a lot of potential buyers, but not the Covingtons."

"What does he do for a living?" Larry wondered.

"I know he has a government security clearance, but it's Mrs. Covington who has all the money. It seems her father is a large government contractor with contracts worth millions, mainly in helicopter replacement parts, and she is Daddy's little girl and right hand man. I assume the husband works for him also and thus the top security clearance."

Bob smiled. "Seems like our kind of people and can't wait to meet them," the other three men all looked at Bob and smiled back.

Marie looked over. "So tell them, Bob, about the speech you will be giving in a few weeks…"

"Don't tell me, Bob, the *New England Journal of Medicine* has finally discovered you?"

“Not quite, Cal, but it seems that the school district of Briarcliff has and I’ve been asked to be one of the motivational speakers for the graduating class of 2017 at the Berkshire School.”

“Bob, that’s awesome, you get to speak to your son’s graduating class.”

“Thanks. I’m very excited and flattered by it. Not sure that Matt is. Just kidding; he was ecstatic because I told him to be.”

“So, Bob, are you already working on your speech to the future of America to inspire them to greatness?”

“Very funny, Cal. I am sure I can plagiarize something off the internet,” everyone was laughing and having a good time as the drinks flowed.

“Tell me, Bob, since I didn’t attend the prestigious Berkshire High, what in the hell is senior motivation night?”

“Diane, dear, for those who attended public school with the general population, I will talk slowly and explain.”

“Fuck you, Bob!”

Everyone laughed as Bob explained that every year the senior class is spoken to by previous graduates who attended the school and what opportunities lay ahead for them if they continued to work hard and suck up to the right people. A grand time was had by all when the evening finally ended well after midnight.

Chapter Two

One of the most prestigious and difficult jobs in all of college academia is Dean of admission. The occupier of this position quite literally holds the future of a young man or woman in his or her hands. In no place in America is that position more powerful or more stressful than it is in Harvard University. Currently, the position belonged to William Gray, a Harvard grad himself. The job had a number of requirements; first and foremost, that of making decisions that were above reproach, because the holder's integrity would often be tested.

Over the years, many parents, often starting when their kids were in the 9th grade, offered William Gray everything from trips to cars and even the use of their vacation homes if he would just push the admission committee and help their son or daughter get into Harvard. William always told him the same thing: the playing field would be level. Their school achievements, academic scores, extra-curricular activities, and outside community service would be the deciding factors, and nothing else. Still, many tried to curry favor with him.

Harvard University prided itself on being open to everyone regardless income or status. The university offered a full tuition ride to many undergraduates who otherwise could never have afforded the steep tuition of $65,000 a year. William himself was one such student, raised by a single mom who could never have afforded it and, therefore, he was very aware of being fair-minded to whoever was accepted. Every year, parents would ask to meet with him personally, and very subtly, the offers would come. On occasion, he would have a little fun with them. One father, knowing he was a serious sports fan, sent him an expensive set of golf clubs, assuming he played. He didn't, and offered the clubs for auction and gave the money to charity, thanking the sender with the enclosed card. *Tom, thank you for your generous donation of golf clubs. They brought over $1,800 for our Research Center. If only you could have gotten me tickets to the Rose Bowl. I live for college football. Your friend, William.*

Dr. Robert Weinstein was up at 5 a.m. on Thursday morning. He had a long day ahead of him. Having showered and shaved, along with his morning coffee, he pulled his Mercedes Benz S-Class out of the driveway at precisely 6 a.m. He was a stickler for punctuality and it was 162 miles to Cambridge, Massachusetts. He knew the trip by heart, having made many a trip up to Harvard to see a game or meet with old friends. It took just under three hours on a good day. It had required some badgering and a few highly placed phone calls, but he had managed an appointment with Dean Gray. Bob enjoyed the ride to Cambridge, although his wife Marie had no idea he was meeting with the dean of admissions. She thought he was meeting some friends. At exactly 8:50, Bob pulled his Mercedes into the parking lot.

"Good morning. Welcome to Kirkland Place. I'm Ann-Marie. How can I help you today?"

"Yes, Doctor Robert Weinstein. I have an appointment

with the Dean."

She glanced down at her itinerary. "Yes, you do, and he's expecting you. Please follow me." Anne-Marie knocked on the large solid oak doors. "Dean, Dr. Weinstein has arrived."

"Please, show him in."

The men shook hands. Anne-Marie backed out and closed the door behind her.

"Please, Doctor, have a seat. I would appreciate it if you call me William."

"You, sir, have a beautiful office." Dr. Bob was totally impressed with the beautiful solid mahogany desk. A large handcrafted yacht sat on the mantel above the fireplace along with pictures of his wife and three kids.

"Thank you. I inherited the place, so I cannot take any credit for the fine craftsmanship and décor."

"Your family on the mantel?"

"Yes, my wife Cindy and the three kids. Adam, the oldest, now 26, Amy, 23, and Kimberly, 21."

"Beautiful."

"Thank you. Yes, I'm a very lucky man, Doctor. What brings you back to Harvard today? And yes, I did a little background on you."

They both laughed. "Then you're aware my son Matt has applied for admission next fall?"

"Yes, I pulled up his file this morning and was looking it over. Very impressive. Having gone through the admission process yourself, Doctor, you know the competition is extremely competitive, but Matt looks like a viable candidate. I spoke with a member of the admission committee last evening. There are still approximately nineteen openings remaining for next year's class and they will be chosen from the final list of sixty-one. I would assume Matt is on that list, but I'm not privy to that information until the final selections are made."

"Tell me, Dean, do you like to travel?"

"Oh, who doesn't?"

"And cruise?"

"For sure. I went to Belize two years ago on a cruise. It was fantastic."

"That's good to hear. Marie and I are planning a two-week cruise next year to Alaska. You and your wife should consider joining us. I know for a fact there are still a couple of openings. The best part about cruising, of course, is there is no cash exchanged on board, so you can just relax and indulge yourself and not worry about any expense."

Dean Williams smiled. "That, my friend, is very tempting. I will have to talk it over it with Cindy. Doctor, you're a very bright man and I believe you probably prefer honesty above all else."

"Absolutely."

"Harvard, you know, having gone here, is not for everyone. The academics are, to say the least, very strenuous, and it takes a certain amount of self-determination to excel here."

"Dean, if you're trying to make a point, please be upfront. We're both adults here."

"Good. Matt is on the list of the final sixty-one, but only because he is a legacy and that means a lot here. His chances are at best average. I believe he will be put on the wait list. I also have no doubt there are a dozen top universities in which he will be accepted with no problem. Harvard, at times, is a numbers game and nothing more. He has a fine academic record."

Dr. Bob let what was said sink in for a few minutes. There was an awkward silence between the two.

Bob finally stood up. "Well, Dean, I appreciate your candor and taking time to meet with me this morning."

"I wish I could be more optimistic, but I wanted to be upfront." The men shook hands and Bob started to leave, then turned to Dean Williams, who was standing behind the desk.

"As a token of my appreciation, Dean, for taking time out of your busy schedule and all, I will be sending something over in the mail."

"It was my pleasure, Doctor. You don't need to reward me."

"Oh, I insist, Dean. You have a great day." Dr. Bob quietly exited the office and closed the door behind him.

***

Dr. Bob pulled his silver Mercedes out on the road and headed for home. He glanced in the rearview mirror at the tree-lined campus and smiled to himself. *Next fall, Matt will be attending here.*

Chapter Three

Peyton Long, tall for a female, with long, flowing brown hair, was coming home from class. She attended Cayuga Community College in Syracuse, NY, where she was studying to become a dental hygienist. She also waitressed at a local pub called the Oyster Shooter. It helped to keep her afloat financially. She shared her apartment with another student. Joy Summers. They got along great and spent many a night polishing off cheap wine and discussing the men in their lives, or the lack of one.

Peyton grabbed the mail and headed up the stairs toward the two-bedroom apartment. She noticed one envelope in particular and threw the rest on the kitchen table and tore it open. *Yes!* she shouted to herself. Talk about timing; money was really tight and her car payment was already ten days past due.

She had known the rules for over a year now and followed them exactly. She grabbed her iPhone and quickly put in the number. There was never any communication except by her answering with a simple text:

Yes, I'm available and will be at the location.

She waited a few seconds and an emoji with a thumbs-up

appeared.

Peyton grabbed a quick shower and put on some music and pranced around in just her shorts and halter top. She got her duffel bag, threw it on the bed, and started going through her clothes, when her roommate Joy arrived. Joy joined her in the back bedroom.

"Well now, someone is in a really good mood for a Thursday. What, no class tomorrow?"

"Oh, I have class in the morning, but I'll be gone for the weekend."

"Is this another one of your mystery getaways that you never talk about?"

"It is and I just can't."

"Be careful, Peyton. No guy is worth getting hurt over."

Peyton smiled and kept putting clothes into her bag for the weekend trip. Joy had no idea where her roommate went on these weekend trips that occurred infrequently and always on the spur of the moment. She knew when Peyton returned from these trips, she had money to spend. Once, she bought a new flat screen TV. Another time, she bought several outfits when only the week before she was scraping to pay the utility bill.

Joy didn't know it, but she needn't worry about her roommate. Peyton Long was raised by a single mom who had her when she was just sixteen. Having a mom that young often felt like having an older sister.

Gwen, her mother, was not your average stay-at-home type. As a young mother, she didn't always have the best parenting skills, and when Peyton was young, Gwen would have her latest boyfriend on more than one occasion spend the night, but she had to admit her boyfriends were always nice to her and treated her well. The most she knew of her biological father was that he was nothing more than a one-night stand after a school dance who came from a wealthy family, who, when pressed, would send her mom money, usually when Gwen threatened to take him to court for back child support payments.

Gwen dropped out of school and worked different jobs to keep the tiny apartment she shared with her daughter. Money was always tight, but they managed.

When Peyton started high school, life started to get a little better. Gwen went back to night school and got her GED and then went on to take classes and became a certified pubic account, or CPA for short. They moved out of the tiny one-bedroom apartment and into a two-bedroom townhouse in a nicer part of town. She never asked, but her mom seemed to change jobs often. She would tell Peyton she had a better offer and took it. The reality of it was Gwen knew her way around the books and would help herself to company funds on occasion. Gwen never considered it embezzlement. She would tell herself: '*This firm is making millions and paying me $40,000 a year*'. She was also smart enough to know when to move on, having taken just enough to fall under the radar of any suspicious auditor.

Peyton Long was raised by a street-smart mom and picked up many of her traits. She knew how the world treated people like her; she would have to make their own way and she planned on doing just that.

***

Robert Weinstein and his friends Larry Sinclair, Roger Palmer, and Cal Estrada were more than college friends who still socialized together; they also owned a couple of businesses together. They were partners in a car wash and the building where Dr. Bob had his medical practice. They rented out the car wash, which seemed like an unusual purchase for a couple of reasons. The first, it was twenty miles away, and second, these were all professional men, but it met a major need of theirs; it was an all-cash business. The four Harvard-educated men thought it was pure genius if they had to wash some money, so to speak.

The wives were aware of their husbands' business ties and mainly didn't question too much about them. They were obviously all four doing well as partners living in exclusive neighborhoods. Private tennis clubs, new cars dotted the driveways, yearly cruises to exotic ports. Cal and his wife recently purchased a vacation home near the water. Money, it seemed, was never an issue.

What the wives were not aware of was the four men's other business they owned and operated under the corporation name Eagle 2 Investments.

It was series of enterprises run by the group, including a medical billing service. Dr. Bob would recommend a physical therapy program to almost all his patients, who loved him dearly and swore by him. Oftentimes, a patient would tell him they felt great. "Of course, you do, but a good PT program will help your muscles regain lost strength because of aging and repetitive motion-on syndrome."

They would smile and say, "Well, you're the doctor. Can you recommend a good PT program?"

Of course he would send them to one of the group-owned clinics. The patients would receive physical therapy — many of whom didn't require it — some for a few weeks and some for several months, depending on how long their insurance would pay. Eagle 2 would bill their insurance company an enormous markup. Of course, it was totally unethical sending patients for care that wasn't necessary, but no one ever questioned the cost or need for care. After all, it was physician recommended.

The clinic, car wash, and commercial properties were all financially successful for the group, but they were small change compared to the group's real money maker, and the idea behind it actually started when they were in college.

All four learned to play poker to help pass the time when not studying and they became very proficient at it. The young college students soon found themselves traveling to Atlantic City on weekends and making some new friends.

One of them was Benjamin Larson, a professional bookie who ran poker games on the side for the mob. "You gentlemen seem to know your way around the game a little bit. I'm Benjamin Larson, or Big Ben for short." Bob, Cal, Larry, and Roger soon were playing with some of the best and learning to say "fuck Atlantic City." These pots were twice the size with no taxes; you win it, you keep it. When the four wanted some excitement away from the stress of their grueling academic schedules, they would spend an evening away from campus playing in some high stakes poker games, sometimes winning and sometimes losing, but it was never boring. They were also keenly aware of whom they were dealing with and made sure to never get in over their heads. This continued off and on during their junior and senior years. Bob Weinstein was headed to medical school and his three friends went on to earn their masters degrees. There was no free time to gamble.

Fast forward nine years and the friends were now married

and all living in Wilton and that was not by accident; they planned on doing business together. The rental properties and the clinic were solid money makers for a good five years running, when Cal had an idea that would change their lives and friendship forever.

"Why not start making book on sporting events? We can cover bets on everything from football to horse racing."

Dr. Bob at first thought the idea was ludicrous, but Cal started to reach out to some former alums from college and business connections. Cal was right; people loved to gamble.

Within three years, they were taking in over a quarter million a month in bets, thus the need to purchase the car wash. When you're dealing in a cash business, you have to show the IRS where the money came from. Their clientele were not the average blue-collar workers plunking down fifty dollars, hoping to make a hundred. They were lawyers, investment bankers, architects — all professional people wagering anywhere from one thousand to several thousand, but even with so-called high earners on occasion, problems would arise and someone would get in over their head and wouldn't be able to cover their losses. This usually happened when the spouse was unaware of the gambling. The group, for all their sleaziness, was not in the business of threatening someone with bodily harm who owed them money but would cut them off from placing any more wagers. The addicted gambler, the kind who just couldn't stay away from the action, would beg for one more opportunity to get even and pay back what they owed. This was when Cal did his best investment counseling.

"We cannot let you make any more wagers until all the back money you owe is paid in full, but you're a professional and a friend. Here is my advice: your car (usually a BMW,

Mercedes Benz, etc.) I'm sure has theft insurance. Rumor has it if you drive into New York City and park in certain areas with the keys left in it by mistake, you know, shit happens." Cal would then just walk away. On more than one occasion, the advice was taken.

Eagle 2 Investments, after only six years in business, was profiting over four million monthly from its gambling enterprise, now with two car washes and several new rentals and almost all of it tax free.

***

"Marie, honey, are you sure about not joining us this weekend for the fundraiser?"

"I am very sure. Listen, I think it's great what the four of you do with your charity, the Crimson raising money for cancer research, but to drive 90 miles and watch you and a bunch of your old frat buddies smoke cigars, play poker, drink until you puke, and tell raunchy jokes, I'll pass."

"Tell me, are Lauren, Susan, and Diane going?"

"Ah, no."

"That's what I thought."

"Have a great time and raise a lot of money. I will be busy shopping and having a nice dinner with my girlfriends. See you Sunday."

If Marie and her friends ever decided to drive the 90 plus miles north to the Wiltshire Hotel, they would indeed find their husbands' cars in the parking garage, the hotel rooms booked in their husband's names, but Dr. Bob, Larry, Cal, and Roger would be nowhere in sight. Dr. Bob booked the same hotel and suite three or four times a year for their so-called fundraiser charity, the Crimson. Once, they had all the wives attend and spend the weekend. They all hated it, just as the men had planned.

The group had some old college friends stop by and they smoked, drank bourbon, and played cards until daylight and the wives hated every minute of it, and that was exactly what they were counting on.

So when the men now went on these semi-annual fundraisers, the wives begged off. Normally, when they went to the Wiltshire, all four of the friends drove together, but Dr. Bob drove separately this time; he had other plans for Monday morning.

***

Cal Estrada pulled his black BMW into the Wiltshire Hotel parking garage along with Larry Sinclair and Roger Palmer. Fifteen minutes later, Dr. Bob arrived.

"Damn, Bob, you're late," chimed Larry.

"Very funny. Tell me, did you wax that bald spot for the weekend?"

"I did, wise guy. They say the fishing's better that way!"

All were laughing and cracking jokes.

"Here comes our ride." A full-size black Escalade pulled up. The driver hopped out and opened up the door for the men and put their luggage in the rear.

"Good evening, gentlemen. My name is Steve and I will have you at Waterbury Airport in about thirty minutes. I just talked with Jack and he will be waiting."

"Sounds good, Steve."

***

Peyton Long pulled her muddy 2008 green Jeep into the park and ride lot. She didn't have to wait long for the red Malibu with the Uber symbol to come in behind her.

"Are you Peyton?"

"I am."

"Glad to meet you. I'm Mark. Can I get your bags?"

"No, I'm good. Just have the one." Peyton climbed into the back.

"Make yourself comfortable. It's about fifty minutes to the airport from here. That package on the seat is for you also. I picked it up at the on the way."

"Thanks." Mark headed toward the airport as Peyton took out her iPhone and put her earphones in and started listening to some of her favorite music.

She took the package and slowly removed the paper. Inside the plain brown box was a nicely wrapped box from Maxine's Lingerie. Peyton knew the landscape by now. This was how her date for the weekend worked. He always left her a package, something he desired her to wear sometimes when they were together. In the past, she had worn a long red wig (he enjoyed pulling her hair while having sex), stilettos, and fishnet stockings, just to name a few.

She was thrilled to see something from Maxine's; they had the nicest nightwear. She smiled to herself as she opened the top of the box so only she could see it, not the driver, in case he was to look in the rear-view mirror. *Well,* she thought to herself, *not something I would ever pick out for myself, but he is a paying customer.* She had been hoping for some expensive silk pajamas.

Peyton, sometime over the next forty-eight hours, would be wearing a red corset, scarf, and matching underwear. *Men,* she thought to herself. *Where do they come up with this shit?*

At 11:00 a.m. sharp, the red Malibu arrived at Waterbury airport. "Thanks, Mark. You're a great Uber driver. I gave you five stars."

"Thank you. Have a great flight. Who knows, maybe I'll pick you up on the return."

Peyton smiled, grabbed her duffel, and made her way through the airport.

The best thing about flying on a private jet was no need to check bags or go through security.

"Peyton. over here."

She knew the voice. It was Pilot Jack Saunders, also owner of the airplane and a genuinely nice guy. He gave her a hug.

"Great to see you again."

"Same here. I love your plane."

They headed across the tarmac and boarded the Gulfstream V1. On her first trip, Jack was nice enough to show her all the features. He was very proud of what he referred to as his baby. It seated fourteen, with all-white leather high backs, flat screen TV, complete with bar, refrigerator, solid oak cabinets, and a gaming table in the back.

"Here they come."

"Hi, Jack." Dr. Bob hugged his old friend, followed by Cal, Larry, and Roger.

"I hope you know how to fly this bird."

"It's my first time, Roger, but I've been practicing on the computer at home!"

"Shit, if that's the case, what can go wrong!"

“Alright, gentlemen, and I use the term loosely, and Ms. Peyton, buckle up. Who wants to ride shotgun?” Cal quickly jumped into the co-pilot seat. Jack looked over as Cal got situated.

“How many flying hours do you have in the air, son?”

Cal thought for a moment. “I actually joined the mile-high club going from New York to Boston. That was like forty minutes!”

Jack just shook his head and laughed. “That’s good enough for me.”

The Gulfstream V1 taxied down the runway. “Tower, Whitebird is ready for takeoff.”

“Stand by, Whitebird.”

***

They sat on the tarmac about five minutes. Roger sat next to Peyton, slyly rubbing her thigh. His friends barely acknowledged her existence. *Assholes,* she thought.

“Whitebird, this is tower. You’re clear for take-off on runway 7. Have a safe flight.”

“Roger that, tower.”

Jack taxied out onto the runway and revved the engines. In a matter of minutes, they were thundering down the runway and lifting off.

“This is your pilot speaking. We have reached an altitude of 10,000 feet. I have turned off the seat belt sign. Please free to move about the cabin. We should be in sunny Miami, Florida in approximately three hours and fifteen minutes. The present forecast there is a balmy 82 under sunny skies.”

“Wahoo!” Loud cheers went up and the men headed to the

bar. Roger looked over at Peyton with a question in his eyes.

"Go ahead; join your friends. We have the whole weekend together." Roger grabbed her thigh again and headed back to his fellow deviants, as Peyton thought of them. She put her ear phones back in and smiled to herself. They hadn't a clue, but she knew all about Roger Palmer and his cashmere-sweater-wearing friends. She had met Roger almost sixteen months ago. She was having a hard time making ends meet, being a full-time student with car payments, rent, and utility bills. On more than one occasion, mac and cheese from the dollar store was dinner.

Peyton finally found a reliable roommate to help with the rent, but she was always counting every dime just to get by. She complained to her friend Heather, who seemed to be doing just fine, even though she was in the same situation.

"Did you ask your mom?"

"I just can't. She has a hard time budgeting herself."

Heather looked at her intently with her blue eyes. She had short brown hair and a small frame. She was the athletic type. "How bad do you want to make it on your own?"

"I have no other option."

"I'm just like you; there is no one I can just call and have some cash to hold me over and I don't want that. You ever hear of Executive Introductions?"

"No. What is it?"

"It's an organization that hooks up young, attractive females like us with older men with money."

"You mean…?"

"Yup, you got it, and don't knock it till you try it. Listen, I spend an evening with the same guy every two weeks. I get first class hotels, fine dining. Hell, he even brings me jewelry on occasion and the best part is, the next morning, I have fifteen hundred dollars in cash on the nightstand, no questions asked."

Peyton was speechless.

"You look shocked. You can't make that kind of money for one night anywhere else. I'll leave you with a contact number."

Peyton didn't do it right away. One Saturday night, she really wanted to meet some friends for drinks. She had exactly nine dollars and change to her name and was feeling depressed about it, so she made the call. That was how she came in contact with Roger Palmer, the balding research chemist. Peyton laughed to herself when she said it because his story to Peyton was that he was a pharmaceutical sales rep. That was part of the deal when she signed on: an agreed-upon amount of money, type of sex permitted, and no other contact unless he called first. They had their first introduction at a really nice restaurant and went to a nearby hotel. It was nothing kinky; he just liked her to wear different outfits on occasion. He knew all about Peyton, where she was from, that she was a student, etc. Peyton was sure he figured this was just some attractive bimbo going to a community college and she played right along. The second time they were together, Peyton wore his old ass out, and while he was sleeping, she took his wallet and her iPhone in the bathroom and photographed everything from his driver's license to his credit cards just for insurance. Peyton didn't think Roger was a bad guy; he treated Peyton well and always at the end of the date slid the envelope into her purse. If it was just one evening, one thousand dollars; these weekend trips to Miami, twenty-five hundred dollars — never a dime more or a dime less. It was strictly a business transaction.

They landed in Miami right on schedule and headed straight over to their usual place, the Emerald Palace, a 5-star hotel that was absolutely gorgeous and right on the beach.

After checking in, the men had their routine — they went straight to the bar — and Peyton had hers — straight to the beach. Roger texted her: *"Let me know when you come up to shower. I would like to join you."* He signed it with an emoji wearing an evil grin. Peyton guessed her guy was a little horny.

She always liked it when he asked her on these trips. She could never afford something like this, and for the next few weeks, money wouldn't be so tight. It had taken some detective work on her part, but over time, she found out who his friends really were and their occupations. It didn't take long to figure out that Dr. Bob was the ringleader, although in front of Peyton, it was just Doc.

Tonight would be a catered dinner in their five-bedroom suite with champagne, cigars, and music until dawn. Peyton stayed on the beach until five pm. and texted Roger, *"Taking my sweaty ass up for to the shower if you want to join me!"*

Roger texted back, *"It's tempting, but I'll wait till I see you in the outfit tonight!!"*

"That works for me." Peyton thought, *once a night or all night, the price is still the same.*

She stripped down and got in the shower. It felt wonderful. Afterward, as she was drying off, she looked at herself in the full-length mirror and liked what she saw. Roger Palmer was getting a hell of a bargain.

Peyton put on the blue silk gown Roger had given her. It came just above the knee, skin tight, with a plunging V neck down the front. She put on a string of white knock-off pearls she owned and headed out to the living area. The caterer was already serving hors d'oeuvres. Roger and his friends were already milling about the balcony with drinks in hand, looking out over the ocean. It was quite a view.

The one thing that always changed when they came to Miami was four new girls, all stunning. Dr. Bob, Cal, Larry, and millionaire pilot Jack Saunders liked variety. Peyton was the only returnee ever. She made her way over to meet them. After all, they would be spending the evening together.

She introduced herself to a petite redhead Amber. "Thank God, someone to talk to. I was starting to wonder if I was in the wrong place."

"No, you're in the right place. Just those four. It's alcohol first, cards second, and then sex, in that order."

She started laughing.

"Your first time here?" Peyton knew it was.

"Yes, and I'm a little intimidated. I mean, this is some place."

"I have to ask, who do you work for?"

"Mainline Consultants, a really upscale name for an escort service, don't you think?" They both laughed, drank some wine, had delicious appetizers, and watched their dates for the evening get trashed.

"I hate to pry, but does Mainline pay well?"

"A night like, this around $900.00. Who do you work for?"

"Executive Introductions."

"I heard of them and was seriously considering it. I mean, it would be nice to have a regular guy and know what to expect. Are you happy with them?"

"Yes, I can't complain. They keep it safe. Not just any guy can join. They do a thorough background check and they keep a copy of his credit card on file. Let's say he tries something you didn't sign up for and he tries to stiff you. They charge his card and cut you a check no questions asked."

"Sounds pretty solid." They talked for the next hour and became friends.

"Well, looks like it's time to turn in for the evening. Roger is signaling me. I'm curious, who is your date for this tonight?"

"Says his name is Cal; probably a lie."

They both laughed.

"No, I can assure you that's his first name. Lucky you, though. I would consider doing him for free!"

"I know, right."

"I can also assure you anything else he tells you is bullshit." They both just smiled and hugged.

"Peyton, do me a favor and text me the information on Executive Introductions. I might be interested. And let's stay in touch."

Roger came across the room and put his arm around Peyton's waist. She could tell the alcohol had allowed him to let his guard down because he never showed any outward signs of affection before.

All four of the girls paired up and went their way. Peyton and Roger finally made their way to the bedroom and Roger slowly ran his tongue down the back of Peyton's neck and unzipped her gown and let it drop to the floor. She was totally nude underneath as per his request.

"You mind going and putting on the outfit?"

She gave him a quick kiss. "Be right back." She slid on the skin-tight corset and red bikini.

Peyton kicked open the bathroom door. On your knees, Mister!" Roger smiled and obeyed.

Afterward, as they lay in bed, he was in the mood to talk — unusual for him; obviously, the alcohol had an effect. "Ask me anything you want tonight, after that performance. It was amazing."

"I do aim to please. Since you offered, here goes. I notice your associates always have a new date for these excursions, but not you, so am I that good or what?"

Roger laughed. "It's funny you should ask. That's a touchy spot with my friends. The deal was always no repeat connections. They keep telling me I'm breaking the protocol and they're serious, but I stand my ground. I like being with you. We click, as they say, and you're great in the sack."

"Thanks, I enjoy your company as well."

Roger also discussed his life as a salesman. Peyton played along, but she knew it was bullshit. She even knew where he worked.

Finally, around 3:00am, Roger dozed off, but he gave Peyton something to think about. His friends, who held a lot of sway with him, were trying have him drop her. She was going to need some insurance in case that happened. She needed the income he provided and had to make sure it didn't dry up.

***

Peyton was surprised when they left for the airport late Sunday evening. Dr. Bob wasn't with them. He was staying behind in Miami with some business to attend to. The plane touched down back in Waterbury around 7:00 pm. Roger was sober now and back to his old self, talking with his boys, as Peyton called them, and pretty much ignoring her. She wasn't complaining; she felt she was a paid lay to him and nothing else.

Pilot Jack, always the gentleman, gave her a hug; Roger nodded and climbed into the SUV they had waiting and drove off.

A few minutes later, the Uber driver showed up and Peyton headed back to her world, class and work. On the way back home, Peyton looked in her pocketbook. Sure enough, there was an envelope. She unsealed it. Twenty-five hundred dollars in cash. Smiling to herself, she leaned back in the seat and put her ear phones in. *You do what you gotta do*.

Chapter Four

"Good morning and welcome to Denver. I'm Wayne. How can I be of service this morning?"

"I have a rental reserved. Dr. Robert Weinstein."

"Yes, here it is. We have a Blue Mercedes all ready to go. How was your flight in this morning?"

"Uneventful, thankfully."

"Good to hear that. Give me one minute to print this out. You're all set. Enjoy your stay."

Dr. Bob stopped by the vending machine and purchased five packs of chewing gum on his way to the car.

He didn't need directions, knowing the route by heart. He had been making the trip three or four times a year and no one knew it, not Marie or any of his friends.

After forty-five minutes, he whipped the Mercedes up the long and winding driveway beautifully landscaped with flowering white dogwood trees on both sides and acres of lush green lawn as far as the eye could see. A light frost had covered it and the sun danced off it like a million lights.

The security guard slid open the window. "Welcome to Meadowood. Can I help you?"

"Yes, Bob Weinstein to see Samuel Bennett."

"Yes, Samuel Bennett, building 4, the Alpine. Enjoy your visit."

Bob put on his visitor's badge.

Before exiting the car, Bob checked himself in the mirror. The toupee looked good with the added dark reader sunglasses and golfer's hat. His own wife would not recognize him. Meadowoods was a facility for those who could afford the very steep-priced home to those with disabilities who could no longer take care of themselves on a daily basis.

Bob smiled as he walked down the hallway toward room 112. It was 10:00 am when he entered the room.

"Good morning. I'm Sam's aide, Ann Watts."

"Nice to meet you." Ann looked to be around fifty with short dark hair and a pleasant smile. They shook hands.

"Bob Weinstein, Sam's legal guardian."

"I heard Sam was getting a visitor today. It's always nice when friends and family stop by."

"Thanks for taking such good care of Sam."

Sam looked up and smiled and went back to eating his cereal.

"It's been my pleasure."

Bob took a seat and looked around the room that had been Sam's home for over sixteen years. It was very nice and neat with a small sofa and kitchenette, TV on the mantel, and books on the shelves. Lots of books and pictures of Sam's parents on the nightstand.

"So tell me, how is he doing?"

"Just great. As you know, Samuel is very regimented. This is cereal time. At noon, he will go out and meet his two friends at the front door and walk the track three times around every time." Bob just smiled. Some things never changed.

"But you know he is very content in his world and we love him here; the whole staff does."

"Do you think he recognizes me?"

"He very well may. When you walked in, he smiled, so he may not be able to verbally communicate it, but yes, I believe he knows friendly faces."

"Does he still say a few words on occasion?"

"He does and it's almost always when he is looking through one of his books. I honestly believe he considers the characters he reads about as his friends."

"I assume he is still reading the same ones?"

Ann smiled. "Of course, his all-about-trains book, then he will look through his one of his space explorers books. I just know one of these days he is going to read out loud."

Bob looked up at Ann. "Wouldn't that be something? You said he had a couple of friends?"

"He does. They're approximately all the same age and have the same abilities. We never say the word 'disability' because we don't look at it that way. We always ask what can we do to help them have a productive day."

"That's why I like this facility for him. I know how well he is treated here because I can only make it out a few times a year. The staff here knows how dedicated you are to Samuel. I've only been on this wing of the facility for three months. You're well thought of."

"Mr. Weinstein, we understand this is his home and we are his extended family. We take Sam on group outings to the mall, the state park — which he loves, by the way — movies. He has a full life here that he thoroughly enjoys. Samuel is always upbeat, just a joy to be around."

"Thank you. That makes me feel better. I brought his

favorite." Bob walked over and put five packs of chewing gum on the table in front of Sam. He looked up and smiled, then took four packs and put them in a single file on the nightstand and left one pack out. Bob shrugged at Ann.

She smiled. "Oh, he will share that one with his friends when they walk the track."

Bob laughed. "He is great, isn't he?"

"Yes, he is."

Ann stayed and answered all of Bobs questions for forty minutes. "Mr. Weinstein, it has been a pleasure and I hope I'm on duty when you visit next time. I'm always available by phone. Never hesitate to call or email me. We're here for you." They embraced and Ann left the room. Bob sat back and watched as Sam flipped through one of his books and asked himself, '*Why wasn't that me?*' They were identical twins at birth, but Sam was always withdrawn in his own world. When Bob was twelve, he would ask his mom why. She would always say *God put certain people on this Earth and their only job is to show love and your brother was chosen to be one of them.* It was the perfect answer. Bob became legal guardian when his parents began to age and could no longer take care of him. His parents found this place and it had been home ever since they registered Sam under his mom's maiden name Bennett.

Bob never questioned why; he always felt it made his mom feel even closer to her special son. Both of his parents were gone over seven years now, so he visited when he could.

Why Bob Weinstein never told anyone, not even his wife, about his twin brother was a secret known only to him.

***

Bob was driving along the freeway and dialed Marie.

"Well, there you are. I was getting a little concerned about you. I got your text. So one of your biggest donors invited you to his place in Vermont?"

"Yes, and wouldn't take no for an answer. It was nice; we just had some steaks and beer, basically hung out and talked a lot of bullshit like guys do. I should be home around noon tomorrow. What's new on your end?"

"Nothing major, but I did see some people walking around the Weatherhill Estate. Looks like we're getting new neighbors."

"Oh, that's right. I will give Cal a call see if it's a done deal and get the low down on them."

"I'm sure they're very nice, Bob."

"Marie, honey, that's why I love you. Always thinking the best of everyone." They chatted for another twenty minutes as Bob made his way to the airport. He would spend the night in Denver and fly back in the morning.

He parked his rental and headed through the terminal and dialed up Cal.

"Bob, where the hell are you?"

"I had a business matter needed attending. I will be back home in the morning."

"Business matter, really? What kind of business, Bob?"

"I'm not bullshitting. It was strictly work-related. Now the reason I called is Marie said someone was walking the grounds at the Weatherhill Estate. Is it sold?"

"Done deal, Bob. We close in forty-five days and you, my friend, will have some new neighbors."

"So it's the Covingtons, right?"

"Correct. Gary and Sara. She was the one with the money."

"Do me a favor and find out exactly what he does for his father-in law. I like to be prepared ahead of time if I can."

"No problem. I will call our guy and get the lowdown. So you had some business to tie up?"

"Nothing serious, just some loose ends. Listen, find out what you can about this guy and get back to me pronto and tell Diane I said hello. She probably thinks I'm an ass for dragging you away again for one our fundraisers."

"Don't kid yourself, Bob. She always thinks you're an ass; no fundraiser needed."

Bob was laughing. "Alright, man. I'll talk to you."

After chatting with Dr. Bob, Cal dialed up a business acquaintance, Geoff Lane, private investigations.

"Cal Estrada, this is a surprise. We haven't talked in some time. What's up?"

"Nothing new. Reason I called, I have a job for you. Need some background information on a new neighbor moving in next to Bob and Marie. Mr. Gary Covington and his wife Sara, but it's Gary we're interested in. The guy has a government security clearance. His father-in-law is some large government contractor. We're just trying to figure out exactly what he does for his father-in-law."

"When you say 'we're' trying, I assume you mean Dr. Bob?"

"Correct, he is going to be Bob's new neighbor. Doc's thinking he might like a little action now and then."

"Absolutely, and with that kind of money, we should encourage him. Send me over all you have on him: social security number, driver's, etc. Give me a couple of days and

I'll be in touch."

"Appreciate it."

***

Dr. Bob and his group had been very successful over the years because they were painstakingly careful about who they let place wagers with them. They always did a background check, and on more than one occasion, people who seemed very wealthy were in fact total frauds, all a front.

Wilton, Connecticut, with all its wealth, could afford the best. They had a professional police force, volunteer fire company with new equipment annually, little league fields that would be the envy of many small colleges. Appearances were very important to Robert Weinstein and his charity, the Crimson, so they made generous donations to all these organizations and many others. Members were encouraged to spend time at town functions and be seen. Photographs of Dr. Bob, Cal, Roger, and Larry handing over checks to the police and fire departments lined the walls of those buildings.

After all, what better way to keep suspicions about your activities at bay than being an outstanding member of the community?

***

"Hello?"

Ann Payne looked up from her computer. "Sorry, I didn't hear you come in. Can I help you?"

"Yes, I'm from the Williams Courier Agency. I have a delivery for Dean William Gray. Is this his office?"

"It is. You're in the right place. I will see that he gets it."

"I'm sorry. It's company policy. This is a signature-required letter."

"Wait here and I'll see if the dean is in."

"Thanks."

Ann knocked lightly and stuck her head into Dean Gray's office. "I hate to interrupt you, but I have a courier out front with a letter for you and signature required."

"No problem. Send them in."

Ann went back out to the reception area.

"This way, sir. The dean will see you."

The courier walked into the office. "Sorry about this; it's company policy."

"I understand; just doing your job." Dean Gray signed the register and the courier handed him a large manila envelope and then left. William Gray glanced at the return address: Dr. Robert Weinstein, 4 Cherry Blossom Lane, Pelican Hills Crest. He looked at it for a minute and then tossed it aside. He was busy on his computer with the admission committee making sure there were no surprises.

At 11:00 am, he finally logged off and was going through his paperwork when he noticed the envelope that Dr. Bob had sent him. He just smiled to himself and thought *when will they learn?* No matter what the good doctor had to offer, it wasn't going to sway him. Dean Gray had actually told Dr. Weinstein a small white lie, something in his position on occasion he felt compelled to do.

Matt Weinstein was never under serious consideration for one of the last nineteen openings for admission to Harvard. In fact, his name wasn't even on the list of the final sixty-one.

Dr. Robert Weinstein was a legacy and that carried a lot

of weight, so one had to be tactful in such situations because donations from alumni were paramount. Dean Gray put his feet on his desk and smiled, wondering what kind of bribe was inside. He recalled being asked about a cruise to Alaska with his wife, and that would be tempting, but of course he would just have to return it with a gracious thank-you note but could not accept. He opened up the envelope and removed some black and white photographs and his suddenly jovial matter was gone as put his feet down off the desk and spread the photos out. Dean William Gray was a very well-respected citizen and family man, but like all men who claimed sainthood, he had a few blemishes and his were laid out in 8x10s across his desk. There he was naked in one with a spike collar around his neck; in another, he was nude, handcuffed, and being whipped by a woman in nothing but a black halter top and tall black boots. In yet another, he was handcuffed from behind his back with the spike collar on and licking a lady's black stilettos as she whipped him.

There were twelve photos in all in which he was nude, being whipped, even him spanking someone, and it wasn't his wife; none of them were. It seemed that clean cut Dean Gray was into S & M. It had been his secret, or so he thought for over twenty years and absolutely no one knew.

How in the hell did that son of bitch get his hands on these?

If he were here right now, I would kill that spineless bastard with my bare hands.

Dean Gray rubbed his forehead and thought to himself, *this cannot get out. I could lose everything*. He looked up at the mantel with the picture of his wife and kids. *Fuck, fuck, fuck,* he thought to himself and then he noticed a letter still in the envelope. The letter read, *Dean Gray, it was so nice to spend some quality time with you. I feel as if we're old friends. I especially admired the photos of your beautiful wife and kids. You're indeed a lucky man. I really didn't know what to get someone who has everything — family, prestige, wealth — but I always heard that a picture is worth a thousand words. This is a wild guess on my part, but I'm thinking right now, you're speechless. I have always admired people of principle, forthright, above reproach; someone like yourself, people who always do the right thing, and that's what I'm counting on. I also have a great wife, and of course my son Matt, who is really looking forward to freshman orientation and wearing the Crimson. Feel free to keep the photos I sent. I have the originals, but safeguard them. It's amazing the material that some people post on social media. I was reminiscing the other day about receiving my fat acceptance letter from Harvard and am so looking forward to seeing Matt's face when his comes. I was wondering, since you wield a lot of power, would it be possible for you to include two tickets to the Harvard-Yale game next fall in with the acceptance letter? Best, Dr. Bob.*

Dean Gray, a small bead of sweat running down his forehead, had a yellow number 2 pencil he was twirling between his fingers. He snapped it in half. *Fuck!*

***

It was Wednesday afternoon and Cal was just heading out for lunch, when his cell buzzed.

"Geoff, how's it going, buddy?"

"Life's a peach, you know that. Listen I got that

background info for you on Gary Covington. It took me a little longer than usual."

"Don't tell me. He is his father-in-law's number one boot licker and yes man."

"Sorry, my friend, but nothing could be farther from the truth. If you're standing, you may want to sit down for this one." They talked for over thirty minutes and Cal Estrada was taking some very deep breaths. He had to call Bob Weinstein and it was not going to go well.

***

"Sandy, what time is my next appointment?"

"Not until one o'clock. Mary Knotts is due in to have her shoulder looked at."

"Very well. Buzz me when she arrives. I'm staying in for lunch today."

Dr. Bob, for all his business ties, had a very well-run medical practice, and by all accounts, was a fine physician. His personal office, just outside the examining room, had all the comforts of home: mahogany desk, leather sofa, a huge built-in TV and sound system. Pictures of great athletes adorned the walls and a prized signed football from the Harvard team the year he graduated when he was a student athletic trainer. The room was also soundproof, a requisite when taking personal calls of a delicate nature.

Dr. Bob was going over some charts and enjoying his BLT sandwich and chips when his cell buzzed.

"Cal, this is unexpected during work hours."

"Didn't mean to interrupt, Bob. I called Sandy at the desk first and she said you were free till one o'clock."

"She's right, and I might fire her for telling you that." He was laughing. "It must be important; you never call me at the office, so what's up?"

"I just got off the phone with our man Geoff and he gave me the lowdown on your new neighbor, Mr. Gary Covington."

"Awesome. I'm glad you called. I was wondering if he forgot about us. What's his story?"

"It seems he does indeed have a government security clearance, but not for working for his father-in-law. Gary Covington works for the Federal Bureau of Investigation."

"You mean the fucking FBI?"

"It seems so. Geoff made sure."

"Let me get this straight. You sold the estate next to me to a fucking FBI agent."

"Bob, honestly, I didn't know. I assumed he worked for the father-in-law like his wife."

"And what the fuck happens, Cal, when we assume?"

"It makes an ass out of you and me."

"This cannot happen. You know that, right? How long do you think that prick is going to be living next to me until he starts wondering what else Dr. Bob does or did you fucking forget, Cal?"

"Bob, what the fuck can I do now that it's sold?"

"When is settlement?"

"Forty-five days from Monday."

"Cal, did you really go to Harvard or is that some fake fucking degree you bought online? Why didn't you do the background check ahead of time?"

"Bob, I'm really sorry. They were just so nice. It never occurred to me."

"No, Cal, you saw that fucking commission check and

were probably thinking about balling his wife." Bob hung up then took his iPhone and threw it across the room, hitting the steel filing cabinet and shattering the phone into a hundred pieces. "Fucking idiot!" he yelled out loud to himself. Dr. Bob threw his head back and stared up at the ceiling. This was going to require some action. He looked at his iPhone, now in a hundred pieces scattered across the polished hardwood flooring. He calmed himself and picked up all the parts and threw them into the waste basket. He walked out to the reception area.

"Sandy, I'm sorry to bother you during lunch, but I need you to do me a large favor."

"Of course, anything.

"This morning, foolish me, I was in the trunk of my car and accidentally dropped my cell phone without realizing it and then backed over it with the car. Needless to say, it was not salvageable. Would you mind running to the phone store and picking me up a new one? I will give you all the information. I just cannot leave the office right now and I'm afraid it might close before I can get there."

"Consider it done. I mean, you're asking me to go shopping," she said with a wicked smile.

"And while you're there, please get yourself a new one."

"Are you serious?"

"Absolutely."

"Dr. Weinstein, you do know they're close to nine hundred dollars?"

"Of course, I have a wife and teenage son," he said with a laugh. "Make sure it comes with a shatterproof case. Just a hunch, but I may need one in the future."

The perky twenty-two-year-old blonde was smiling as she left for the phone store. "I tell everybody I have the kindest, most generous, most sincere boss in the world."

Chapter Five

Peyton Long hadn't heard from Roger Palmer in over a month but wasn't concerned. She was actually feeling good about life. Her "just in case her sugar daddy dropped her" insurance plan had fallen into place easier than expected and it was time to cash in the policy.

"Peyton, are you heading out again on one of those last-minute weekend getaways?"

Peyton smiled at her roommate. "Joy, no, I'm not. This is strictly a business trip."

"A business trip?"

"Yes, I have an opportunity to make some money, so I'm going for an interview."

"Overnight? Are you taking a job where you'll have to move? I need to know."

Peyton was laughing. "Relax. Nothing like that. I still have to get my degree. This would be something I would be doing from home, but it's almost a four-hour trip and I don't feel doing all the back and forth driving, that's all."

"You have me curious, girlfriend, but good luck to you. I hope it goes well."

"Thanks. I'm throwing a couple of things together so I can

get an early start in the morning hoping, it being Saturday, the traffic will be light."

Joy headed out to the kitchen and couldn't help but wonder what type of business did interviews on a Saturday. She figured Peyton was just telling her a line of crap and was probably going to spend the night at a hotel. Joy was convinced Peyton was seeing a married man, but it was none of her business. She knew in these circumstances someone always got hurt and it was usually the girlfriend.

***

"Good morning. You're listening to WSTM. 57 on your dial. Thanks for spending Saturday morning with us. I'm Gary Styer here in the studio on this brilliant sunny morning in Wilton. The annual run for the cure is taking place today over on the athletic fields of Berkshire High that is scheduled to kick off around 1:00 this afternoon. Stop by our tent and say hello. Will be doing a live remote from there. In the meantime, let's get back to some classics from the 70s."

Peyton Long turned off the radio and put the window down on her green Jeep, the dried mud falling off the tires as she rounded the corner. A huge fountain was in the center of town surrounded by mountains of shrubbery and the large gold-plated sign on the wall with water cascading over it. *Welcome to Wilton.*

This is impressive, she thought. Brick sidewalks, street lanterns on every corner, and gift shops lined the main street with park benches to sit on. She laughed to herself. *In my hometown, they would have stolen those benches.*

She pulled into a parking spot and took out her iPhone and

typed in “114 Heritage Court, Wilton, Connecticut.” Approximate travel time, eight minutes. She took a deep breath to compose herself and then backed out of the parking spot. She drove ever so slowly through the winding streets of Wilton, finally coming to Heritage Court. *Holy shit*, she thought. *Who can afford to live like this?* Every residence was an estate with long, winding driveways, manicured lawns that looked like they belonged on a golf course, in-ground pools, and tennis courts. BMWs and Mercedes Benzes lined the driveways. On occasion, someone would pass her Jeep and stare for a second, but then keep moving. She felt totally out of place.

She went past 114 Heritage Court twice just looking down the driveway lined with white dogwood trees. On the third trip, she stopped at the bottom and took another deep breath, not sure she could go through with it.

***

“Bob, I’m going into town. You need anything?”

“No, just relaxing enjoying the game.”

“Okay, I shall return in a couple of hours. I will leave you and your second love to yourselves.”

“Second? Very funny.”

Marie walked over and gave Bob a kiss. She was only gone a short time when his cell buzzed.

“Is this Bob Weinstein?”

“The one and only.”

“It’s Ben Logan.”

“I can’t believe it.”

“How long has it been, Bob?”

"Twenty plus years, maybe more since we spoke. I still miss those card games with your guys, all the bullshit, alcohol, and hell, on occasion, we even won a couple of bucks from you."

"A couple, my ass. You and your frat buddies were damn good players, and I'm told it's now Dr. Robert Weinstein. Is that right?"

"It's true, also married; I got the house and my son's off to college next year."

"Where does the time go? How about your friends? You guys stay in touch?"

"We do see each other infrequently, but Ben, you know how it is once you're married. You lose touch."

"Yeah, that's a shame; you four were like brothers. You still playing any?"

"No, not anymore. The medical practice takes all my time."

"Bob, the reason I called is a gentleman by the name of Geoff Lane tracked me down and said you were wondering if I was still involved in special services, and if by chance I was, you would like me to get in contact. Is that true?"

"Yes, Ben, I did ask Geoff to reach out and make that request. Something recently landed on my desk and I would like it to go away."

"Bob, that's what our specialty is. People have issues and we solve them. Tell you what, let's meet for dinner next Wednesday at Sparks Steak House and you can treat an old friend to the best New York strip and beer in the state and we'll catch up and discuss some business. Does 7:00 work?"

"That sounds good to me, Ben. I will reserve us a table in the back. Thanks for getting back to me so quickly. See you then."

***

Quarry Head State Park is tucked away among the wealthy estates of bucolic Wilton where, decades ago, millstones were mined and hauled by oxen to the grist mills, where they were used to grind rye and corn. Today, the park is used by joggers and bikers and is known locally for its great hiking trails.

"Come on, Lewis; come on, Clark." The two large yellow labs darted up the bank.

"So you coming, old man?" Ellen Parkin looked back at her husband, Derek, who was hustling to keep up with his marathoner wife. Ellen was five foot three inches of solid muscle from running all the time. Her short black hair bounced and she smiled, showing pearl white teeth as Derek made his way up the hillside, all six foot four, one hundred ninety pounds of him in good shape, but not in Ellen's league. Derek's tongue was sticking out in fake exhaustion. "I was getting worried for a minute there. Thought I would have to call 911 and come rescue you.

Derek smirked. "Very funny, but I wasn't the one last night asking for mercy, unable to keep up, was I!"

"You wish, Mister!" She punched him in the chest. "Should we keep going?"

"I can hang. Where to?"

"Should we hike the Devil's Path and see the gorge this time of year? The trees are spectacular along the path."

"Now those nice people from the park service put that cable across the path with the sign to keep out, didn't they?"

"Honey, that's like a Q-tip. It says right on the box not to put it in your ear, so everyone does."

Derek laughed. "Yeah, let's do it. Besides, it looks like Lewis and Clark already made the decision for us." The yellow labs loved the park and were running full steam ahead up the trail and under the cable onto Devil's Path.

They hiked up the stone path with all the trees bursting out in their autumn colors. Red and orange leaves dotted the landscape Ellen grabbed Derek's hand and smiled as they walked.

"What's up, guys?" Lewis and Clark were barking up a storm from the top of the hill overlooking the gorge.

"They probably spooked up a rabbit," Derek remarked as he laughed.

"Or a deer," Ellen chimed in. Lewis was wagging his tail feverishly and really barking now.

"You go ahead up. I don't have the energy to run."

"Okay," Ellen gave Derek a kiss. "I hope you have better stamina for later," she goaded and took off up the hill. "What is it, girl? What ya see?" She put her arms around the yellow lab. "Oh my God! Derek, get up here now!"

Hearing the desperation in her voice, Derek, racing on adrenaline, climbed the steep path in no time. "What is it?"

"Look!" Ellen put her hand around his waist and pointed at the bottom of the gorge.

There, lying some three hundred feet down at the bottom, was what looked to be a female body.

"Oh my God! Oh my God!" Derek replied. "Listen I'll make my way down. You run back for help." Ellen was half-crying and shaking. "Ellen, go. Lewis, Clark, go with her." Ellen darted down the path with the labs right on her heels. Derek slowly made his way down the skinny path that ran adjacent with the gorge. No way anyone could walk straight down the face of it, all smooth rock and almost straight down.

Derek was covered in sweat, even though the temperatures were in the low sixties, part from nervousness and part was sheer panic. He slipped twice on the way down, once landing flat on his back.

Finally landing at the bottom, he made his way over to the body. He quickly took her hand and tried in vain to talk to her. "Hey, can you hear me? This is Derek. Grab my hand if you can hear me." He got no response. He checked her pulse and felt nothing. Derek was doing his best to maintain his composure. The young female looked to be in her twenties, wearing a jogging outfit and a purple bandana around her long brown hair. Her face and arms were badly bruised, no doubt from the fall. Derek knew things didn't look good, but he quickly composed himself to try and do what he could for her. He gently held her hand, but he couldn't completely control his emotions and tears started running down his face.

"Listen, it's going to be fine. Hang in there a little longer. Help is on the way."

His flannel shirt was drenched in sweat as he tried to comfort her best he could, still holding her hand and talking to her. It had been over twenty minutes, when he heard Lewis and Clark barking at the top of the gorge. Soon Ellen appeared and right behind her a park ranger, who looked over and saw Derek with the fallen jogger.

"Wait here for the paramedics. I'm going down with your husband." Ellen nodded and the ranger made his way down the tree line.

Ellen yelled down, "Paramedics are on the way. Derek nodded, still holding the young girl's hand. How is she?" Ellen yelled.

"I'm not sure. She's not responding."

The ranger made his way over to Derek. "David Shaw. How is she?"

"I can't tell. No response from her."

The ranger took off his hat and held the young girl's wrist, hoping for a pulse but couldn't feel anything. He too was becoming emotional, but maintained poise. If he was to be of help, he needed to remain calm and render first aid until help arrived.

After what seemed like an eternity, the sirens of the ambulance could be heard roaring up the pathway. The paramedics made their way to the bottom and started to assess the young trauma victim. Derek and the Ranger Shaw stood back and watched, feeling helpless but hoping for the best.

After twelve minutes, the lead paramedic Thomas radioed up to the waiting ambulance driver to lower down the scoop stretcher basket. He didn't want to wait for a chopper.

"Call Mercy General. The accident victim, approximately twenty years of age, has severe trauma to her extremities and possible internal as well as head injuries."

"Roger that. Basket on the way."

"Is she alive?"

The young paramedic looked up at Derek. "Sorry, I'm not a doctor. My job is to assess, stabilize, and get her to the hospital as quickly and safely as possible." The ranger and Derek both knew what that meant. A paramedic cannot pronounce someone deceased. That had to come from a board-certified medical professional.

They watched as the two paramedics gently placed the young girl into the basket and strapped her in and then looked at Derek and David Shaw.

"I don't want to waste any time. Can you help us with the basket?"

"Absolutely." The two paramedics carried the end of the basket with Derek and David at the front as they slowly and methodically made their way up the hillside hugging the tree line for support. It went smoothly and without incident. The crew, once reaching the top, worked quickly to stabilize and move her into the ambulance. In a matter of minutes, they were off, sirens roaring.

They all stood silently, even Lewis and Clark, as the ambulance sped down the dirt road.

"On behalf of the park service, Derek, I want to thank you and Ellen for what you did today.

Ellen walked over and gave him a hug. "I wish we could have done more."

Ranger Shaw looked at Ellen. "I know what you mean. That stupid chain. There must be a way to keep people off that trail. It's just too narrow for jogging."

Derek, Ellen, and the labs made their way back to the parking lot and barely talked. Witnessing the possible death of a young person was heartbreaking. The lab Lewis, sensing Ellen's sadness, began to rub up against her. She looked down at him and smiled as tears rolled down her face.

Chapter Six

Wednesday evening was the Berkshire High School class of 2018 motivational speakers' night. The auditorium was decorated in the school colors, maroon and white. Members of the senior class had been seated and were talking among themselves or on their iPhones. Up on stage were the six guest speakers for the evening. The gavel came down on the podium.

"Good evening, senior class of 2018."

"Good evening, Principal Bakken," came the reply from all 151 of the graduating class.

"I welcome you to motivational speakers night, a tradition here for over 40 years. It's something I personally look forward to. Tonight, we have gentlemen from all walks of life who at one time were sitting right where you are. They have come here to share their stories of success, and in some cases, failure, and how they overcame failure to succeed. So let's have a warm welcome for all our guests. It is my pleasure to introduce the first speaker of the evening, Robert Weinstein, better known to us locals as Dr. Bob." There was loud applause for Dr. Bob.

"Thank you, Principal Bakken, and you, Class of 2018, for inviting me here this evening. This is quite an honor."

There was more applause. "Thank you. You are too kind." The class settled down as Dr. Bob began. "As you are all aware, my son Matt is in your class and he asked me tonight when I was speaking to volunteer to go first. That way, if I'm really bad, by the end, they will forget my speech."

Everyone laughed.

"Of course, that's not really what happened back stage. Principal Bakken had us all draw straws and I got the short one." There was yet more laughter.

"Let me ask you something, Class of 2018, what is the most important thing in life?"

Someone yelled out "Money!" and everyone laughed.

"Who said that?" A hand went up. "Come up on stage, young man." The student made his way onto the stage. "And your name?"

"Mark Wagner, sir."

"Glad to meet you, Mark, and you said 'money.' Let me see here… I'll take this five-dollar bill from my wallet… Here you go, Mark!"

"Thanks!" Everyone was laughing as Mark stuck the five-dollar bill in his pocket. "Just kidding, Dr. Bob. Here you go." He tried to hand the money back.

"No, you keep it, Mark." Dr. Bob looked out at the class. "You see, a five-dollar bill or any denomination — it could be a hundred-dollar-bill — it wouldn't matter. Money has no conscience; anyone can obtain it. What I'm looking for money cannot buy. Thank you, Mark. Go back and join your classmates." Dr. Bob was pacing the stage. "Any other guesses?" A hand went up. "Yes, the young lady in the second row."

"Is it achieving goals?"

"No, but a good answer." Several more tried; all were wrong.

Dr. Bob paused for a few seconds and stared at the student body. It was so quiet; you could hear a pin drop. He had gained their attention. "The correct answer is one word. Integrity. No money can buy it and you cannot inherit it; you must earn it. The qualification of being honest, of having strong moral principles; it's a personal choice, of course, but integrity is something we all should aspire to, unless you're a dishonest, immoral scoundrel." There was some laughter at this remark. "It's a personality trait we admire in people since it means that person has a moral compass that never wavers. This is extremely important as you go through life as you make new friends and develop business interests. People have to know you're trustworthy. Integrity in one's self is earned over the years by always doing things the right way, not the easy way. History tells us the men we have admired who led our country during its most turbulent times — the Lincolns, Roosevelts — men of that stature were not necessarily the best students, but people followed them and never wavered because there was never any doubt about character. Ask yourself when we watch a sporting event and the official makes a call we don't like, and one side is always not going to, why is it we don't question his integrity? We might question his eyesight," there was laughter, "because, over the years, game officials have earned our trust. Think about this: if a game was deliberately fixed by an official taking a bribe and the public found out, they would never sell another ticket because we trust the game is unbiased. That is why integrity among everything else in your life is paramount. I urge you to work for it every day, take no shortcuts, always try and do the right thing, and you will be rewarded in a way no amount of money could ever hope to buy."

Dr. Bob spoke for another twenty minutes about decency to always remember those less fortunate than yourself and lend a hand up to someone climbing the ladder. "Remember, we all start at the bottom. Class of 2018, thank you again for this evening. I wish you the best of luck in all your endeavors. Stay safe and Godspeed." There was thunderous applause.

At 8:15, the last speaker for the evening took a seat and Principal Bakken was at the mike.

"I cannot begin to thank all of our guest speakers enough for a very inspiring evening, Class of 2018. Let's show them our appreciation." All one hundred fifty students stood and gave a standing ovation.

"That concludes our program for this evening, but as we all know, part of the tradition is waiting out in the lobby where our wonderful kitchen staff has prepared all sorts of desserts for us to enjoy while we mingle and you can meet our guests in person and feel free to ask their advice."

"Dr. Bob, is that you with the cherry cheesecake?"

"Well now, isn't this a surprise. Loz, I didn't see you come in."

"I snuck in the back and sat with the other parents."

"And where is your better half?"

"At home on his computer. I told him I had a few errands to run and would be about an hour. What's your schedule?"

"Give me twenty minutes and I'll meet you at our spot."

Loz licked her lips. "I will count down the minutes." She walked off.

"Hi, Dr. Bob, not sure you remember me. I played little league with Matt years ago."

"You look familiar, but I'm stumped."

"Tim Jenkins, sir."

"What? You were a scrawny little shortstop."

"I know, right." Tim now stood over six feet and was a solid one hundred ninety pounds.

"So, young man, where are you off to after graduation?"

"US Naval Academy, sir."

"Wow, that's terrific. Your parents must be very proud."

"They are, thank you. I very much enjoyed your speech tonight. It hit home with me. I have to run, but I wanted to say hi. Tell Matt I was asking about him."

"I will do that if I ever find him." Dr. Bob mingled among the guests, shaking hands with some students and chatting with some teachers he had known for years and talking about the future of the high school. Enrollment had dropped. Dr. Bob quipped, "We need to get these young people busy and I don't mean with homework!" Everyone laughed. Dr. Robert Weinstein was truly admired at the Berkshire School.

***

"Joey, you almost done in there?"

"Keep an eye out, bro. I'll just be another minute. Matt, it's ready; all sliced and diced brought to you by Merchants credit card, for when you really want to get away."

Matt took a dollar bill from his wallet and rolled it up, cleared his nostril, and snorted the line of coke. "Oh my God, Joey, that's the best damn coke around. We'll be wired tonight."

His two friends Joey and Louis were next and all three did a line.

"Joey, dude, that is so fucking good. How much did it set you back?"

"Does it matter?" All three were laughing.

"We better get back up there. I gotta see the old man before he leaves."

"Hey, your old man did a nice job tonight."

"Thanks, yeah, he's all right, but like all parents always wanting to know my shit. I cannot wait to graduate and get out on my own." The three made their way back to talk with their classmates.

***

"Principal Bakken, I must be on my way. Thanks for a great evening. I thoroughly enjoyed it."

"Dr. Weinstein, thanks for being part of tonight. Your speech was very good and I speak on behalf of the administration. It means so much when our former graduates who have been successful come back here and talk about life experiences. It carries a lot of weight with young people."

"Thank you. It was nice coming back here; a lot of good memories." He shook Principal Bakken's hand. "I have to leave. I have another appointment this evening. If you see my wayward son Matt, tell him I will see him later at home."

"I will."

Dr. Bob pulled his silver Mercedes into the parking lot next to the navy blue Land Rover. The parking lot was pitch black when his driver's side door opened and Loz got in.

"Sure you don't want me to come over to the Land Rover? It's a little tight in here."

"I can't. That fucking nitwit is always taking my car. You

never know; we may leave a stain or something incriminating."

Both were laughing. "If we do, it's all your fault."

Loz just stuck her tongue out at that one. "Bob, I don't have much time." And with that, Loz pulled her skirt up and slid onto Bob's lap. They made love right on the driver's side seat. Afterward, she slid over to the passenger side. You're a good lover, Bob. We should practice more."

"What we need to do is be discreet as we have been. Did you transfer the money?"

"I did just as you said. $9, 900 dollars. That brings the total, by the way, to almost half a million."

"Excellent."

"I'm curious, why always $9, 900?"

"Because by federal law, banks must report to the IRS any deposit or withdrawal of ten thousand dollars or more. Hopefully, when the time is right, I will move it offshore and the IRS will no longer be a problem."

"Sounds a little bit high risk to me and exciting."

"Trust me, if I'm not careful, the only thing exciting will be the day some judge sentences me."

"I have to get going before that dipshit husband starts calling me." She leaned over and gave Bob a kiss.

"Hey, don't leave these here." Her blue bikini underwear was on the gearshift knob. "I don't think Marie would understand."

Loz smiled and stuck them in her purse. "I will be in touch." She gave Dr. Bob a wicked smile and exited the car.

Chapter Seven

Lead Detective Laura Brockington was a five-foot-eleven tall blonde with green eyes and a disarming personality, which came in handy while working in a male-dominated field. Of course, being physically attractive with an athletic body never hurt. She was well known in police circles, having helped solve one of New York's most publicized crimes, the so-called Silk Stocking killer case that captivated the country and held the city of New York on edge for eighteen months.

The decision to leave Manhattan was not easy, but the opportunity was too good to pass up and she was ready for a more stable life. Now a resident of Syracuse, at twenty-nine, she had bought a house with her long-time boyfriend and marriage was being discussed.

Detective Brockington's new partner was Detective Ed Wade, age fifty-eight, in good shape for someone his age. Ed stood just over six feet tall and was a little overweight at one hundred ninety-five pounds with dark receding hair and a quick sense of humor. When asked by Detective Brockington if he would have a problem working under a younger detective and female at that, his reply was, "As long as you don't mind working with someone smarter and better-looking." She knew right then they would get along just fine.

The two detectives found themselves at the city of Syracuse county morgue. The chief medical examiner had left her a voicemail asking her to stop by. They had never met in person but had spoken in the past by phone.

Thomas Roberts was sixty-eight years old, but could easily pass for fifty-eight. He stood medium height and was around one hundred eighty pounds, but solid, like he worked out regularly and actually looked taller in his white lab coat. He had been chief medical examiner for Syracuse for almost twenty years. After some introductions, they got down to business.

"I was surprised to receive your voicemail. It's not every day the county coroner asks you come by."

"Well, it may be nothing, but when you do this job as long as I have, sometimes things just don't seem right. Let me show you what I have and you can tell me your thoughts." They went into the part of the morgue where the deceased were kept and autopsies performed. "I assume you're both used to this." Brockington and Wade both nodded. "Good. They brought this victim in Sunday afternoon, and honestly, because of the work load, I couldn't go over the coroner's report from Wilton until Tuesday. He pulled back the sheet to reveal the body of a young girl. "The victim is twenty years of age from Syracuse, New York. Her name is Peyton Long, and from my brief interview with her mother, was a college student."

"If you don't mind, Chief, I'm going to record as you talk in case I need to refer later."

"I would expect nothing less. The victim fell to her death while either hiking or jogging in a state park in upstate Connecticut. She was brought in here on Sunday. She had sustained from the fall internal bleeding, also severe bruising to her arms and legs. The cause of death is listed for now as internal bleeding and a hematoma. I found some bleeding had taken place in the cranium. For fall victims, you look for certain indicators to confirm that indeed was the cause.

"But one of the things that caught my attention not listed in the autopsy from Wilton, when someone falls, whether it be three feet — or, in this case, three hundred feet — you instinctively put your hands out to grab on to anything and to brace yourself. Ms. Long's hands, after falling that distance, look like they could be in photo shoot; not a scratch. More impressive, not even a broken nail; quite a feat.

"Ever notice, detectives, when someone who is heavily intoxicated falls, they tend to not get badly hurt because they relax and roll with it, as they say? Was she intoxicated? Not according to the toxicology on my end three days later. Unfortunately, they had not done one up there, listing cause of death, as accidental. Of course, three days later, any alcohol or narcotic taken either intentionally or unintentionally would be out of her system."

Detective Brockington walked alongside the body of the young girl and was visibly taken aback. "You never really get used to seeing a young victim. Anything else raise your suspicion, Chief?"

"Yes, two things. The first one, the clothes she was wearing when she fell. I have them bagged up and tagged. I'll let you make your own judgment. Also, and this really raised a red flag with me and I'm not sure she even knew it, but Ms. Long was about six weeks pregnant."

"What?"

"You heard me correctly. Obviously not showing yet, but

make no doubt, she was with child. That's why I wanted you to come by; a young female over 200 miles from home out jogging alone in some remote park and falls to her death."

Detective Brockington nodded. She got the implication that maybe she wasn't alone. "Tell me about the mother."

"I don't judge, Detective. Everyone handles grief in their own way; some very outwardly and cannot control their emotions. Others suffer enormously inside. Ms. Long's mother, I assume, leans more toward the inward type, shall I say.

She was upset when first viewing the body but very quickly composed herself and confirmed it was indeed Peyton. She then thanked me and was gone in less than fifteen minutes from the time she walked in the door."

"You can cover the body, Chief. I would like to have those clothes to take back with me. Ed, looks like we have some work to do." Detective Wade smiled and so did Chief Medical Examiner Roberts. Something didn't pass the smell test and they both knew it.

Ed was driving back to the precinct. "So what are your thoughts on this?"

Detective Brockington thought for a minute. "Once we're back, I want you to find out where Peyton Long was living and we'll pay a visit, then check to see where she was staying in Connecticut, see if she was meeting someone. That's a long way from home to go for a jog."

Back at the precinct, the two detectives made their way to the evidence room, and donning neoprene gloves, carefully laid out the jogging outfit Payton was wearing when she fell. The lavender and white outfit was not the type you would purchase at your local Target. This was more upscale. There were grass stains on the knees and top along with some slight tears on the zip-up jacket. Nothing unusual for a fall of that distance.

Next, they removed a pair of sneakers from another Ziploc. Detective Brockington turned them to look at the bottom. “This is curious: no gravel stains, dirt marks — nothing to indicate she was out running.”

Detective Wade disagreed. “That doesn’t necessarily mean anything. Some of my friends are serious runners and they’re anal-retentive about their footwear. She may have been the same way.”

“Okay. If you say so.”

“What else you have?”

“That’s it.”

“What?”

“Except for her undergarments. They tested her panties and a bra for semen and got nothing. Ed, where are her personal belongings, you know, pocketbook, driver’s license, registration card, and the biggie, her damn cell phone, and don’t tell me some twenty-year-old college student doesn’t have a cell. It’s like part of their arm. This is bullshit, Ed. Where is the car she was driving impounded at?”

“I’m not even sure what the hell she was driving. I assume it’s back at her residence.”

“We need to go over the car. She has a cell somewhere. I want it.” Ed nodded and then unzipped the nylon jacket. Inside was a small pocket tee-shirt Peyton had been wearing and he removed a small piece of paper from the tee.

“Look at this.”

“You find something?”

“A sales slip from Janzen’s Market for a bottle of water

and a pack of cupcakes for $2.85 located in Wilton, Connecticut."

Brockington looked at the sales slip and smiled. "Purchased on the Saturday before Peyton was found. I believe, Ed, we're heading to Wilton, Connecticut, wherever the hell that is. I need to clear this with the chief before we go any further. Do me a favor in the meantime. Don't forget, I need Peyton's address and see if she had a roommate. It's tough, but we need to get some background on Peyton. I would like to interview her mother as soon as possible."

"I'll make some calls. Laura, this is kind of a ridiculous question. You don't think there is any chance the vehicle Peyton was driving is still at that state park, do you?"

Laura looked dumbfounded. "That's a damn good question. Find the name of that park and the ranger who found her now."

Ed Wade nodded and made a bee line back to his desk. Detective Wade had Peyton Long's autopsy report in front of him, detailing all her personal information name, date of birth, etc. Using it as guide, he made a quick call to the Department of Motor Vehicles (DMV), and as usual, they were very accommodating to the police department. The DMV confirmed Peyton Long owned a 2006 Green Jeep tagged in Syracuse New York RT-0485. He then found a number for Quarry Head State Park and made a call.

"Quarry Head State Park. How can I help you?"

"Yes, I'm trying to reach Ranger David Shaw."

"Speaking."

"Great. Mr. Shaw, my name is Detective Ed Wade. I work for the Syracuse, New York Police Department. Recently, you had a falling victim at your park. Her name was Peyton Long.

I was told you helped with the recovery?"

"That's correct, Detective."

"Mr. Shaw, I have a favor to ask."

"Go ahead."

"I need to know if the green Jeep the young girl Peyton Long was driving is by chance still at the park?"

"I can check. We only have three main parking areas. Give me the tag number and I'll take a look and call you back."

"I really appreciate it, and if it's there, would you mind checking to see if its unlocked? Sometimes joggers have a tendency to throw their keys under the floor mat because they don't like carry them while running."

"Be glad to."

Detective Wade waited patiently by the phone. In less than twenty minutes, Ranger Shaw confirmed the Jeep was indeed still there, the keys under the mat. Detective Wade had David Shaw lock the Jeep and take the keys back to his office. Unbelievable luck with that one; he also found out that, yes, Peyton had a roommate, Joy Carson, who would be glad to meet them at the apartment. Things were moving smoothly, but locating Gwen Long took some time. She still lived in Syracuse but left no street address, only a P.O. box. Detective Wade spent three days of badgering the phone company to finally get her cell number, which was pretty much useless because everything went straight to her voicemail. And she was not returning any calls.

Detective Brockington found herself sitting across from her boss, Police Chief for the City of Syracuse, Gary Spence.

"Detective Brockington, let me understand this. You want me to let you go to Wilton, Connecticut to check the circumstances of a female jogger who fell to her death."

“I know it sounds farfetched, Chief, and when the coroner called me, I thought the same thing, but this just seems too tidy, as they say.”

“Detective, you have a record to stand on second to none, but you realize this isn’t Manhattan? We serve 150,000 citizens more or less in the city, but our metropolitan area covers 600,000 with a force of 545 men and women and to tie up two detectives on a possibility, you’re asking a lot. Have you had a chance to research Wilton, Connecticut?”

“No, sir. I was going to do that after interviewing the mother of the victim and her roommate.”

The chief was smiling. “You’re going to be quite surprised at what you find. We’re talking Rockefeller-type money and power. Detective, I trust your instincts. I’ll allow it for now. If you reach a dead end, you’ve got to pull the plug and move on, and I would like a progress report every two weeks.”

“Yes, sir, and thank you.”

***

Marie Weinstein was having a breakfast of coffee and bagels and reading the news on her iPad. “Bob, did you read the story about the young girl jogging over at Quarry Head State Park?”

“I overheard one of my patients talking about it. They said she fell?”

“Yes, jogging on that damn trail they call the Devil’s Path. They just released her name and picture. Peyton Long, 20, from Syracuse, New York. Look at that sweet smile, Bob. What a shame.” Marie handed Bob her iPad.

He had been reading the paper with one hand and coffee

in the other. Dr. Bob put his paper down and looked at the picture. He knew that face instantly, not the name — he'd never really cared. Ever so slowly, he read the article maintaining his calm demeanor. "Marie, you're right; such a tragedy." Bob forwarded the article to his e-mail and gave Marie her iPad back and went back to reading the paper, or so Marie thought. One thousand thoughts were racing through Dr. Bob's mind at the moment. *What the hell was Peyton Long from Syracuse doing up here? Roger was not meeting her up here, was he? Could he be that fucking stupid? Accidental fall?* "Honey, listen, I know we planned on spending the morning together, but I really have to finish up some files back at the office."

"That's fine; go do what needs to be done and we'll have dinner together."

"I knew you would understand." He gave Marie a kiss and headed for his Mercedes. He had Roger on speed dial before he had his seat belt fastened.

"Good morning, Bob. You're up and about early."

"You anywhere near your laptop?"

"Yeah, I'm at home. What gives?"

"I sent you a news link. Check it out and call me back in five."

"Okay." Roger quickly opened his laptop and found the news link Dr. Bob had sent him.

Roger Palmer was still in his pajamas and t-shirt and drinking his coffee when he opened the link. He was stunned, immediately recognizing the girl on his iPad as his former part time lover Peyton Long. He sat his coffee down on the nightstand next to the sofa. He was in total disbelief. Roger read the article and couldn't believe it. Peyton died from an accidental fall less than five miles from Wilton. He was feeling a sense of grief coming over him; he had never been in love with her, but he liked her.

"This is unusual, you having coffee out in the living room." Roger looked up from his iPad. Lauren, his wife, had come in and he hadn't even noticed her.

"Yes, I know. Just felt like putting my feet up this morning and reading my e-mails in comfort."

"That's nice. Anything new and exciting?"

"Not really. Same old garbage, mostly junk mail."

Lauren looked very attractive in her short tennis skirt and top. She leaned over and gave Roger a kiss. See you this evening. I'm going to the club to play."

"Okay."

"I should be home around six for dinner." Lauren, with tennis bag in hand, headed out.

Roger quickly called back Dr. Bob.

"What the fuck is going on, Roger?"

"Bob, I have no idea."

"Have you been seeing this girl regularly?"

"Honestly, Bob, I haven't seen or spoken to her since Miami."

"How in the hell do you explain some bimbo from Syracuse you were balling finds her way 250 miles north to go jogging and ends up dead less than ten miles from Wilton? Defies common sense. Roger, if something happened, I can't help you unless I know about it."

"Bob, I have no idea what she was doing in this area. There is always the possibility she had another male friend in the area. It's not like she even knew my real name or where I lived. This is probably a sad coincidence."

"I hope you're right." They spoke for another twenty minutes. Dr. Bob was convinced that Roger had not seen Peyton since their tryst in Florida, but he still felt uneasy about it after the fiasco with Cal selling the neighbors' house to an FBI agent. He felt his friends were getting a little sloppy and that was how people ended up in prison.

Chapter Eight

It had been seven days since Peyton Long was discovered at the bottom of a gorge in in Quarry Head State Park and Detective Brockington and Wade had been on the case only three days but were having a hard time interviewing Gwen Long. She refused to answer her phone or return their calls. They were meeting Joy Carson at the apartment she had shared with Peyton. They found her to be very open and friendly and greatly saddened by the loss of her friend.

Ed was taking notes as Laura did the questioning. They got all the basics out of the way. “First, how long have you known Peyton?”

“Fourteen months.”

“Did Peyton have a steady boyfriend?”

“Not that I knew of and we talked guys all the time.”

“You both attend the same community college?”

“Yes, I’m going for radiology and I believe Peyton was also studying something in the medical field, but I’m not sure.”

“Did you ever go running with Peyton?”

“No, never. I honestly didn’t know she was into that.”

“How about hiking together?”

“No. And I read about her falling while out jogging. I was

surprised. I never knew."

"Have you ever met her mom Gwen?"

"Just briefly. She stopped by once to drop off a check or something. Peyton introduced us. She seemed nice."

"I want you to really think about this one. Did Peyton have any unusual habits or do anything out of her daily routine?"

"Yes, we shared a lot of stuff. Girl talk. But one thing she did she wouldn't talk to me about. On occasion, she would just pack her duffel bag and leave for two or three days at a time and always on spur of the moment. I privately wondered if maybe she was seeing a married man, but I never asked her because it was none of my business."

"Anything else?"

"Yes, after these weekend getaways, she always had extra money when she got home. Once, she bought that flat-screen TV; another time, a new sofa. I remember the sofa purchase because the week before we were scrounging to pay the damn utility bill."

Detective Brockington glanced over at Ed Wade. They were both thinking the same thing: Peyton Long was seeing someone who was financially stable. The only questions were 'who' and 'was he the father?'

"Did Peyton have a laptop?"

"For sure, but I haven't seen it around lately. Like most of us, she used her cell phone for everything."

"Have you seen her cell lately?"

"No, I'm sure she had it with her when she left for the weekend. No way she would've left that behind." They spent another forty-five minutes with Joy and found her to be very honest and forthcoming.

"Joy, would you have a problem if we were to take a look

at Peyton's room?"

"Not at all. I haven't heard from her mom about her stuff. It really saddens me. She was such an outgoing person with everything right in front of her. I know detectives don't come and ask questions about an accidental fall. If that's not what happened, Detective Brockington, she deserved better. She was a good person."

Laura smiled. "Yes, she did." The two detectives spent another hour going through Peyton's room and taking a few photographs. Nothing unusual for a young college girl: a lot of make-up, costume jewelry, lots of shoes — no hiking boots — and suspiciously, no running shoes. Most serious runners had at least two pairs if not more. Detective Brockington started to clean out all the drawers and lay all the clothes on the bed, everything from socks to underwear and then everything in the closet. Detective Wade had finished going through the nightstand and walked over.

"What gives with the clothes?"

"What's missing, Ed?"

He shrugged. "I give up. What?"

"I thought she was a runner; not one pair of running shorts, no sports bra, no other running outfits, no headbands — nothing that an avid runner would have. Make a note when you get back; find out the price of that jogging outfit she was found in."

"You got it."

They were hoping to find an address book or possibly a daily log — anything that would give them a couple of names to start with. They didn't have much to go on.

"Joy, thank you so much for your time and helping us out. I know this is a tough time, but if you think of anything, no matter how insignificant, call me or Detective Wade. Please contact me if Gwen Long shows up." She gave Joy a hug as they left.

"Let's head back to the precinct."

"So what's our next step?"

Brockington looked over at Wade. "I think we should get some background on the town of Wilton before we head up there. I'm thinking we leave Friday morning and plan on coming home Sunday. Sorry to your spoil your weekend."

Wade smiled. "You know me, Laura, world traveler that I am. This was my weekend in Vegas, but for you, I will give it up."

"And your wife Linda?"

"You kidding me? Once I tell her, she'll be on the first flight to Chicago to visit our daughter."

"I would feel better about this if we could have spoken to Gwen first, but I'm sure with everything else she's dealing with, taking time to meet with us is far down on her list."

"Don't think I'm an unfeeling jackass, Laura, but I hope you're right."

"Meaning?"

"Think about it. You lose your daughter in a tragic accident and the police want to meet with you about it. Speaking as a dad, I would want to know why detectives keep calling my cell and leaving me voicemails."

Laura shrugged. "You make a valid point."

***

Gwen Long was well aware that Detectives Brockington and Wade wanted to meet with her. She had gotten all their voicemails and she had no intention of reciprocating. She was indeed very distraught over the loss of Peyton. She also knew, like herself, that Peyton was a bit of a risk taker and street tough. Gwen never believed for a minute that Peyton died from an accidental fall. She knew her daughter was not the jogging type. She was more into yoga and meditation. She was no jock. The last thing Gwen Long needed were detectives snooping around her background. They might get suspicious as to why she was on her sixth job as a CPA in a little over two years.

Thursday morning found Gwen Long on her way to the First County Bank of Syracuse. She had received a certified letter from them.

To Gwen Long: First off, from the people and staff of First County, let us offer our sincere condolences on the loss of your daughter Peyton. We like to think of ourselves here as family. If at any time you have questions or we can help in any way, feel free to contact us. You are receiving this letter as required by law in the State of New York. Anyone owning a safety deposit box must have on record an heir in case of loss of life. Peyton Long has listed Gwen Long as her heir. Please bring with you along with this letter two forms of identification, one of which must have a current photo ID. Once again, with deepest symphony, Rod Newhouse President First County Bank of Syracuse.

To say that Gwen Long was surprised that her daughter would have a safe deposit box would be an understatement. What in the world, she thought, could Peyton possibly have owned that would require a safety deposit box? She was a twenty-year-old living week to week like most college coeds.

"Welcome to First County. I'm Beverly. How can I help you today?"

"I received this certified letter in the mail."

Beverly looked at the letter. "Please follow me, Ms. Long. Our manager, Mr. Hendrick, will help you." Beverly walked into the manager's office. Sorry to bother you, sir, but I have a Ms. Long out front." She showed him the letter and he followed out of the office.

"Good morning. I'm Guy Hendrick, Ms. Long. Please come into my office and have a seat. I'm very sorry for your loss." Gwen nodded thank you. "This is just a formality, but by law, I have to ask, may I see a copy of your driver's license and one other piece of identification?"

"I understand." Gwen produced her driver's license and a recent utility bill with her name and address.

"Thank you. I will make a quick copy here. Give me one minute and you can have these back." He left for a few moments and then returned. "There you are, and if you will follow me to the viewing area." Gwen followed him down a narrow corridor into a small room with a long table and chairs. "Ms. Long, have a seat and I will return with your box." Guy Hendricks returned with a long metal safety deposit box. "Here is your key and please take all the time you need. Afterward, if you decide to remove all the contents, let us know and we will close the account. If you decide to keep it open, we will be happy to serve you and make some changes to the account."

"Thank you."

Guy nodded. "You're welcome." He left the room and closed the door. Gwen was nervous, not sure what to expect as she turned the key to the long gray box and lifted the lid. Inside, she found three items. One was Peyton's high school class ring from Ridley with her initials inscribed on the inside.

Gwen laid it aside and pulled the two remaining items: one was a small black and white notebook, the kind you would write reminders to yourself. Next to that was a prepaid cell phone, also known as a pay-as-you-go phone. There is no contract; you paid in advance for a certain amount of data or minutes. When you hit the limit, you paid for the service to buy more time. Gwen knew all about the no-contract phones. She had one for years while struggling to get by and would often have to shorten Peyton's time talking with her friends so as not to run out of minutes. Gwen opened the small notebook. Inside was a list of names. Dr. Robert Weinstein, Lawrence Sinclair also known as Larry, Roger Palmer, Cal Estrada. Next to each name was their street address and city. It seemed they all lived in Wilton, Connecticut. Gwen had never heard of Wilton or knew any of the names in the small notebook. She turned the page. A note read: '*If you are reading this, I have moved on either physically or emotionally. Either way, I'm leaving you with this information to do with what you seem appropriate. Since I could not afford a real insurance policy, I thought this would be the next best thing. The names listed in the notebook will correspond with the voicemail I left on the cell telling you my time spent with them, where I spent it, including all times and dates and my contact at Executive Dating Introduction to verify I knew one of them intimately. I ask that you please be careful. These people are not what they seem and I'm not sure what they are capable of. XX, Peyton*'.

Gwen didn't know what to think; she was totally confused. Hopefully, the cell phone would help clear things up. She turned on the phone and went right to the voicemail, and for the next fifteen minutes, she learned about a life her daughter had been leading and could not believe it.

Gwen learned all about relationship with Roger Palmer and working for Executive Dating Introduction. One part really troubled her as she listened to the voicemail for a third time. "*Roger Palmer and I have been carrying on this arrangement for several months. He seems nice enough, but make no mistake about it, Dr. Robert Weinstein is making all the important decisions among the four. I overheard them speak of a fake charity they run, the Crimson. They use it as a front for some shady business they're all involved in. Not sure what kind of business. When I walked in from the other room, they quickly changed the subject. In the notebook, you will find their home address, job titles, and what they actually do for a living and not the bullshit they told me. I'm convinced their wives have no idea the double lives they're leading, but then again, maybe they don't care. The main reason for this, Dr. Bob, as he is referred to, would like to see me out of the picture, so I figured I had better take out some protection for myself. I will be visiting Wilton in the very near future with some very big news for Roger Palmer. I'm sure he will not be pleased, but if you play the game, sometimes it costs! Feel free to use this information as you see fit, but I urge caution. People with this kind of money and power can be unpredictable.*"

Gwen stopped the voicemail. She had listened to it six times already and her head was spinning. What had Peyton fallen into? Gwen had known from the coroner that Peyton was indeed pregnant at the time of her death. Could this Roger Palmer somehow be involved? Who was this Dr. Bob and what role, if any, did he play in this? Gwen was asking herself all these questions. She knew the right thing to do would be to call those two detectives, Brockington and Wade, who kept calling her, and give them this information. Obviously, that was why they kept blowing up her cell. Gwen leaned back in her chair and stared up at the ceiling for the longest time, looking for answers. She leaned forward and looked at the cell and notebook and decided maybe she should do some research on Wilton and see what it had to offer. It might just be her kind of town.

Gwen carefully put the small notebook, cell phone, and class ring in her purse and closed the box. She stopped by the branch manager's office on the way out.

"Thank you, Mr. Hendricks, for everything, but I believe at this time I will be closing the account and taking the contents of the safety deposit box with me."

"I understand. If we can be of service at any time in the future, please don't hesitate to call me directly. Here is my business card." Gwen smiled, took his card, and exited the bank. The cool, fresh air invigorated her. She needed to get home; she had homework to do. *Where is Wilton Connecticut and what have its residents done to my daughter?*

***

It was 7:00 Friday morning when the Ford Escape left the city of Syracuse.

"How far did you say?"

Detective Wade looked over at his partner. "I didn't, but Mr. Google estimates around 240 miles or four and a half hours, more or less."

"Well then, sir, that being the case, I'm changing the station." Laura smiled and put on her favorite country station.

Wade looked at her. "Really not a sports fan?"

"Talk radio, Ed? You need to take Linda on a vacation."

They both laughed.

"So where did you book us? Someplace special, I hope. We're on the company dime, right?"

Brockington smiled. "I got us a four-star resort, including a massage," she laughed. "I wish. Our allowance for the weekend is $155.00 a night and I had to beg for that. Then he asked if we could share a room."

Wade looked over. "Hey, I'm okay with that if it means saving the city money, of course."

Brockington gave him the old "nice try" look. Men, they were all the same. "Okay, but I will have to call Linda get her approval first."

Detective Wade smiled. "That's all right. Sometimes I snore. We should stick with the separate rooms."

"I thought so. The good news is we will be staying at the lovely Stamford Hotel with a shower, TV, and hopefully, Wi-Fi. I did make sure, yes, free coffee in the lobby."

Wade glanced over. "Oh, what a luxurious life we lead. You did research on Wilton?"

"Ed, that town is flush. It has the one of the largest per capita incomes in the US."

"Sounds like the kind of place a college student living week to week eating Ramen noodles would be found hanging out." Detective Wade smirked. "Nice girl from the local community college drives over 240 miles just to jog in a state park no one's ever heard of. I mean, Quarry Head State Park isn't on anyone's bucket list. Just happens to drive into Wilton for a bottle of water?" Neither detective was buying that story. "So after we check in, where is our first stop?"

"Quarry Head State Park and go over that Jeep."

Detective Wade had arranged in advance to have Ranger

David Shaw meet them. After all, he was there when the body was recovered. Laura found him quiet, unassuming, and friendly, kind of like an older uncle. "Wade, you have the gloves?"

"I do." He handed Laura a pair of nitrile gloves. "David, can I have those keys now?"

Ranger Shaw handed Ed the keys to the Jeep. "You guys don't mind if I hang around and watch, do you? I promise not to get in the way."

Laura looked at David. "I want you here afterward. I need you to take us to the gorge and show us exactly where Peyton's body was found."

Ed unlocked the doors to the Jeep. "I'll take the front. You can start in the back. You have an evidence bag?"

Laura nodded that she did, and for the next ninety minutes, they collected every gum wrapper, pencil, pen — anything that wasn't nailed down — but no cell phone. Ed pulled the green duffel bag from the rear and went through it; nothing out of the ordinary.

"Dammit, Ed. She had to at least had a purse with credit cards and a driver's license. Let's go over it again. Let's try some fresh eyes; you go over the back and I'll do the front seats and dash."

"Works for me."

Laura had her flashlight and was looking under the dashboard when she noticed a slit in the carpet. Under the driver's side seat, she lifted it up and thought to herself, *this is one smart girl.* "Ed, I got the purse!"

"Where was it?" Brockington lifted up the slit in the carpet and there lay a lavender purse.

Wade smiled. This girl was street smart. They laid out the

contents of the purse. Nothing special: credit cards, driver's license, a few family photos, a First County Bank of Syracuse monthly calendar, and $68.00 in cash — not much, but a start. They logged everything they found and ziplocked it.

Laura looked over at Ranger Shaw reading the paper. "Sir, you have been very patient waiting for us, but we're ready to go and see the gorge."

"Not a problem. I appreciate you letting me hang out. Not every day I get to see two detectives in action. Hop in. I'll drive up to the path and we'll hike from there." Brockington and Wade got in the Explorer and made some small talk with Ranger Shaw, who had spent his whole life in the area.

"Tell us about the town of Wilton, David."

"I should warn you, they tend to only like their own, if you get my drift. If you're not driving a BMW or similar, they won't exactly roll out the welcome mat for you, but it's a beautiful town. You will not believe how immaculate it is. Mansions everywhere, pools, huge fountain in the center of town, but hell, they won't even allow a fast food restaurant to open. That's damn near un-American." Everyone laughed. "I guess they figured if they did that, us burger-buying types might converge on their sanctuary."

The trio made their way up the trail toward the gorge. "So, David, why do the locals refer to this as the Devil's Path?"

He looked at Laura and laughed. "You heard that?"

"No, actually, I read it in the paper."

"Well, you know what they say: don't believe everything you read. That's just a name the locals gave. The real name is Old Gorge Road. The Devil's Path name came from years ago. Young couples would sneak up there with their blankets and look at the stars and whatever else and the joke was, *Yeah, we had a good time, but the Devil made me do it.* Of course, those days are long gone. With cell phones and internet, young people don't need to be as creative, but they also missed out on a lot of fun. Well, from here we park and walk up the trail to the gorge."

Detectives Brockington and Wade were impressed, looking out over it. "Quite a view from up top looking down. David, how wide would you guess the path is?"

"No need to guess. At the widest, it is nine feet, six inches; at the narrowest, up around the turn, three feet even. I know because I get asked that a lot. If you notice, Detectives, along the edge, there is a lot of loose gravel. If you're not careful, it is very easy to lose your footing. We believe that's what happened to that young girl."

Laura looked at him. "That may be true, but why jog that close to edge when there is plenty of room in the middle of the path?"

"Maybe like us, she was enjoying the view."

"David, would you take Detective Wade down to the bottom and show him exactly where Peyton was found?"

"I would be glad to."

"Ed, get plenty of photos. While you do that, I'm going to walk this whole path and take some photos from up here." Laura remembered what the coroner had said about Peyton's hands having no scratches of any kind and he was right, there being plenty of small trees and brush to grab on to as she was falling. The path had plenty of room for anyone to jog if that indeed what she was doing up here. After close to an hour, Ranger Shaw and Wade made their way back up top.

Laura looked at Ed, who was a little sweaty and dirty. "Well, anything?"

“Just a lot brush and weeds. I got photos of where she was found and the surrounding area.”

“David, would someone not familiar with this path be able to find it?”

“Not really; just the locals are aware of it. Visitors to the park tend to take the marked trails so they won’t get lost. I mean, this is really off the beaten path, as they say. Chances are very good this wouldn’t be your first trip up here.”

Detectives Brockington and Wade, along with Park Ranger David Shaw, spent close to five hours at Quarry Head State Park. “David, you have been a huge help today and we appreciate it. Ed and I are going to head back to the hotel for a nice shower and dinner and call it day.”

“It was my pleasure, and if you’re looking for a good Italian meal close by, I recommend Casa del Sol on Market Street. Very good and won’t break the bank and for you. Detective Wade, they have over twenty beers on tap.”

Brockington and Wade both smiled. “We’re in.”

Chapter Nine

"Lauren, you must be stronger with your backhand. Try a more fluid swing. You're lunging at the ball."

Lauren Palmer nodded as her private tennis coach Lars continued to hit balls across the net to her. She enjoyed tennis, but more importantly, she liked belonging to an exclusive club like the Ball and Thistle Racket Club. This was where the wealthy — and there were many in Wilton — liked to spend their free time. The initiation fee of $250,000 plus yearly annual membership fee of $25,000 entitled members to the pools, both indoor and outdoor, lighted outdoor tennis courts and indoor courts for winter, a masseuse on the premises at all times, a beautiful oak bar where no money ever changed hands; you simply showed your card and drinks were billed to your account. Of course, when a glass of Chardonnay went for $18.00, that was good business for the club. When patrons didn't see the bill in front of them, they tended to spend more.

After her morning lesson, Lauren had her usual deep tissue massage, and then, after a shower, she made her way to the bar. For lunch, a salad and a glass of wine. She could never get Roger to join the club. He was not the athletic type, so while she spent time at the club, Roger pursued his favorite pastime, skydiving, something he could never talk her into trying. "Lauren," he would say, "It's such a rush; it's almost better than sex. When he would say that, she had to keep a straight face because, for her, sex with Roger was about as exciting as watching paint dry.

Lauren met Roger through a friend and thought he was nice enough but wasn't really in her league. She asked her friend Rebecca, "Why the date? He isn't really my type."

"Of course he's your type: a research chemist making six figures."

Lauren Dilworth immediately fell in love. To her, it was a marriage of convenience. No, she wasn't in love with Roger, but as they say, the job paid well and had great benefits.

"Is this seat taken?"

Lauren smiled as the gentleman sat down next to her. "I didn't think you were going to show."

"Tony."

"Yes, sir, what can I get you today?"

"I'll have an old-fashioned and refresh the lady's wine, would you please?"

"Coming right up."

"I got your text, but I had a morning appointment I needed to keep."

Tony poured Lauren a fresh glass of wine and her friend the old-fashioned.

"I assume that Roger is busy this morning?"

"Skydiving as we speak, so I don't expect him home until after two at the earliest." As she casually but cautiously slid her hand onto his thigh, they made small talk for another fifteen minutes. Lauren finished her second glass of wine, got up, flashed her pearly whites, and left. More than one head at the bar glanced over as she walked away. Lauren Palmer was a head turner. She knew it and she used it to her advantage.

"Tony, if you would be so kind, sir, I'll have one more."

Tony nodded. "One old-fashioned on the way."

***

It was just after 1:00 pm Saturday afternoon when the white Ford Escape pulled into the Wilton Town Police Department. Detective Laura Brockington thought it would be the right thing to do to pay a courtesy call on the chief of police and inform him why they were in town. Detectives Brockington and Wade had spent the morning riding around the town and getting a feel for it. What they felt was money and a lot of it. They were thoroughly impressed by the police barracks; everything was immaculate, from the brick paved entrance way to the tile floors that glistened. They were met at front desk by the sergeant, who directed them to the office of Eric Snow, Chief of Police.

Chief Snow had been in command for over twelve years in Wilton, coming from the State Police Force in Tennessee. He stood just under six feet tall and was stocky. He looked to be in his early sixties with thinning dark hair that was quickly receding. "Welcome to Wilton, Detectives," he said as they shook hands. "Please have a seat. I was surprised but pleased to get your e-mail last night. I do appreciate that, letting me know you're in town. I'm not real sure what you're looking to accomplish."

Detective Brockington did the talking. "Chief, it's like I said in the email. We're basically covering all the possibilities about Peyton Long."

“Yes, I kind of understand that. But first off, she fell while jogging over eight miles from Wilton and I know the park backs up to the town line and the residents here consider it their own, but it’s really not part of Wilton, so why are you here?”

“Chief, don’t you find it strange that a young girl would drive over 250 miles to go jogging in some obscure state park that most people never knew existed?”

“Did you ever consider, Detective Brockington, that maybe that’s her thing, running in different areas?”

Detective Wade was up looking at all the black and white photographs lining the office walls. Chief Snow looked over and smiled. “You like those?”

“I do. Friends of yours?”

“Absolutely. They are residents of this close-knit community. Those photos were taken doing different fundraisers for the police department. People here give generously and appreciate the work we do. It makes for a great partnership. One group in particular, the Crimson, donated last year alone over $200,000.”

Detective Wade nodded. “Very impressive.” He came and sat back down.

“Chief, I know for a fact that Peyton Long was indeed in Wilton. Ed, can I have the receipt?” He handed Brockington a slip of paper and she showed to the chief, who looked it over and shrugged.

“This shows what exactly?”

“It proves the day before she ended up at bottom of a gorge, she was here in town at Janzen’s Market making a purchase of bottled water and a pack of cupcakes.”

“So, Detective, she was out jogging and got thirsty.

Nothing unusual about that."

"They have bottled water and snacks at the park ranger's office and it doesn't cost $3.00, so like you said, why drive eight miles into town?"

The chief was becoming noticeably annoyed with where the conversation was heading. "Detective Brockington, I know of your background and the fact that you helped to break one the biggest cases in New York City last year. I congratulate you on that, but nothing much happens here in Wilton. Oh, I get the occasional rich kid stopped for a DUI driving the BMW that he owns at the ripe old age of sixteen and his parents come in and plead their case that little Johnny is heading to Stanford or some other Ivy league school next year and this needs to go away if possible, and you know what I do, Detective? I smile and I look at my fat pension that this town provides and little Johnny gets to go to Stanford next year. I'm not sure what you're hoping to find here, Detectives, but there is no crime wave taking place in Wilton. I'm sorry that young girl lost her life while jogging, but accidents happen even in the best neighborhoods."

Detective Brockington got the message there was nothing here for her to find and she should move on. Chief Snow had seriously underestimated her. Brockington rose to leave. It had been less than half an hour. There was no need for further discussion. "Thanks for taking the time this morning, Chief. I know you're busy."

"It was my pleasure, Detectives, and tell the fine men in blue back in Syracuse I send my best." They all shook hands and parted ways.

Once back in the Ford Escape, Wade looked over at Brockington. "What in the hell just happened?"

"I believe we were informed that the very wealthy never commit any crimes." They both started laughing. "It's safe to say we're getting no cooperation from the local police department."

"So where do we go from here?"

Brockington looked over at her partner. "Do you think it was an accident?"

"No way, and I did a price check on that jogging suit Peyton was found in. The average was $195.00 and the sneakers $165.00. For someone on her budget, no way she paid for it."

"Let's go into town and park. I would like to walk around Main Street and get a feel for the town."

"While we're doing that, I'll make some calls and have Peyton's Jeep towed back to Syracuse. We're missing something and I know it's right in front of us."

***

It was 1:30 am when the call came in. "Station 51 Ladder 42, fire and smoke reported at 6 Cherry Blossom Lane, Pelican Hills Crest." The fire house roared to life.

Marie Weinstein was sound asleep when she was startled by the sounds of fire engines and bright lights roaring past her home. She still wasn't sure what all the commotion was about. After all, in Pelican Hills, it was normally so quiet in the evenings, you could hear the crickets after dark.

It was dark in the bedroom and she didn't want to disturb Dr. Bob. She went over and opened the large double doors to the bedroom balcony. Down below, several neighbors in bathrobes and slippers were running past her house and then the roar and sirens of fire trucks barreling down the road, lights and sirens blaring. She hurried onto the balcony and looked to her left. She could not believe what she was seeing. "Oh my God!" She went running back into the bedroom. The sounds of sirens and Marie's scream woke Dr. Bob.

"Marie, what the hell is going on?"

"Bob, it's the Weatherhills' estate. It's on fire!"

"What?" Bob quickly ran onto the balcony, and there to his left, the estate just two acers away, he could see the flames shooting skyward from the residence.

The sounds of sirens, flashing lights, and bullhorns could be heard.

"Let's go! I want that ladder up on the roof now!" came the screams.

More neighbors came running past to see what all the commotion was about. They gasped with disbelief as they watched from a distance.

Two more fire trucks came roaring past, more lights and sirens piercing the crisp night air.

"Are you coming?"

"No, I think I'll watch from here. You go ahead down with the rest of the neighbors."

Marie quickly threw on her robe and slippers and Bob watched as she made her way down the driveway to join the rest of the onlookers.

Dr. Bob went back into the bedroom, put on his thick robe, got a bottle of brandy and a cigar from his nightstand, and returned to the balcony. All the neighbors watched in horror as the flames shot from the roof of the Weatherhills' estate and then heard a huge explosion and the sounds of glass shattering. The intense heat had blown out the glass doors and windows.

Now the mansion was now fully engulfed.

"Come on, men, give me more water on the other side. Let's go here! Come on, more hose, men. Hustle, hustle, get that damn ladder truck overhead now. Let's go!" came the commands through the bullhorn.

The spotlights shone on the mansion, not that they were needed; the fire alone lit up the sky. There must have been two dozen firemen and they fought valiantly, but it was becoming obvious to everyone who had gathered to watch it was a losing battle for all the noise, commotion, and yelling from the bullhorn. You could have heard a pin drop among the onlookers, who were stunned as they watched this beautiful home burn.

Dr. Bob stretched out in his lounge chair, lit a nice Cuban cigar, and then poured himself a brandy. He watched from his chaise lounge with the lit cigar, inhaled, then his exhale blew smoke rings into the dark sky. He smiled to himself and then sipped his brandy.

Dr. Bob's dinner at Sparks Steak House with his old friend Big Ben Logan had been expensive, $50,000 to be exact, but FBI special agent Gary Covington and his wife Sara would not be moving into 6 Cherry Blossom Lane next week, not next month, not ever.

***

Sunday morning at eight o'clock after getting his morning shower, Dr. Bob made his way down to the kitchen. The smell of bacon and eggs was already underway, as Marie always made Sunday breakfast. Dr. Bob grabbed a cup of coffee and walked down the long driveway to retrieve the Sunday paper.

He looked across the perfectly kept green lawn and saw the yellow tape stretching all the way around the Weatherhills' estate, the smell of burnt embers still in the air.

Where once stood a palatial estate with neatly manicured hedges and gorgeous white dogwood trees was now nothing more than a hollowed burned-out building waiting to be bulldozed.

Bob sat down at the breakfast counter and Marie joined him. "Toast, Bob?"

"Sure." Marie buttered his toast and sipped her coffee while they ate.

"I still cannot believe last night that beautiful home ruined. Thank the good Lord no one was home." Bob nodded in agreement. "What could cause such a fire?"

"I have no idea. Like you, just so glad no one was home."

"Bob, what happens now? I mean, the house was sold, right?"

"According to Cal, I believe he said settlement was scheduled for sometime late next week, and if that's the case, then the house still belongs to the Weatherhills."

"Oh, that's terrible for them and that new couple. I think their last name was Covington. And I was so looking forward to having new neighbors. It would have been nice. We could have had them over and gotten to know them. We may have hit it off."

"I feel the same way." Dr. Bob opened up his paper and started to read the sports section and drink his coffee. Everything at 4 Cherry Blossom Lane was just fine.

***

It was Monday morning and Dr. Robert Weinstein was heading to the office when he noticed the Weatherhills walking around their burned-out home. They had been neighbors for over twenty years and Bob felt the need to stop. He pulled his Mercedes into the driveway and immediately Phillip and Kate made their way over.

Bob got out and all three hugged. “Phillip, Kate, I don’t know what to say.” Tears were running down Kate’s face.

“What happened?”

“We just got in from Florida this morning, Bob. We’re just in shock. The Wilton Police called me in the early hours of Saturday morning and told us about the fire.” Kate walked over and gave Bob another hug. “You men talk. I’m going for a walk around the old neighborhood. I need to gather all this in.”

“What was the cause, Phil?”

“They told me from the investigation that it looks like the whole fuse box panel just exploded, probably from some sort of wiring malfunction, causing it to overload.”

“But didn’t you just sell the house?”

“No. Settlement was in ten days, ten stinking days.”

“So now what happens?”

“We have to wait for the insurance adjuster, all kinds of paperwork. We’re talking at least six months before all this is settled and we’re paid, and to top that off, I will lose close to a quarter million! From the selling price, the Covingtons were paying top dollar and now this. Unbelievable.”

“Phillip, I don’t have words to tell you how sorry I am. Just so glad you and Kate were not home.”

“I know I should be thankful no one was hurt, but we loved this home. To see it like this… They will want this leveled in three weeks tops. Gone like that!" Phillip snapped his fingers.

Dr. Bob put his arm around Phillip. "I know in my heart this will work out for you and Kate."

Phillip smiled. "Thanks, Bob."

"I'm curious. I met them once; what will the Covingtons do? Any idea?"

"I talked to him yesterday. Told me he was sorry and they may move to Hartford now. I lose all the way around."

"Phillip, you and Kate are now in Florida and I was hoping to strike up a new friendship with the Covingtons." They spent another twenty minutes talking about old times.

Dr. Bob said his good-byes and pulled his Mercedes out of the driveway. He made his way through Wilton. He had one last stop to make before going to the office.

"Good morning, Dr. Weinstein. This is a nice surprise."

"Thank you, Sharon. Nice to see you again. Is Cal in this morning?"

"He is."

"Don't bother to buzz him; he always likes to see me. I'll just barge in."

Sharon smiled. "Okay with me." Dr. Bob often wondered about Sharon and Cal. She was quite a looker, tall with shoulder-length brown hair and a great smile.

Cal looked up from his computer as Bob walked in.

"I would say I was surprised to see you, being how busy you've been lately."

Bob sat down on the adjoining sofa. "Now is that any way to greet your partner? I thought for sure you would be giving me a big hug."

Cal just looked at Bob and took a drink of coffee. "You

know this is some serious shit that went down."

"It's business, Cal. I couldn't take the chance. I live in a nice neighborhood and to let some outsider move in could depreciate the property values."

"Very funny. I hope you know what the fuck you're doing and covered everything. We don't need some arson investigator snooping around."

"I did, my friend, and let's not forget, if you had covered everything beforehand, this never would have been necessary, so let's put it to bed and move on. How is Susan?"

"She's fine. Thanks for asking."

"Listen, let's get together for dinner this weekend. We'll go to that new place La Bec's. Supposedly really good and the wives can get drunk and we'll take advantage of them. Who knows, with enough wine, we can talk them into swapping for one night. I mean, they're both attractive."

"You know, it's hard to believe you're a doctor, because you're one sick fuck!" Cal was laughing. "Count us in. I'll have Susan make reservations."

Bob went over and gave his partner a hug. "Nothing to worry about. I only hire the best."

Chapter Ten

Three weeks later

The white Escape pulled next to the curb with Detective Ed Wade at the wheel and Detective Laura Brockington riding along. it had taken some time, but with the help of the Department of Motors Vehicles, they had managed to find the townhouse of Gwen Cox Long, 22 Bernard Blvd. They were nice townhouses, middle class, and the surrounding neighborhood safe with little crime. They had been parked for over an hour when a black Jetta pulled into the parking space. The two detectives exited the car and approached the Jetta. The occupant was on her cell, when she saw the two detective approach, and quickly hung up. She put her window down.

"Can I help you?"

"Yes. Ms. Long?"

"Yes."

"I'm Detective Laura Brockington and my partner Detective Wade." They showed their IDs and she exited the car.

"I've have gotten your voicemails, Detectives, but to say this has been a very trying time would be putting it mildly, which is why I haven't returned your calls."

Laura nodded. "Perfectly understandable, and I hate to intrude at a time like this, but if we could just have twenty minutes of your time to help us clear up a few things, it would be greatly appreciated."

"Of course, although I don't know how I can help."

"We just need a few questions answered that maybe you can help us with."

Gwen nodded slightly and shrugged her shoulders, obviously annoyed, but she agreed. They followed Gwen into her townhouse and had a seat on the green sofa. The townhouse was nicely decorated, a lot of artwork on the walls with a built-in brick fireplace and wood floors that shined. Gwen took a seat across from the detectives.

"You have a lovely home," remarked Laura.

"Thank you. Can I get either of you something to drink?" Both declined but thanked her. Detective Brockington would ask the questions as Detective Wade took notes.

"Ms. Long—"

"Please, call me Gwen."

"Gwen, did you know that Peyton was pregnant?"

"Not until the coroner told me, and yes, I was surprised."

"Did you know of anyone Peyton was dating at the time?"

"No, Peyton and I didn't discuss her love life. She never confided in me who she was dating."

"So, besides being a full-time student, Peyton worked?"

"She did, as a part-time bartender. I think it was called the Oyster Shooter, but I'm not positive. It was a college bar."

"Did Peyton have any friends in Wilton she may have been visiting?"

"Not that I knew of, and honestly, I never even heard of

Wilton until this, but I understand it's a very wealthy community."

"Was Peyton always into jogging?"

"I knew she cared about her looks like all young people, so I assume it was something she took up recently."

"We were unable to locate her cell phone. I assume she had one?"

"Of course."

"Would you be able to provide us with her number?"

"I don't see why not, but Detective Brockington, why all these questions when my daughter died from an accidental fall?"

"The State of New York requires that any resident who dies out of state for other than natural causes, we have to fill out this inquiry. Basically, dot all the I's and cross all the T's, just a formality."

"I see. I understand the Syracuse Police Department has possession of Peyton's Jeep. Any idea when I can retrieve it? I would like to get that matter settled with the insurance company and the bank."

"Yes, I'll have Detective Wade check on that and give you a call this week."

Gwen smiled approvingly.

"When was your last conversation with Peyton?"

"Just guessing, I would say the Friday before she was found, just one of those short I-love-you phone calls."

"Did Peyton say anything about going for an interview?"

"Not to me." They asked Gwen several more questions and she mostly answered in three words or less. The interview had been a waste of time and they couldn't figure out why her answers were so stock. Detective Brockington was sure Gwen

Long knew something, but she had no intention of sharing it.

Gwen Long certainly didn't buy the old line about the State of New York required it, but played right along. She was very attractive and more intelligent than she was letting on.

Back in the car, Wade looked over at his partner. "So what are your thoughts on the grieving mother?"

"You took the words right out of my mouth. Ed, when we get back, take that cell number she gave us of Peyton's and see if you can find out when it was last used from what location and who that call went to. For the life of me, I don't understand her lack of cooperation and her attitude. Very matter of fact."

Ed agreed. "She was pleasant, but distant."

***

Roger Palmer was excited as he drove through Wilton. It was Friday morning and he had the day off. Lauren had decided to come and watch him jump, as he called it. Skydiving was Roger's one true passion.

"Honey, I've made over 300 jumps. We could do a tandem with the GoPro on. It would make an awesome video."

Lauren laughed. "You're out of your fucking mind if you think I'm jumping out of an airplane. I don't care if you made over 3000 jumps, as you call it. I will wait on the ground with my iPhone and will film you to the best of my ability with my two feet planted safely on Planet Earth."

"Lauren, I guarantee you. One jump and you will want to do it again. The rush you get, it's unbelievable."

"I'll take your word for it." As she smiled, she asked, "Do you know how safe it is?"

"I mean, that's always the question people ask me. Do you

realize there are an estimated three million jumps per year and the fatality count is only twenty-one? That's like 0. 0007% chance of dying from skydiving compared to 0. 0167% of dying in an automobile."

"That's impressive you would know that statistic. So tell me, how many people died while on the ground watching people jump out of airplanes?"

"You're such a smart ass." Roger was laughing as he whipped his white Mustang into the small airport and grabbed his gear. Lauren gave him a quick kiss and got on the trunk of the Mustang.

It was a nice clear day, nearly 65 degrees, with no wind, which made it feel warmer. Lauren had on a white nylon jacket and tight blue jeans. She flipped her sunglasses down and stretched her legs across the trunk and leaned back against the glass. She read through the emails on her iPhone. She wondered how a man who was so boring in bed could have such a dangerous outlet for his hobby.

"Hello."

Lauren sat up quickly. "Hello."

"Sorry, didn't mean to interrupt you. Tyler Drake. I work here at the airport. I noticed Roger's car. It's a gem."

"Thanks, no, you didn't interrupt at all. I'm Lauren, Roger's wife."

"Glad to meet you. I assume Roger is jumping today?"

"Yup, not me." She smiled. "I'm just here to clap when he lands." Tyler laughed. "Do you jump?"

"I have but not much anymore, but I know most of the guys who jump. I met Roger a couple times just in passing."

"So you work here doing what exactly?"

"I do several things around the airport, but my main job

here is I pack parachutes."

"No way, are you serious?"

"I honestly do and everybody has the same reaction when I tell them that." Lauren slid her legs down off the back of the Mustang and let them dangle over the edge. She found Tyler Drake ruggedly attractive with dark black wavy hair, tall with a nice build, not a muscle-head, a diamond stud earring in one ear with green eyes and she liked the way he filled out his jeans.

"I always thought a machine packed the parachutes. Now I feel really stupid."

"Don't. Everybody thinks that. A few of the guys will pack their own, but mostly they pay someone like me to."

"So where did you learn how to do that?"

"I was in the Air Force and it was part of my training. I also worked in communications. That was a few years back. Needless to say, packing chutes is one of the rare jobs where you're never allowed to make a mistake."

Lauren laughed. "That's true. I never thought of it like that. I find it fascinating," she said as she bit her lower lip, obviously flirting.

"Listen, if you like sometime, come by and I will show you how it's done."

"I would love that."

Tyler smiled, took a pen from his pocket, and wrote down his cell number. "Feel free to text me anytime. I'm usually here a few days a week." Lauren took the number and stuck it in her jeans pocket. "I have to get to work. It was very nice meeting you."

"Likewise." Lauren watched as Tyler walked across the parking lot and slid back up the trunk and leaned against the glass and thought to herself *maybe this outing wasn't such a waste of my time after all.*

***

Over the years, the charitable group the Crimson had raised money for several causes in Wilton. Occasionally, an outside organization would offer financial support for their cause. It was usually several hundred dollars. They would use the donation as a tax write-off. Dr. Bob or another member of his group would receive the check, shake some hands, and take pictures for publicity, and that was pretty much it.

Dr. Robert Weinstein was at the Kobe Japanese restaurant for one such occasion, having received a certified letter offering his foundation $5,000 toward the renovation of a local landmark. The letter was sent from Gwen Cox Associates and Dr. Bob was more than happy to meet for dinner and accept the funds. He found Gwen Cox attractive. She looked to be in her early forties with short reddish-brown hair on her petite frame with wire-rimmed glasses and a nice smile. They had a private booth in the back and were having drinks, Dr. Bob with a glass of chardonnay and Gwen with a margarita.

"I have to ask, how did the Cox Organization hear about the Crimson and why our charity?"

Gwen smiled. "Let's discuss business after dinner, shall we? Tell me about your medical practice."

Bob was pleased; he loved to talk about his practice and how it got started.

"So, the name the Crimson arose from your days as a student at Harvard?"

"Correct." Dr. Bob filled Gwen in on his practice and his

need to give back to the community that had given him so much. The Crimson charity was his way of doing so.

"That is quite a success story and the fact that your college friends are part of this charity is just remarkable. You and your friends should be proud of what you have accomplished."

"Thank you. We feel an obligation to give back."

Gwen raised her glass and clicked hers with Dr. Bob's. "So do I." They enjoyed some Asian cuisine and quiet conversation. Gwen asked the waiter for another round of drinks then asked not to be disturbed. The waiter nodded politely. "Dr. Weinstein, you asked me earlier why I chose the Crimson charity to donate and the answer is simple. Really, you chose me."

Dr. Bob had a look of confusion on his face. "I don't follow."

Gwen smiled. "Maybe this will help." She took an 8x10 color photograph from her purse and laid it on the table. "This, Doctor, is my daughter, Peyton Long."

The good doctor recognized the face immediately and took the glass of chardonnay he was enjoying and set it down. The smile had disappeared from his face and was replaced by a look of apprehension, but as always, he remained calm in the moment. "This is your daughter? Have I met her?"

Gwen looked him straight in the eye. "First off, Doctor, let me assure you I'm not wearing a wire or any other type of recording device and I will understand after I tell you a few things in the next few minutes if you decide not to say a word. I know all about your charity the Crimson and how it's used as a front to conceal your business enterprises. "You see, Dr. Weinstein, my daughter Peyton was extremely smart in ways that academics like yourself wouldn't understand. Before she suddenly died, she had the wisdom to rent a safety deposit box at the First County Bank of Syracuse and left me few items, two of which I think you will find of immense importance to the future of your charity, not to mention your own and those of your group." Dr. Bob still wasn't saying a word, but he could feel tightness in his chest. Gwen took a cell phone from her purse and a small notebook. She opened it up. "Doctor, that is your home address and your office address. Next, the home addresses of Cal Estrada, Lawrence Sinclair, also known as Larry, and Roger Palmer." Gwen then went to the cell and held it in her hands. This takes me back, Doctor, when I was a struggling single mom. I'm sure you have no idea what a pay-as-you-go phone is, but at the time, it was what I could afford and now it seems my life has come full circle. On this phone, Peyton tells me all about Roger Palmer and his bullshit story of being a pharmaceutical rep, when of course, we know he is a research chemist. About the weekends in Miami at the swank Emerald Palace Hotel, and of course, your lovely dates for the evening. Now you're thinking what married men do in their private lives is their business and you would be correct. But here is where it gets interesting. I bet you didn't know because it wasn't on the evening news that at the time of her death, Peyton Long was six weeks pregnant. I didn't know that either until the coroner told me. Here is another little caveat for you to think about. Two Syracuse detectives, a Laura Brockington and an Ed Wade, made several attempts to contact me. I put them off for a while, but you know how damn persistent they can be. It seems they cannot understand why a young college student would travel over 250 miles to go for a run on some trail that most locals wouldn't even know how to find. They know she visited Wilton. It seems she stopped at the local convenience store, Janzen's, for a snack and a bottle of water, and by sheer coincidence, that receipt was inside her shirt pocket, not the pocket of that four-hundred-dollar jogging suit she was wearing. I assume someone didn't check her pockets.

"Doctor, you see my predicament. I happen to think that Peyton was in town to break the big news of her being with child to your colleague Roger Palmer, and being a happily married man, I'm assuming he was less than thrilled. Understand, on my part, this is just pure speculation.

"I guess the right thing to do would be to inform those nice detectives about this phone and address book, but I'm inclined not to do so for several reasons.

"You see, Doctor, I understand that my daughter Peyton was no saint; she decided to date a married man for money. She's not the first female to do so and she certainly will not be the last. So I have a proposal I think will help us both in this situation we find ourselves in. I see no reason to ever inform those detectives of this information. I would feel good about it for a while and they would do a very thorough investigation and who knows what all they might uncover. They would send me a nice letter of appreciation. They might earn a promotion, and two weeks later, I'm back working 9-5 every day, and honestly, it's getting a little tiring. It would be nice to spend more time at the beach.

"And that's where the Crimson charity can help me. Since there are four members, I was thinking if each could find within their hearts to donate, say, $500,000, I'm sure all this would go away, no phone, no address book. It will be as if Peyton never visited Wilton or ever heard of Roger Palmer." Gwen turned her glass of wine up and finished it. She looked across the table at Dr. Bob. He didn't even acknowledge she had been talking. He turned his drink up, finished it, and sat it down on the table.

Dr. Bob got up and put on his coat. "It was a pleasure meeting you, Ms. Long. I'm sure we'll talk in the future."

"Looking forward to it, Doctor, and, please, dinner is on me tonight. You have a safe ride home."

Gwen watched as Dr. Bob exited the restaurant. She ordered another drink. She was in a celebratory mood. It seemed the prospects of an early retirement had just improved dramatically.

***

Dr. Bob Weinstein backed his silver Mercedes out of the parking spot. It was already dark, as night had settled in. The restaurant parking lot was well-lit as he drove around twice to make sure, and he was right; there was only one license plate from New York State on a black Jetta. He took his iPhone and used the camera to snap a picture of the tag. Bob smiled to himself. *Carelessness,* he thought, putting on some soft jazz. He was prone to moments of uncontrollable anger, but very few people knew it, not even his closest family members. He would soothe his anger in private with soft jazz; it always seemed to calm him.

He drove along the parkway, finally coming to the archway of Mayfair Biotec with the billboard greeting "Researching Your Tomorrows Today."

It was quiet. Everyone had left for the day. The guard house was empty, but sure enough, just as he thought, there sat the pearl white Mustang belonging to Roger Palmer. It was very dark; the street lights were on and the night air was still.

Robert Weinstein parked and listened to the soft jazz play for another minute and then turned down his radio and exited the Mercedes, but left it running. He went the rear and popped open the trunk of his car and grabbed the Louisville Slugger baseball bat he had since college and walked over to the pearl white Mustang and thought to himself, *Roger, you fucking idiot*, and then the sound of breaking glass shattered the quiet of the night. First the windshield and then the headlights. The rear window was next, glass shattering and lying everywhere. Bob then smashed in the driver's side door. For another five minutes, he smashed everything he could — taillights, side mirrors — and then he very calmly returned to his car and put the baseball bat back in the trunk.

Dr. Bob slid into the Mercedes and turned his soft jazz back on and looked over at the dream car that Roger Palmer was so proud of. It looked like it had been broadsided by a cement truck. Bob looked at himself in the rearview mirror, combed his hair, and quietly left the parking lot.

Chapter Eleven

It was Thursday morning and Roger and Lauren Palmer were sharing breakfast before he headed off to work. "I still cannot fucking believe it. Who the fuck destroys a beautiful car just for the hell of it?"

"Honey, relax and finish your coffee. It's like the police said, probably just a bunch of high school punks with free time on their hands. The insurance company will pay."

"You don't understand. It's not the money. It's a guy thing. Fucking assholes. So you're dropping me off this morning, correct?"

"Of course. My lesson isn't until ten; I have plenty of time."

"Yeah, I wouldn't want you to be late for your lesson."

"What do you mean by that?"

"Sorry, I'm just really pissed about the car."

"Do you need a ride home?"

"No, I'll have one of the guys drop me. Did you talk to Marie?"

"Not recently."

"Bob wants to have a guy's-only night at his place this Saturday to discuss the business. Some shit about taxes and

Marie thought you girls could go out for dinner while we're busy."

"Sounds fine by me. I'll give her a call later. Honey, I was wondering watching you jump the other day. How long does it take to get your parachute ready?"

"I have no idea, now that you mention it. Never gave it much thought. I pay someone to do it. What made you ask that?"

Lauren looked across the table at him and smiled. "I worry about you."

Roger smiled back. "Thanks. We better get going; I have a meeting this morning with the New Director, Chip Conlan. Rumor has it he was such an asshole at the main headquarters in Pennsylvania, they threw an office party the day he left."

Lauren got in the driver seat of her Land Rover wearing her short tennis dress with white sneakers. She knew the guys at the club liked to check her out, so she made sure she looked good. Roger didn't notice and it used to piss her off that he never complimented her. Now she knew it was because he was just a nerd who probably preferred watching *National Geographic* to looking at women. She looked over and he was half asleep. "Roger, are you falling asleep?"

"Sorry, I'm beat this morning. I couldn't fall asleep last night. I go to the medicine cabinet to get a sleeping pill and the damn bottle of Restoril was empty. I thought for sure I had two left. I'm really careful with that shit."

"Honey, now think for a minute. Who else takes them but you?"

"I guess I miscounted. This has been one fucked-up week already and it's only Wednesday."

Lauren pulled into the parking area and gave Roger a kiss.

"Have a good day. I'll make a nice dinner tonight."

"That sounds good. Have fun at your tennis thing." Roger exited the car and she thought to herself, *it's nice to have a husband with blind loyalty*. It was the key to their marriage.

***

"Doc, I appreciate the call. I didn't even realize it had been two years since my last physical."

"Don't thank me, Chief. I had nothing to do with it. My office manager Sandy was going over our patient records and noticed." Chief Eric Snow of the Wilton Police sat on the edge of the examining table as Dr. Robert Weinstein took his blood pressure. "That should about do it. From what I see, everything looks good. All your vitals are well within range. I should have all your bloodwork back in about a week. If there is anything, I'll call you."

"Sounds good." The chief sat up and started to button up his shirt.

"Chief, I heard about that young girl falling out at the park while jogging. Such a tragedy."

"Tell me about it. That was a real unfortunate accident, and get this, Doc. Two detectives from New York drove all way up to Wilton to question me about it. What a wasted trip."

"Two detectives? For what purpose?"

"Who knows? Just wasting taxpayer time and money. One was some hot-shot detective pretty well-known in police circles, but I set them straight. I told them the only crime in this town is if someone spends less than $50,000 on a car." Both men started laughing.

"That's pretty funny, Chief. I still don't understand why

they bothered you. Quarry Head is almost eight miles from Wilton."

"Doc, I told them the same thing. It seems the girl stopped by Janzen's Market for a bottle of water on Saturday. When they found her Sunday morning, she had the receipt in her shirt pocket."

Dr. Bob looked up from filling out his medical chart. "Just sorry to hear about it."

"Yeah, Doc, me too."

"Well, that does it for today. Just stop by and see Sandy on your way out."

"Oh, you can be sure of that!"

Dr. Bob just nodded, making sure to keep with his professional appearance at all times. He went into his office and closed the door. He walked over along the back wall of his office. He had put up a nice full-size dart board. He removed the darts from the case and walked back exactly seven feet, nine inches where he had a tape mark. He took one dart, and with all his strength, fired it into the dartboard.

Gwen Long had not been bluffing; she knew all about Roger Palmer and Peyton. Police detectives had contacted her. He fired another dart into the board. Everything they had worked for was in jeopardy all because Roger Palmer insisted on breaking with protocol and seeing the same girl more than once. Bob Weinstein was a stickler for details, and now, for the second time in less than three months, he found himself having to clean up someone else's mess. He fired another dart into the board. He then regained his control and went out to the waiting area.

"Sandy, you can send in Ms. Harvey now? I'm ready for her."

Sandy smiled. "I'll bring her right back. Is Chief Snow okay? He's a family friend?"

"Yes, he called me last night. Was feeling some angina in his chest, so I had him come in for a check-up, but everything was fine."

"Good to hear."

***

Detective Laura Brockington was down in the motor pool watching the professionals take apart the green Jeep owned by Peyton Long. It was Thursday afternoon and Gwen Long had arranged for someone pick it up Friday morning. Laura waited patiently, as they had basically removed everything. She approached the head mechanic, Mark.

"Anything?"

"Sorry, Detective. Nothing. We even took the dashboard apart. Is there anything special you're looking for?"

"I was hoping maybe we missed something — address book, phone number, anything."

"It's probably nothing, but we did find the payment book for the Jeep." He handed Laura a zip-lock bag.

Laura took out the book. Still four payments owed to the First County Bank of Syracuse. "I appreciate your effort."

"Anytime, Detective."

The payment book itself was of little value and they had hit a dead-end. Laura made her way back upstairs. She stopped by her partner's desk. "Ed, any word on that cell number Gwen provided of Peyton's?"

"Yeah, she was a big help. I spent over three hours making calls and practically begging the phone company for information. Of course I got the old 'you need a court order.' Finally, one reasonable guy called me back to let me know I was wasting my time. That number belongs to one of those pay-as-you-go phones and hasn't been used in over eighteen months. Gwen Long gave us bullshit."

Unlike TV and the movies, real life detectives are often working anywhere from two to four cases at one time, Chief Gary Spence had been lenient on the Peyton Long case, but Laura Brockington had been around long enough to know she needed something quickly before this case would be put on the backburner.

"Ed, grab your coat."

"Where we off to?"

"The First County Bank of Syracuse. I'll explain on the way."

At 11:00 a.m., Detectives Brockington and Wade found themselves meeting with the branch manager of First County Bank of Syracuse Guy Hendricks in his office.

"Yes, of course I know the name. Such a sad situation, the loss of such a young person. I did not know her personally. We honestly have thousands of customers."

"Mr. Hendrick, we were going through the 2008 Jeep owned by Peyton and came across this payment book. It seems she still had four more payments until it was paid off."

Guy Hendrick looked at the book. "Yes, that's one of ours. There is the possibility since she took out a bank loan, she may have taken the insurance offered on it in case something like this occurred and that would pay it off."

"I'm sorry, that's really not what I meant. Is there a chance that Peyton also had a checking account here?"

"Give me five minutes. I can find out. Be right back."

"Ed, what gives with the checking account?"

"Joy said whenever Peyton took one of her weekend jaunts, she always returned with extra income. Maybe we'll get lucky and her sugar daddy paid by check."

"Damn, I never thought about that. If we could only be so lucky."

Guy Hendrick returned and sat down. "Sorry, Detectives, no checking or saving account; just the safety deposit box."

"Peyton Long had a safety deposit box?" Laura asked, questioning what she heard.

"Yes, just last week, her mother Gwen, being named as the beneficiary, came in and removed its contents. I know what you're thinking, Detectives, and yes, it's unusual for such a young person, but you never know what someone considers valuable."

Detective Brockington had just stumbled onto something and she knew it. "Does the bank have a copy of its contents?"

"We do — it's the law — but as you know, there are specific provisions as to who can view it, and without a court order, I cannot let you."

"Did Gwen Long come alone?"

"She did and was very pleasant, considering the circumstances. If it's of any help, under the law, since she closed the account and took the contents, we must hold a photo and written copy of everything removed for five years. Of course, you can always just ask Ms. Long. She may be willing to show you."

"You said it would require a court order?"

"Afraid so. Banking laws are very strict regarding privacy. Wish I could help. Is there anything else?"

"Not at this time, Mr. Hendrick. Thank you for your time.

You have been very helpful." He stood and shook hands with the detectives.

On the way back to the precinct, Ed Wade was incensed. "You do realize when we spoke to Gwen, she had already been to the bank and didn't say a damn thing about any safety deposit box."

Brockington concurred. "Of course, the question is why all the secrecy? What use would a college coed have for a safety deposit box?"

Ed remarked, "Whatever it is, Gwen Long isn't fucking sharing."

***

"You ladies have a fun night out." It was Saturday evening at Robert Weinstein's residence. He had invited his partners over for an evening of business and pleasure without the wives, presumably to discuss tax issues. The men all kissed their wives good-bye and watched as Marie Weinstein, Susan Sinclair, Lauren Palmer, and Diane Estrada all piled into the Land Rover and headed out.

Roger remarked, "We are four lucky bastards. Not too many wives would put up with our bullshit."

Dr. Bob remarked, "Let's not kid ourselves here. Those four all like the green. Watch that disappear and see how their attitude is." All the guys started laughing.

"Damn, Bob!" exclaimed Larry. "Give yourself a little credit. I'm sure Marie would love you just as much for only $200,000 a year and an inground pool." All the guys laughed. "So, Bob, what's with the tax situation?"

"Let's go down to the game room. We can discuss as we

play and indulge."

Dr. Bob's game room was indeed very impressive: a full-size slate pool table and oak bar that seated eight with high-back padded chairs, a huge built-in hi-def TV, and fireplace on a marble inlaid floor.

"Why don't we play a game of eight-ball? I'll take Roger first."

"Feeling cocky tonight, Doc?"

"You just rack 'em there, pal, but first, let's have another round." Dr. Bob poured everyone another round of drinks. "You break, Roger." As his companions sat around the bar, Roger lined up the cue ball and broke the stack with pool balls rolling around the table, but nothing went in.

"You're up, Doc, and you have choice."

Dr. Bob lined up his shot and knocked it into the corner pocket. A round of jeers went up.

"Don't worry, Roger," yelled Cal. "That's just home-field advantage."

The good doctor walked around the table looking for his next shot, his cue in his right hand. He picked up his glass of brandy with the other hand and downed it and gently sat the glass on the side of the pool table. "About that tax situation I brought you here to discuss tonight and the reason I asked the wives to leave… we have a major complication and it's really not taxes. I wish it were that simple. Roger, does the name Gwen Long sound familiar?"

"No, never heard of her."

"That's very interesting because she knows all about you. It seems that not only were you fucking her daughter Peyton, you got her pregnant." There was total silence in the room. The guys at the bar were speechless.

“What the fuck you talking about, Bob?” Roger yelled. And with that, Dr. Bob took his pool stick, and with an anger none of his friends had seen before, pressed the much taller Roger against the wall with his pool stick across Roger’s chest.

“Do you realize what the fuck you have done to us!” Dr. Bob was seething as Cal and Larry rushed to his defense and restrained Dr. Bob, pulling him off Roger. They all looked at him; they had never seen their friend like this.

“Bob, what the hell is going on with you?” Larry asked. “And what the fuck is this all about?”

With sweat rolling down his forehead, Dr. Bob made his way over to the bar and poured himself another drink. Dr. Bob filled in his partners on his dinner with Gwen Long and how the detectives from New York had paid her a visit. “They also paid a visit to Wilton. They don’t know who got Peyton pregnant, but they believe whoever the sperm donor was wasn’t quite ready for fatherhood and that’s how she ended up at the bottom of the gorge.” The looks on his friends’ faces were of disbelief. None them for one second thought Roger capable of anything so heinous.

Roger himself was so flush in the face, he looked close to passing out. “I never laid a single hand on that girl. We had no contact since Miami.”

“No, but you had to keep fucking the same girl, didn’t you?” yelled Bob, his blood still boiling. He then took his pool stick and cracked it in half across his leg and threw it behind the bar. “This is so fucked up!” he yelled. “And it shouldn’t be. All you had to do was follow protocol like the rest of us. That’s why we had the fucking rule of no return engagements, but not you. Of course the fucking rule didn’t apply to Roger.” There was a long silence Larry and Cal poured themselves another drink. You could hear the ice hitting the bottom of the glass.

Cal looked at Bob. "So now what?"

"Well, Gwen Long knows everything about us — where we live, where we work. She claims to have financial knowledge of our charity the Crimson. It seems that Peyton Long, the community college girl, was a lot smarter than we gave her credit for. She wasn't just some young piece of ass. She left behind a notebook and cell phone with times, dates, and places she spent with us, all our real names, our wives' names. She was taking mental notes on everything we did. I believe when the time was right, she planned on blackmailing us, but of course she never got the chance. You know the old saying the apple doesn't fall far from the tree, and that's where we're at. Gwen Long wants two million dollars to make this go away. She is no Suzy Homemaker; this bitch means business."

Cal spoke first. "You saw firsthand the cell phone?"

"Everything — the cell, small notebook — she flipped open the pages and there were names, dates, places, and a vivid description of a mole on the side of Roger's inner thigh right next to his dick. She has more than enough to cause us all a lot of problems, very serious problems."

"Then we pay her. We have the money."

"Oh really, Roger." Dr. Bob looked at him incredulously. "You really think it's that fucking simple. We just hand over two million and she goes away? I have news for you, Roger and everyone else in this room. Gwen Long will never go away as long as she's walking on God's green earth. What do you think happens, Roger, when two years from now, after she blows through that two million, do you think for one minute she won't be back at the National Bank of Bob, Cal, Larry, and Roger? Gwen Long is a long-term problem we need to make short term and the sooner the better."

Roger looked straight at Bob. "You cannot be serious. What kind of people do you think we are? Yes, we do some shady shit for money, but that's where we draw the line." Bob walked around the pool table. "Let me ask something. What we are looking at if they start snooping around our finances on tips from Ms. Long?"

"Let's see, maybe they find income tax evasion, money laundering, wire fraud, and then of course, there's still that minor inconvenience called a body. Tell me, Roger, how do you think you would do in a state penitentiary for the next forty years, and that's if you're lucky." Roger just looked away. "How about you, Cal? You're a pretty athletic guy; hell, you could probably play on the prison baseball team. Of course, you understand they're all home games. Larry, they might let you teach class. Hell, I mean, you're an economics professor, but you have to understand you're going to be taking a rather large pay cut. Look around this room. Is there one of us who would last six months in prison?"

Silence.

Finally, Larry spoke up. "Bob, just so there is no misunderstanding on our part, what in plain English are you asking us to be a part of?" All three men stared at Dr. Bob.

Bob took the white cue ball and rolled it across the pool table and knocked the black eight ball into the corner pocket. "Gwen Long needs to go away. If not, it might be us."

No one wanted to ask what they were all thinking. Cal broke the ice. "How?"

"I have an idea that's foolproof. Ever hear of castor

beans?"

"You talking about ricin?"

"That's right. Roger, you should be familiar with it as a chemist. Why don't you fill everyone else in?" Cal and Larry were seated at the bar. Dr. Bob stood behind with the bar with his drink, staring intently at Roger, who leaned against the pool table with his arms folded.

"First off, it's illegal to own a lethal dose of ricin powder for humans. The size of a few grains of table salt, it's absolutely deadly."

"Can it be detected?" Dr. Bob asked, even though he already knew the answer.

"It's virtually untraceable in humans unless someone did a full autopsy and tested for it. People who come in contact with it are usually bedridden within days, sometimes hours, depending on the individual, as their vital organs start to shut down."

Dr. Bob smiled. "And tell us, Roger, what is usually the determining factor in someone's cause of death from ricin?"

"It's rarely ever found. Most victims are pronounced deceased from septic, which can come from any number of factors."

"Thank you, Roger, for that was very informative."

"It's a moot point, Doc. It's illegal to own so much for your foolproof plan."

"Roger, you're a research chemist. I have no doubt you could obtain it without raising suspicion."

"I won't do it, no way."

Bob looked at him, his eyes piercing. "You don't get it; you're the fucking reason we're in this mess."

"Bob's right, Roger."

"Oh, really, Cal. Like you're some fucking saint."

"No, I'm not, but I have no desire to spend the rest of my life in a 10x6."

"How about you, Larry, you're awfully quiet. You okay with this?"

"Nobody is okay with this, Roger. If you have another idea, let's hear it."

"Am I fucking imagining this? We're talking about premeditated murder. There, I said the word." Roger was pacing the floor. "Even if I could get it, and I can't promise you I can, who the fuck is going to do this?"

Bob looked at him. "Let me worry about that. How long will it take?"

"At least two weeks and that's no guarantee. When are you meeting with her?"

"She's supposed to contact me. I can bullshit her, telling it's going to take some time to put that kind of cash together. I'll push her for three weeks." Still glaring at Roger, he said, "I don't care whose ass you gotta kiss. Make it happen."

"Hey, anybody alive down there?" Marie yelled down from the top of the stairs. "Hey, honey, the wives are back."

After the women made their way down the stairs, they all went over and gave their husbands a big kiss.

"What do we owe this to?" Cal asked his wife.

Diane, flipping her long auburn hair, put her arm around her husband. "We were just discussing you guys on our way home and saying how lucky we all are you guys are like brothers and that means we're all friends. It's so much fun, especially when you have one of your stupid fundraisers out of town for the weekend and we can just spend, spend, spend!" Everyone started laughing. Diane stuck her tongue down Cal's throat. “So, Mister, what’s a lady have to do get a drink around here?”

“Coming right up!” The group settled in at the bar for a nightcap with their wives unsuspecting of what had gone down earlier in the evening. There was friendly banter among the group, but a line had been crossed. What had been a lifestyle of beautiful women, exotic trips, and luxury homes had gone way off the rails and no was quite sure how it was going to end.

***

Tuesday morning, three days after their meeting to discuss Gwen Long, Robert Weinstein was making his way to the office when he pulled up next to Wilton Police Officer Roy Yardley, who was having a breakfast sandwich in his patrol car.

“Good morning, Doc. To what do I owe the pleasure?”

“Roy, I hate to ask, but I need a favor.”

“Doc, you name it. All that you guys have done for the department, just tell me.”

“I have an old acquaintance I would like to drop in on and surprise. I’m just assuming she’s still living in Syracuse somewhere. I have her tag number. I got it from an old photo. It would shock the hell out of her if I just showed up unannounced.”

“Hell, Doc, that’s easy enough. Let me have the tag number. Should take less than five minutes.” Patrolman Yardley entered the information into his database. “Here it is, Doc.” He handed the readout over. “That tag is registered in Syracuse, New York to one Gwen Cox Long, age thirty-eight.

Hey, Doc, she is quite a looker if you don't mind me saying. And the address is 22 Bernard Blvd. Syracuse."

"Roy, I really appreciate this."

"Not a problem, Doc. Glad I could help you out for a change and good luck surprising your friend."

"I'm sure she will be. Thanks again." He drove off.

Robert Weinstein wasn't sure when Gwen would contact him or where she would want to meet, but he always liked to be prepared, and if he had his way, this would be their last meal together.

Chapter Twelve

The White Plains Motor Lodge sat inconspicuously along Rt. 15 in Trumball, Connecticut. It was well-kept, very neat and clean, and was mainly used by businessmen for an overnight stay. Lauren Palmer and her shoulder-length blonde hair walked past the mirror. She had on a white robe and nothing else. She turned to Tyler Drake. "Be right back. Just want to freshen up a bit, then maybe we can go round two if you're up for it," she said with a wicked grin.

Tyler and his six-foot frame were stretched across the bed. "So tell me, how the hell did you find this place?"

Lauren was washing her face. She took the hand towel and dried herself. "I couldn't exactly book us a place in Wilton, now could I? I mean, talk about small town gossip."

"Is there anybody in that rich enclave who isn't related?"

"What, you don't approve of the accommodations sir?" And with that, she doffed her robe and crawled onto the bed next to him.

"You kidding? I love it, but when you texted me about meeting and I put the address in, I was like, damn, forty-five miles."

"So was it worth the trip?" she said while licking her lips.

"Forty-five miles for you? I would have driven at least forty-six!"

Lauren started to laugh. "So tell me, does Tyler Drake live in Wilton?"

He started laughing. "Let me share a little insight with you. Anyone who physically works in Wilton, outside of doctors and other professionals, does not live there, so to answer your question, I have a townhouse about twelve miles south of Wilton in Darien."

"Were you ever married?"

"I was for six years; we just weren't a good fit. We're still friends. She remarried and here I am. So you know my story. What's yours?"

"Roger and I get along fine. He is extremely bright and likes to discuss things like the international trade agreements and the mining of gold in South Africa. I just nod and say 'sure, honey.' I have no idea what in the hell he is talking about, of course. Roger is on his laptop more than he is on me, so I assume the porn site he visits must be really good." Lauren laughed.

So you married for money," Tyler said with sarcasm. "I find that very offensive! Very sorry. I was just joking around."

Lauren started smiling. "That's all right. You're right. I did, and I don't regret it for one minute."

They spent another twenty minutes sharing their backgrounds and their likes and dislikes, and two hours later, checked out of the White Plains Motor Lodge. In the parking lot, Tyler put his arm around Lauren's waist.

"Will I see you again?"

"What are you doing?"

"What?"

"You can never touch me in public."

"I'm very discreet. We're forty-five miles out in the middle of nowhere."

"I don't care; that's my rule. If you see me in Wilton, don't approach me. As for us getting together again, maybe, but don't text me unless you're answering mine. I can't take any chances of Roger ever finding out." Lauren Palmer turned her back to Tyler Drake, got into her blue Land Rover, and drove off. Tyler Drake thought to himself, *she is one very attractive lady*. But there was something about her that made him uneasy; it was if she had two different personalities and hers could change quickly. Men who are like that are labeled controlling; women are called trouble.

As she cruised down the turnpike toward Wilton, Lauren Palmer got on her Bluetooth. The voice came over: *Bluetooth is now connected: call 215-212-6400 dialing*. The caller on the other end picked up. It was a personal cell phone, the number given out to a few select individuals.

"Lauren, what's up? I need you to use your connections. I need some background information on an individual."

"You have a name?"

"Tyler Drake. Lives in Darien."

"Can he be beneficial to us?"

"Not at the moment, but if he can be of use, I can handle him, but I need some leverage."

"Text me Tyler Drake's cell number and his address. Give me a week, and I'll be in touch. Take care." That was the end of the conversation.

***

It was Friday evening at the home of Doctor Robert Weinstein and the mood was festive. One young Matt Weinstein, to the astonishment of everyone but his father it seemed, had been accepted to the 2023 Class of Harvard University. The fire pit out back was glowing and the grill was covered in steaks and ribs as the well-wishers came by to offer their congratulations, from relatives to neighbors. The alcohol poured. Matt and some of his fellow classmates also indulged under the watchful eye of his dad, who allowed it for this very special occasion but also took all their car keys. No one under twenty-one would be driving home tonight.

Marie Weinstein was ecstatic and honestly stunned that her son was off to Harvard. She didn't believe Matt would be accepted. She was on her third martini and looked beautiful in a long black one-piece gown, her brown hair blowing slightly in the night air. She went up behind her husband, Dr. Bob, who was in his usual spot manning the grill, flipping steaks and drinking beer with his friends. She put her arms around his waist. "I should never have doubted you."

Dr. Bob turned and kissed his wife. "It was all Matt."

Marie smiled. "I don't know how you do it sometimes and I'm not sure I want to."

"My dear, it's all in how you talk to people."

***

"Good morning. Dr. Weinstein's office. This is Sandy. How can I help you today?"

"Hi, Sandy, my name is Gwen Cox. I'm a sales rep for a medical equipment company and a friend of Dr. Weinstein. Would you be sure and tell him I called? I can leave a number."

"I will be glad to. Go ahead with the number. Thank you so much. Have a great day." Sandy wrote down the number, like so many other messages the doctor received during the day, and thought nothing more of it. Finally, around 2:00 p.m., there was break with no patients in the waiting room. Sandy took the messages into Dr. Bob's office as was the routine and went over who had called and how she should handle each one. Most were for follow-up visits for her to schedule and the usual calls from pharmaceutical sales reps trying to meet and make a sale. Dr. Bob listened as Sandy went through the notes. "Doctor, I had one call. Here is the number said her name is Gwen Cox. She's a sales rep for medical equipment and said she was a friend."

Dr. Bob, with his usual nonchalant attitude, said, "Gwen called? I have not heard from her in some time. I will handle this one myself." They went through the rest of the scheduling.

At three, Sandy returned to her desk, closing the office door behind her. *Very clever,* Bob thought. *Just call the office just like another sales rep.*

He had not talked to Roger in three days. Roger was still working on getting the castor beans. Dr. Bob had a plan. He called Gwen back and made arrangements to meet for dinner at the same Asian restaurant and to go over how this would work. After all, you cannot just hand someone two million in cash.

Dr. Bob waited until 6:00 p. m. to call Roger, who was relaxing in his den at home. He saw the name and hesitated to answer before picking up. "What's up, Bob?"

"I had a call today from an old friend. We're meeting for dinner soon. I was just touching base to see how our procurement was coming?"

"Needless to say, I had to take a lot of precaution to bring something like that into the research lab without raising suspicion."

Bob thought to himself, *now you decide to take precautions, idiot.* "That's fine. When do you expect shipment?"

"Seven days by private courier."

Bob knew his relationship with Roger had become strained over what had gone down, so he changed the subject and asked about Lauren and if he had gone skydiving lately; just small talk for another ten minutes. "Roger, sounds good; just text me when the product arrives."

Roger put his recliner back and wondered where it had all gone wrong; he was a man with a conscience and it was starting to bother him.

***

Thursday evening, Robert Weinstein found himself once again at the Kobe Japanese Restaurant sitting across from Gwen Long.

"I'm glad, Doctor, that we can be professional about this." Gwen was indulging with a White Lady martini and Dr. Bob his usual, an old-fashioned.

"Likewise. There's no reason we can't come to an agreement that is beneficial to both parties. I brought this along as a show of good faith." Bob handed her a small black briefcase.

Gwen smiled. "Well, this is unexpected, but I appreciate the gesture."

"It's a small down payment of twenty-five thousand, all

in small denominations."

"I would like to reciprocate, Doctor." With that, Gwen handed over the small black and white notebook with all the names and addresses of the group.

"I am working on fulfilling your request. As you can guess, it's not something that one can access quickly, but I believe I can have it ready in about ten days. My associates and I have serious questions about our transaction. First and foremost, how do we make this transaction discreetly? Second, when we do receive the full contents of the safety deposit box? My partners also raised the issue of how can we be sure we will not be approached in the future for more funding?"

"Those are good questions, Doctor, and straight to the point. I like that. For the first, once you inform me everything is in place for the transaction, I will send you an email with the bank account where it can be wired electronically. It will not be in this country, so no need to worry about the IRS asking questions. Once I have proof of the transfer, I will mail the package overnight by bonded courier with signature required. As for future funding, trust me, Doctor, and don't take this personally, I hope to never see or hear of you or your friends ever again."

Dr. Bob smiled, as did Gwen. There was a definite sexual chemistry between them, and if he hadn't been planning her demise, he would be tempted to seduce the petite reddish-brown-haired lady who was his equal when it came to the intimidation game. "I'm fine with everything, but there is nothing to stop you from simply keeping part of the package. I will transfer half the funding, the other half after you complete your end of the bargain."

Gwen took a drink of her White Lady. "Touché, Doctor. I

admire your creativity. I believe we have a deal."

Doctor Bob finished his old-fashioned. "You will have to excuse me for not staying for dinner. I have other business to attend to."

"I understand, and tell your associates Gwen sends her thanks for their contributions. Without them, none of this would have been possible, especially Roger for his very special donation."

Robert Weinstein sped down the freeway in his silver Mercedes, topping out over 100 MPH. He needed to blow off some steam. Finally, he put in his favorite Jazz music, which helped to relax him. It was After 9:00 pm when he texted Loz. *I'm at the place now.*

Reply back: *On my way. Be there in 10. Had to stop at the store for a few items to make my excuse for going out legit.* Dr. Bob and his female companion had had a relationship for almost two years. Their meeting was not random. They met every Tuesday once a month on a week night so as not to raise suspicion between their spouses. Bob was parked. It was totally dark. As he sat in his car listening to Jazz, another car pulled car pulled in and immediately dimmed its headlights.

"Sorry, I made it as quick as possible."

"It's fine. I have no place to be. Marie never checks."

"I have to be careful. He never questions when I run to the store as long as I bring back fresh doughnuts." She was laughing as she said it; she leaned over and kissed Dr. Bob, who immediately removed her dress. Afterward, as she was putting her clothes back on, she kissed him again. "Bob, I could be more creative if you were to buy a larger car."

"I have no complaints. Besides, this makes it more of a challenge."

"You're telling me; that damn gear shift is a pain in the ass and I mean that literally." They both laughed.

"Listen, we need to start moving larger sums of money."

"I thought you said anything over ten thousand gets the attention of the IRS?"

"It does, so I set up an overseas banking account. We can transfer it all without any problems. How much do we have presently?"

"Close to half a million in over six different banks."

"Good, we'll move it all but leave five thousand in each account. I will get you all the information."

"Is there anything going on I should be aware of?"

"When the time comes, I will fill you in. Right now, the less you know, the better off you are."

"You know, whatever it takes, you can count on me."

"I do, and that's why I trust you."

"I better get those fucking doughnuts home before he falls asleep." She kissed Bob good night and exited the car. Dr. Robert Weinstein, family man, headed home to his wife.

***

It had been four days since Roger Palmer had dropped off the castor beans to Bob. Without telling Lauren, he decided on the spur of the moment to take the two-hour drive north to his hometown of Ridgefield, Connecticut, situated in the foothills of the Berkshire Mountains. It was 10:00 on a clear, sunny morning. Already joggers were out running and people were working in their yards raking leaves and trimming hedges. It was, for all intents and purposes, small town America. He drove past the Ridgefield High School, home of the Tigers, where he attended. Unlike Dr. Robert Weinstein and the others, Roger had attended a public high school. He looked across the athletic field where he played soccer for four years, an admittedly average player. He loved every minute of it, even practice, because it allowed him to fit in. He was just another kid, not the awkward nerd with the extremely high IQ.

After the incident with his Mustang, he decided to have it restored to its original condition. While it was being repaired, he had leased a bright red Chevy Corvette. He drove through the center of town and past Gibson Ice Cream where he and his best friend growing up, Tim, would hang out front hoping to meet girls. He laughed to himself; they never stood a chance, two geeks together thinking they were cool with their baseball caps on backward and horned-rimmed glasses. Tim even had one of those stupid baskets on his bike to carry his books.

On past Tom and Harry's barbershop and finally turning down Maple Street, he pulled up to a nice well-kept brick rancher the green yard and, shrubbery still immaculate, just how his dad kept it. He could still hear his dad telling him, "Always take pride in your home; it shows you have pride in yourself." He could still picture his mom hanging up fresh laundry to dry outside, something unheard of anymore. The basketball set in the driveway was gone, replaced by a small tricycle. Evidently, the new owners were a young couple just starting out. Roger remembered his Dad telling him they bought the house as a starter home, but over the years, fell in love with it and just couldn't bring themselves to move. His parents were regular people — his dad an electrician, his mom the school nurse — loving parents who doted on him and his older sister Sara, who taught them values of caring for other people, especially those less fortunate. He sat and was reminiscing for almost twenty minutes, finally pulling away from the life he had lived so many years ago. He was feeling overwhelming guilt wondering where it had all gone so wrong, how he could have gone so astray.

He drove three blocks to the Saint Mary's Catholic Church where he attended growing up. He parked the Corvette and gazed up at large red brick church with its huge steeple pointing toward the sky. Slowly walking up the long grey steps to the entrance, he opened the large wooden doors. He walked in and could hear the choir rehearsing in the nave, the principal part of the church. He quietly took a seat in the back as they sang 'Morning Has Broken'. They were very good, he thought.

"That's all for today, people. Let's try again for Wednesday evening say around 7:00." The choir members exited as he contemplated his future and an elderly priest slid in beside him.

"I hope I'm not intruding?"

Roger looked at the aging priest, who looked to be in his late eighties with his warm smile. "Not at all. I grew up in this church many years ago and I was in town, so I thought I would stop in and visit."

"That's wonderful; it's always nice to come back home, isn't it, no matter where life takes you." The elderly priest and Roger chatted for another ten minutes.

"Well, I have an appointment to keep, but I would be remiss not to mention if you're available on Sunday, I give a terrific sermon. Feel free to attend." They both laughed.

"Thank you, Father, but I will be back home." They shook hands and the priest departed.

Roger sat alone looking at the altar and then noticed a

young woman exiting the confessional. Roger thought for a moment and then decided to go himself. He entered the booth and sat down. The small window slid back.

"How may I help you, my son?"

"Bless me, Father, for I have sinned."

"How long since your last confession, my son?"

"I honestly cannot say. Too long."

"That's fine; you found your way here. In life, my son, we often stray off the path of goodness. Sometimes we come to a fork in the road and we take the wrong path. Did you take the wrong path, my son?"

"I have, Father. I have committed mortal sins, including greed and adultery, and would like to repent."

"Temptation is everywhere and can be hard to resist. We know the awesome power of goodness but not the power of evil and that's how it works, by luring us in. It takes all of our human effort at times not to succumb to the dark side. The fact that you are acknowledging your sins is the key to a fresh start and a better life not only today but in the future. As I hear you speak, I have this feeling your shoulders are carrying a tremendous burden. Is there anything else weighing heavily on you?"

"Father, I know of something about to take place that is the severest of mortal sins, but I'm torn internally about what to do."

"There is an old saying as true today as the day it was written. 'These are the times that try men's souls.' In confession, my son, we have the opportunity to repent and recover the friendship with God. At this moment, you have placed yourself in his presence and have acknowledged your sins, but in order to grant absolution, you must do the right thing and go and notify those who can change the outcome immediately. Do you understand? Hello? Are you still there?”

Roger had quickly exited the confessional and was walking down the church steps. He stopped at the bottom and looked up again at the steeple pointing toward the heavens and asked himself again what happened to that twelve-year-old with the nerdy glasses who loved hanging out in the garage with his dad, shooting baskets in the driveway while his sister roller skated. Roger got in his car and thought how he had more material things than his parents ever dreamed of having, but for the first time, realized they had so much more.

Chapter Thirteen

It had been over a week since his meeting with Gwen Long and Robert Weinstein found himself once again at Sparks Steak House waiting for his old friend Ben Logan alias Big Ben.

"Bob, my old friend, how are you?"

"Ben, doing great. Have a seat."

"This is a very pleasant surprise. I don't see you in twenty years and now twice in four months and for the best steak dinner in the area. I'm flattered. Especially considering the beautiful wife you have at home." They were both laughing. "Good evening and welcome to Sparks. I'm Thomas and I will be your server this evening. Can I start you out with cocktails?"

"Ben, what's your pleasure?"

"I'll have gin and tonic on the rocks."

"Very well, and you, sir?"

"Old-fashioned."

"I will bring those right out. While you're looking over the menu, the house specialty tonight is the King Surf and Turf. It's a fourteen-ounce lobster tail topped with Crab Imperial and an eight-ounce filet mignon topped with a crab cake with a brandy peppercorn cream sauce that goes for $135.00."

"That sounds excellent, and since Bob is treating, I'll have it."

Bob grinned. "Make that two."

"Thank you, gentlemen. That makes for an easy order." The waiter returned promptly with their cocktails. The two old friends made some small talk discussing sports and gambling, Dr. Bob reminiscing about how much he missed the action. They enjoyed another round of drinks and the waiter brought their dinner.

"Doc, this looks incredible."

"The food here is amazing."

Ben cut into his filet. "So tell me, Doc, what's this all about?"

"Ben, you did such a professional job last time, I have a job opportunity I thought might be of interest to you."

"Always willing to look at a business opportunity, Doc, for the right pricc, of course."

"That goes without saying."

"So what are we looking at?"

"I have an old acquaintance who recently came back into my life and has caused me some personal conflict I need resolved."

"How?"

"It would require two trips to her residence. On the first one, I need photographs of all the items in her medicine cabinet."

"And the reason for the second visit?"

"I will need you to replace an item."

"That's it?"

"Pretty much. Needless to say, this must be done discreetly."

"I have just the guy. Tell you what. I'll do both for twenty g's. That would be five for my associate and fifteen for me."

"Price is not an issue. I came to you because this must be done discreetly with no mistakes and you're a pro. I respect that."

"I'm flattered and thank you for coming to me first. You haven't a thing to worry about. Doctors, lawyers, politicians, professional people seek my services all the time. They have issues and I resolve them. Tell me, where is this client?"

"Syracuse."

"Wow, long way from home."

"Is that a problem?"

Ben started laughing. "In case you haven't heard, Doc, we have offices worldwide. Hell, once I had to track an individual to fucking Trinidad. Bastard thought he could skip out without paying. I go wherever business takes me."

"What kind of time frame are we looking at? I need the those photographs pronto after that the second visit, within five days. Can it be done?"

"After we finish dinner, you give me the address, and within forty-eight hours, you will have the information, providing, of course, our financial exchange takes place."

"Would you like me to wire it again?"

"Exactly."

"It will be in there tonight."

Big Ben smiled. "Cheers." They toasted their business arrangement.

Dr. Bob drove straight home from the meeting and went immediately to his den, and within ten minutes, had transferred twenty thousand dollars to the bank account of Ben Larson, Men's Tailors. Dr. Bob then contacted Gwen Long. She had finally agreed to give him a cell number. Bob was sure it was from a disposable one. He texted her: *All financial considerations are in order waiting for deposit information.* Send.

It didn't take long for Gwen to respond: *Please make financial contributions to the Long Trust Fund. Here is the bank routing number: XX3444-5757-009988 Bank of Zurich.* Dr. Bob smiled to himself; he had to hand it to Gwen Long. She didn't miss a trick. There was no way of tracing any American deposit made by wire to a bank in Switzerland. Minutes later, after a few key strokes, Gwen Long was Switzerland's newest millionaire. Dr. Bob turned off his computer and went to bed. All he could do now was wait for his package to arrive.

***

It was 1:00 pm on Friday afternoon. Robert Weinstein had just finished with the last patient for the day and was going over his files when his office manager Sandy knocked on the door and peeked in. "I'm sorry to disturb you, sir, but I have a messenger service here who refuses to let me sign for a package. Says he needs your signature."

"Not a problem." Dr. Bob followed Sandy out to her desk where the courier waited.

"I'm sorry, sir, company policy. It's a requirement."

"I wish everyone was so competent. Life would be so much less complicated with that." Dr. Weinstein signed and took the small white box. "Sandy, you're free to go. We're pretty much caught up for the day."

"Great, I will see you in the morning."

Dr. Bob returned to his office and locked the door behind him. He sat at his desk and tore open the box and there it was, just as Gwen Long had described it: a small go phone, the kind you pick up for ninety bucks at any retail outlet. Bob put his feet up on his desk, turned on the cell, and then pressed 1 for the voicemail, and for the next fifteen minutes listened to Peyton Long describe her relationship with Roger Palmer, their time together in Miami, and the fact that she was going to visit him with some very big news. Robert Weinstein cringed when he heard his full professional name and address of the office where he practiced. Dr. Bob could picture the statuesque Peyton Long in his head, her long brown hair and blue eyes as he replayed the voicemail several times. One line set his blood to boil.

"Nothing gets done without Dr. Bob's permission. Nothing." The voicemail continued on. "I find it quite amusing that all four of these of these so-called Harvard men believe their own brilliance with their fake last names and professions. I had every one of them pegged in less than a month. It never ceases to amaze me that no matter how high a man's IQ, a girl with a great body can own him."

Dr. Bob turned off the cell phone for the last time. He had replayed it six times. There was more than enough information on that cell if those detectives started doing some research could destroy everything they had worked for the last twenty years. Bob got up, went to his medicine cabinet, and unlocked it. He removed a manila envelope; looked harmless enough. Before opening it, he donned a surgical mask, neoprene gloves, and a long white lab coat, making sure to leave no skin exposed, including safety glasses. He tore open the envelope, and using surgical scissors, he cut open the thick plastic bag, and then, being painstakingly careful with tweezers, he removed eight castor beans and placed them in his mortar bowl. Then, using his medical skills with a scalpel, he delicately sliced open the beans, removing the outer shell. Next, he took his thick ceramic pestle and ground the inside of the beans into a fine powder substance that resembled table salt. Small beads of sweat were forming on his forehead now. In its deadliest form, ricin, as it is commonly referred to, was ready.

***

Mobster Salvatore Marino was sitting in his rented white van at 22 Bernard Blvd., listening to his radio, when his cell phone lit up. The text read: *She has arrived at work.*

That was all he needed to know about Gwen Long as he donned his fake cable shirt and tool belt. He walked briskly up to the townhouse. With a skill set unmatched at breaking and entering, he was inside in a matter of minutes. Normally, he would go straight for the bedroom and the jewelry box. This was a first he wasn't taking anything; instead, he was there to take photographs. Weird, he thought, but for five thousand dollars, who was he to question how people spent their money.

He quickly made his way to the bathroom and observed how everything was placed in the medicine cabinet before removing each item and photographing them, from prescriptions to tampons. Next, so as not to raise any suspicion, he replaced each item exactly as he found it. Within twenty minutes, he was back in his van and texting Big Ben

Larson *See attached* and sent the photos. Ben texted back *Good job. I will let you know when for the return engagement.* Sal thought to himself, *the sooner the better. I want the other half of my money.*

***

Roger walked in from work and grabbed a beer from the refrigerator and stared out the picture window. He watched as Lauren made her way up the driveway.

"Hello, anyone home?"

"Upstairs," came the reply. Roger appeared at the top of the stairs.

"Hi, babe, with the beer already? I like that. Maybe I'll join you." Lauren made her way to the fridge, took a beer, and joined Roger upstairs. "So how was your day?"

Roger shrugged. "Not bad, but the new guy Conlan won't last. The guy's a real jackass. He's a fucking micro-manager with no concept of what he's doing. Behind his back, they're already taking bets when they ship his ass out. And what did you do today?"

Lauren walked over and flashed her nails. "Nice, right?"

"Very."

"They have this new girl working there. She is amazing, worth every dime."

"If you don't mind me asking, how big was the dime?"

"Roger, really, it was like seventy with a tip. What is up with you lately? You seem really preoccupied."

"I took a little trip last week, spur-of-the-moment deal, and went back to my hometown. It brought back a lot of good memories. Just small-town nostalgia you would find boring,

I'm sure."

"That's not true. I like hearing about your youth in Wrightsville, but look where you're at now."

"That's Ridgefield, honey. Glad you were paying attention."

"Oh, give me a fucking break, will you? Lately, you have been in zombie land, and I'm sorry I didn't remember the name of your hometown, but I'm listening now. So how was it?"

"I really enjoyed it. I went past my old house, past the high school, and then I went over to the church I was raised in and went inside and did something I hadn't done in over twenty years."

"Roger, you didn't steal from the collection plate, did you?" Lauren was laughing.

"No, I actually went to confession."

The look on Lauren's face said it all; the laughter stopped immediately. "Honey, confession, really? I mean, you can talk to me."

"I know that, but they say confession is good for the soul and it had been a while."

"Does this have anything to do with your mood lately?"

"Yes, yes it does."

"Roger, you know whatever you tell in confession stays there. The priest can't say anything to anyone about your discussion."

"I'm well aware of that, but why bring that up?"

"I'm just making conversation, that's all."

Lauren was visibly shaken by Roger's admission, but he had no idea why. "Are you okay?"

"Yes, it's just not every day your husband tells you he

went to confession." She finished her beer and got another one.

"I'm your wife, Roger. You can tell me anything. Trust me, I will understand, but I can't help unless you confide in me."

"I appreciate that, but this is something I have to deal with. Can we change the subject before this turns into an argument?"

"Fine, I'll make dinner in about an hour, but I have to run to the store for a few items."

"I can come with you."

"No, relax. I won't be long." She kissed Roger, grabbed her keys to the Range Rover, and headed out. As she was backing out of the driveway, she was cussing to herself. *Fucking Ichabod Crane idiot, talking to a priest. He's going to ruin fucking everything.* Lauren made a quick turn into the shopping center, slammed the car into park, and got out her iPhone and started texting. *I need that background information on Tyler Drake ASAP*: send. She waited for a response and then sent the same text again marked *Urgent*.

I got your first message was waiting to confirm that the information was available. I just received it and will forward it to your private e-mail. Is this something I should be concerned about or can you handle it?

Lauren texted back: *I'm not making any moves right now, but I want an option if I have to move quickly. We have come too far anyone to screw up our long-term goal*: send.

Chapter Fourteen

Two Weeks Later

Salvatore Marino watched from his white van as Gwen Long pulled her black Jetta into the accounting firm of Harkness and Way. He watched her go into the building, waited five minutes, then made the seven-mile trip to her townhouse, 22 Bernard Boulevard. Once again, with his cable shirt and tool belt, he made his way up the stairs and was inside with the flick of a wrist. He quickly made his way to bathroom medicine cabinet. Big Ben's words to him: "Replace her tampon box with the box I'm giving you. Count the number of tampons in her box, then remove the same amount from the box I'm giving you that are missing, but only take the ones from the back row and then leave." He did exactly as instructed. The tampon box from Gwen's medicine cabinet was missing three, so as instructed, he removed three from his box and placed it back in the cabinet and took Gwen's with him. Salvatore Marino was nothing more than a small-time mobster running illegal bets, loan-sharking, and theft. The tampon exchange had him baffled, but he had been around long enough to know that Gwen Long was in someone's crosshairs and it wasn't going to end up good for her.

***

It had been a little over two months since Joy Carson had lost her roommate and friend Peyton Long. She still had moments of deep sadness and depression but was trying to move on with her life. She still had the apartment they shared, but so far had not found a reliable roommate.

Joy was on her computer when the buzzer rang from below. "Who is it, please?"

"Amber Conway. I was looking for Peyton Long."

Joy didn't know what to think. "I'll be right down." She opened the door to a very attractive petite redhead.

"Hi, so sorry to bother you, but Peyton gave me her address and said if I was ever near Syracuse to just stop by. Is she home?"

"I'm Joy. Come on up."

They entered the apartment. "This is very nice."

"Thanks, have a seat."

"I don't want to intrude if Peyton's not home. I'll come back later."

Joy smiled sadly. "Let me get us some iced tea and we can talk." Amber took off her coat and sat on the sofa. "Here we go."

"Thanks, I love iced tea. I assume you're Peyton's roommate?"

"Yes, when was the last time you spoke with Peyton?"

"It's been several weeks. We used to text and then suddenly it stopped, but I understand people get busy and time just goes, but she helped me land a great job."

"Amber, I don't know how to say this, but unfortunately,

Peyton recently passed away."

"What? How? She was so young."

"The police believe she fell down an embankment while jogging."

Amber started crying uncontrollably. Joy came over and put her arm around to try and comfort her. "She was just so nice to me. I mean, I was a total stranger and she treated me like we were best friends right away. How could this happen?"

Within the hour, Amber composed herself enough to talk. Joy held her hands. "How did you meet Peyton?"

Amber smiled. "We met in Miami. We were at the same party and she introduced herself."

"Peyton was in Miami?"

"Yes, it was business."

"I didn't know Peyton was involved in outside business. She never spoke of it."

"How well did you know Peyton?"

"We were roomies sharing alcohol and guy stories, but nothing about a business venture."

"I probably should just let it go. What she did in her private life she obviously didn't want to share."

"Please tell me. It might help explain why she was in Connecticut when she fell."

Amber took a deep breath. "Alright, but please don't judge her. She was doing what was necessary."

Joy looked perplexed. "I would never."

"The first time I met Peyton was in Miami. I was there working as a high-end escort. Peyton was there with her sugar daddy."

"Really?"

"Yes, really."

Joy took a few minutes to comprehend what she had just heard. "I'm surprised to say the least, but honestly, now that I look back at everything, that would explain a lot. Peyton would tell me on Friday night she would she would be gone for the weekend and start packing at a moment's notice."

"That's how it works; sometimes they give you notice and sometimes it's like are you available to go away this weekend. Peyton and I were in Miami at the time. I was working for an agency that didn't really respect us. That's when Peyton told me about Executive Introductions about how they take care of their associates plus the fact that through Executive, you would meet some very affluent individuals who might become your regular or sugar daddy, as some refer to them. That has a lot of perks; they start to buy you nice things from clothing to jewelry, they take you to the best restaurants, stay at the finest hotels, and of course the money is significant."

"That's amazing. I never would have guessed in a hundred years, but now it all comes together: the last-minute getaways Peyton would go on, coming home with extra cash. I honestly thought she was seeing a married man on the side."

"Trust me, they're all married, so you were right on that part. I believe, by the way she spoke of her date that night, he was her regular guy. Before joining Executive, the dates I went on, guys never used their real names, often lied about their real profession, but the worst part, management didn't do a good job of screening their clients. I met some real winners, let me tell you. Peyton seemed to know all about her date and the friends he came with. They were business partners and were all from the same area. How she knew that, I have no idea, but I had this gut instinct she didn't really care for any of them except for someone named Jack and her date. If I recall, his name was Roger. He was tall."

Joy was smiling. "This is pretty unbelievable. All I can say is wow! It's just amazing to me that Peyton had this almost double life. The girl I knew who drove around in an old Jeep with torn blue jeans who drank cheap wine and made bad pasta stepping out with the rich and powerful. I wonder how she got started."

Amber shrugged. "I have no idea. The home office is in Manhattan. That's why I'm in New York. I have a meeting with them tomorrow. I have their business card." Amber started going through her purse. "Here it is. I have an extra. Would you like one?" Joy took the card.

Executive Introductions. 200 E Street Suite 3 Manhattan, New York.

Their motto: *We Will Exceed Your Expectations*. In small letters at the bottom of the card: *Total discretion guaranteed.*

Joy looked at the card. "Thanks, but I could never…" and started to hand it back.

"Please keep it. I have another one. A year from now, who knows? Trust me, I said the same thing and here I am."

"I wonder how they choose who gets to join?"

"Oh, you would definitely qualify. You're beautiful."

"Thank you. I mean, the men?"

"I know they're very selective. They do a total background check. Any red flags at all, even a DUI, and it's a no go. One date told me the joining fee for the men is $25,000, and of course, whenever you go on a date, they get a fee. I'm sure it's a nice one, but to these men, it's pocket change. My last date was my third time with this guy who flies me in to Toronto, Canada. From there, we take a limo to Niagara Falls with our hotel room overlooking the Falls and all I have to do is what millions of girls do for free every night." She was laughing when she said it.

Joy also was laughing. "I'm glad you stopped in, Amber. It makes me feel a little closer to Peyton."

The two young women had another glass of iced tea and more tears for another thirty minutes.

Three days later, as she was going through the checkout line in the supermarket, Joy went to pull out her ATM card and the card that Amber had given her fell out. She picked it up and placed it back in her wallet. She hadn't really given it any thought until now. Joy finished loading the groceries into her car. She sat in the parking lot and looked at the card. It was probably nothing, but what the hell. She said if anything at all came up to call her.

"Hello, you have reached the voice mail of Detective Laura Brockington. I'm not available at the moment. Please leave your name and number where I can reach you and I will return your call promptly. If this is an emergency, please dial 0 now. Thank you and have a great day."

"Hello, Laura, I'm not sure if you remember me. My name is Joy Carson. I was Peyton Long's roommate. We spoke a couple of months ago. You left me your card and said to call if I thought of anything else. It's probably nothing, but call me when you have time. Thanks. Bye."

***

Detectives Brockington and Wade were out investigating a robbery and had just finished up. Wade looked over. "Let's grab a pizza before heading back to the office. I'm starved."

"That sounds good."

Detective Wade had his foot up on his desk, reading his email and enjoying his pepperoni pizza while Detective Laura Brockington was going through her folders. "So, Laura, you eating today? This is really good."

"I guess I'd better."

"I warned you to never bet me on football."

"You got lucky; that's all." Laura grabbed a slice and went back to her desk. There were at least a dozen folders scattered across her desk, all marked as an open case or pending. At times, it was overwhelming. The folder for Peyton Long was marked "status open: cause of death: undetermined/suspicious."

"Where we off to after lunch?"

Brockington said, "Sixth Street, but let me check my voicemails first." As usual, Laura Brockington had fourteen voicemails to go through. Most were just routine and then this one. "Hi, Detective Brockington, this is Joy Carson." The name immediately grabbed Laura's attention. She listened to the call and wrote down the number.

"What's up?"

She looked over at Wade. "I just got a call from Peyton Long's roommate." She grabbed the folder and flipped through it. The case had gone cold. They had run out of places to turn and needed a break.

"Grab your keys. We're making a house call."

Within the hour, Detectives Brockington and Wade were sitting in Joy Carson's apartment.

"I cannot believe how fast you came over. I hope I'm not wasting your time."

"Joy, when I said 'anything,' that's what I meant. Tell me what you have."

Joy Carson went over everything that Amber had shared with her. The two detectives were beside themselves. Detective Brockington did all the talking. "Did Amber by any chance tell you her last name?"

"No, I'm sorry. I didn't want to pry and she didn't offer."

"That's okay. Did she say where she was from?"

"No, I assumed she was from Miami."

"Could you give me a brief description?"

"She was about five foot two, maybe, with pretty short red hair and very attractive."

"Any tattoos or anything that stood out?"

"No, I'm sorry. I was just so interested in her story about Peyton. She was petite and pretty."

"Amber told you she thought that Peyton's date in Miami was her regular guy?"

"That's what she said. She was pretty sure he was her regular date because Peyton seemed to know all about him and his friends."

"His friends?"

"She told Amber they were in some kind of business together, but she didn't recall what it was."

"Do you recall how many friends were in Miami?"

"She didn't say, but Amber had a date with one of them that night and she remembered Peyton telling her don't believe anything he tells you. It's all bullshit."

"So Amber stops by to thank Peyton for being a good friend and introducing her to something Introductions?"

"That's correct. Peyton told her they treat the associates very well, with a lot of respect, and do an extensive background check on all clients."

"Did Amber happen to mention where their office was?"

"Not only that, she tried to recruit me. I told her it wasn't for me, but she gave me their business card just in case."

"And you have the card?"

"Wait here. I'll get it."

Brockington and Wade looked like they had just hit the lottery.

"Here you go. Keep it. I have no use for it."

Brockington looked at the card. *Executive Introductions 200 E Street Manhattan.* It looked like Detective Brockington would be going back to her old stomping grounds for a visit. "I was wondering, did Gwen Long ever stop back to clean out Peyton's room?"

"I actually did it and packed up all her stuff. It was so hard. I went through two boxes of tissues and Gwen came by and took her things. Don't think bad of her because of that. It was really hard for me to do. I'm not sure she could have."

"No, not at all, and I'm really sorry for all you have been through, but the information you gave us today will be very extremely helpful." Detective Brockington hugged Joy on the way out, as did Detective Wade.

As they were leaving, Detective Brockington looked out the window. "I feel so bad for that girl."

"Me too. She seems like a really nice young lady. I assume were going to Manhattan?"

"First thing in the morning. It's a good four-hour ride. Let's plan on leaving around seven."

"Fine by me. I'm always up at five anyway. I'll drive down, but once we hit the city it's all yours."

"Not a problem. I know Manhattan inside and out. I never thought I would miss the daily hustle, but I do."

"And Syracuse?"

"Very nice. It's just different. I'm still feeling my way around, but I love the fact that I can stop in for a beer without needing to take out a loan to pay for it." They were both laughing.

"It's that bad?"

"Trust me, it's worse. If you can grab lunch for twenty bucks, it's a great deal. That's why when I worked in Manhattan, like everyone else, I commuted."

Eleven o'clock on Thursday morning, Detectives Brockington and Wade found themselves on the 12th floor of Park Tower West at the front desk of Executive Introductions. They introduced themselves then provided proper ID. They were escorted to the office of Scott Montgomery, CEO. Scott looked to be early forties, tall and thin with a small beard and a diamond stud earring in his left ear, looking every bit the executive with a silk tie and custom-made pinstripe suit.

"Detectives, please have a seat." Scott went to the door. "Dawn, please hold all my calls. I must admit, I'm a little shocked. Two detectives from Syracuse. That's a little ways from home base, is it not?"

Brockington replied, "It is, but I think you may be of some help to us."

"If I can."

"Mr. Montgomery, I know a lot more than you think about Executive Introductions, and honestly, we didn't drive over 250 miles to question your business, but an incident occurred about three months ago. One of your associates, Peyton Long, died from an accidental fall and we're investigating it."

Scott Montgomery leaned back in his high back leather chair, looking across his oak desk. "Detective, at Executive, we provide a service for men of means who don't have time to meet eligible females. We arrange that and we are quite in-depth about who we take on as a client. I can assure you all our work is above board from our clients to our associates and please call me Scott."

"Okay, Scott, like I said, Peyton Long was found at the bottom of a gorge and we're not convinced it was an accident. She worked for you, and to your credit, the only reason I'm not breaking your balls right now is you treat your associates fairly. That carries a lot of weight with me. I need your help. I want the names of the clients that Peyton Long was dating."

"Detective, this is a privacy issue. My clients depend on total anonymity and they get it."

"I understand, but here's the thing. I have a young woman who may been murdered and her killer may be one of your clients, which means he very well may be dating another one of your associates right now."

Brockington stood up and walked toward Scott Montgomery, who was seated behind his huge oak desk and looked down at him. "I don't care about your sugar daddies or their fucking money. I don't care about their privacy. I care about a young girl who died way too soon, so here are your options. Honestly, I don't usually bargain, so consider this your lucky day. I'm going to take my partner Ed here for the best pizza and craft beer in all of Manhattan, then I'm going to kick his ass in a game of pool. That should take about an hour and a half. When I come back to your empty office, I expect to find a nice folder with the information I requested on your desk you accidentally left by mistake and I found it. That's the best-case scenario for everyone. If that doesn't work, then I will get a court order, drag your ass before a judge, and you can explain your business to him. I don't believe he will be quite as understanding as me. To make matters worse for you, if that happens, you just know someone is going to tip off a reporter and we both know the New York media just loves stories about the rich and their sex lives, especially if it involves the murder of a young attractive coed and some wealthy businessman."

"Ed, you ready for an ass-kicking? Let's have it, and trust me, no mercy. Did I mention loser buys? I have a credit card. We're good."

Ed then reached across the desk to shake Scott's hand. "It was nice meeting you."

"Have great day." Scott shook Ed's hand then sat back down looking very stoic.

Laura smiled. "Scott, it's been a pleasure." With that, the two detectives walked out of the office and made their way to the elevator.

On the way down, Wade asked, "So you think he fell for it?"

"I hope so. I don't have shit to take him before a judge."

They were on their second beer and playing pool at the Long Island Bar and Grill.

"You were right; this is really good pizza and the beer is awesome."

"This was our favorite watering hole on Friday nights. One of the few places in Manhattan that don't require a coat and tie. Told you I'd kick your ass." Brockington was laughing.

"In my defense, you did have home field advantage."

"Right, it's a fucking pool table. Pay up, pal."

"Glad to; this was great."

They made their way back over to Park Tower West and

pulled into the parking garage.

"Wait here. Be right back," Brockington said with a smirk.

"Good luck."

Less than ten minutes later, Brockington was back. "Look what I found, this nice folder labeled *Confidential: Peyton Long*. I love it when the public is so cooperative with law enforcement. Tell you what, Wade, why don't you grab some shut eye while I get out of the city and then you can drive us home while I look over the folder."

"That works for me." The two detectives didn't arrive back in Syracuse until after 8:00 p.m. Wade pulled into the police station parking lot. "I'm one tired SOB."

"It was worth the trip. The folder was very enlightening. I'll give you the lowdown in the morning. Get some rest. You look like you had your ass kicked."

"Very funny. See you in the a.m."

Detectives Brockington and Wade were at her desk going over Peyton Long's file. "The good news, Wade, is Peyton has only been on six different dates with Executive Dating, and to make this better, only one with the first name Roger, according to my notes. Amber was sure the way Peyton talked he was her regular guy."

"That's right; she did say Roger."

"It only gets better. According to her dating folder, she was the date of one Roger Palmer, who just happens to reside in Wilton, Connecticut. Here is the photo and biography."

Wade grabbed the folder as Brockington leaned back in her chair and just smiled and sipped her coffee. "Roger Palmer: Age 47, occupation: Research Chemist. Six foot three with receding hair line." Wade looked over at his partner. "Not exactly Screen Actors' Guild material, but that's just my opinion." Wade looked again at the photo attached. "This is going to sound strange, but I swear this photo of Roger Palmer looks familiar." The folder listed he was a Harvard Graduate and was married, but no mention of the wife's name. "So where do we go from here?"

"I'll talk to Chief Spence and show him what we got, see if we can spend some quality time in good old Wilton."

"How do we handle Roger Palmer without him getting suspicious and lawyering up? All we have at this point is our own suspicions and some circumstantial evidence, nothing concrete."

Laura pondered the thought for a moment. "Maybe just the fact that two detectives from Syracuse show up on his doorstep and ask if he knew Peyton Long will probably send him into cardiac arrest. We'll see if he volunteers to answer a few questions."

"I guess the first thing we do is make a trip down the hallway. Ladies first."

Brockington smiled. "I haven't been called that in some time."

Detectives Brockington and Wade found themselves sitting across the desk from Police Chief Gary Spence. They were quiet as he read the folder containing information about Peyton Long. He laid the folder down. "This is good work, Detectives. Looks like you might have something. What is your next step?"

"Sir, we wanted go up to Wilton again for maybe two days, see if we could spend quality time with Roger Palmer."

"Do you think Mr. Palmer will answer your questions?"

"He might. We don't know for sure this wasn't a freak

accident. We harbor some serious doubts. We're hoping his demeanor will tell us a lot."

"I'll allow it, but you both have court appearances on the docket for the next two weeks. Brockington, you have three scheduled and Wade two; these are your cases. You have to go or the D.A. will have my ass." Brockington looked perturbed to say the least. "Detective, it comes with the territory, so clear your schedule now. The both of you for three weeks from Monday; that's the best I can offer."

Brockington rose. "Thank you, sir."

Wade nodded. "Thanks, Chief."

"Dammit to hell. Sometimes I hate this job," Brockington muttered as she and Wade made their way back to her desk.

"Relax, Laura. Three weeks will fly by and Roger Palmer isn't going anywhere."

"You're right, but it still sucks if that fuck did this; every day he breathes fresh air is one day too many."

Chapter Fifteen

"I was starting to think I was a lousy lay or something. I hadn't heard from you in over a month." Lauren Palmer smiled as she walked nude across the White Plains Motor Lodge motel room as Tyler Drake sat up in bed wearing his boxers and gold chain. "I'm thinking you're pissed at me for touching you in the parking lot last time."

"Yes, sorry about that. Sometimes I'm a bitch. I have to be careful. No public displays, even out here." She walked over and kissed Tyler. "Don't worry. I plan on spending more time with you. Let's plan again for the same time next week if your schedule permits."

"What schedule? I work for myself, more or less."

"Oh, that's right. The parachute thing you do. I find that fascinating."

"Trust me, it's not that exciting."

"Do you know whose parachute you're doing?"

"Yeah, that's how I get paid. The money is decent, but right now, it's not where I need to be."

Lauren smiled and threw her legs over Tyler and pushed him back on the bed while running her tongue across her red lips. "I have an instinct about relationships and it's telling me this is going to beneficial for both of us."

Tyler looked confused. What relationship? She was a married woman having an affair. He just went with the moment. He kissed her deeply as they made love. Afterward, as they lay in bed, she asked, "So tell me, do you know Roger on a personal level?"

"Not really. Most of the guys who jump kind of all hang out together. If we pass, he just nods and keeps walking. We may have spoken a dozen words in two years."

"Roger's company is sending him to India for two weeks, so we can hook up a few times if you can handle it," Lauren said with a wicked grin.

"I can more than handle it."

"I'm flattered."

"When you didn't call, I just assumed I was a one-night stand."

"What kind of lady do you take me for?" She was laughing. "I have to get going."

"Damn, it's getting late."

Lauren went into the bathroom and quickly dressed. "Sorry to rush out right after. That's how it is. I will text you early next week."

"I'll look forward to it. I assume right here?"

"Yeah, I feel safe here. It's a drive, but I can totally relax and not worry."

Tyler was still in bed. Lauren leaned over, kissed him, and was out the door. Tyler Drake stared at the ceiling in the small motel room. He had a lot on his plate. He didn't give much thought to Lauren Palmer. He had dated married women before. Usually, they just stopped calling and he moved on. Lauren seemed to want more, but he wasn't sure what she was looking for, and right now, she was the least of his worries.

***

"That was the longest three weeks of my life," Brockington remarked as she loaded her bags into the white Ford Escape. "For what? Two of my cases plea bargain and the one case that goes to trial, I spent a grand total of twenty minutes on the witness stand and the next day the DA cuts him a deal."

Detective Wade was laughing. "Is this a great country or what? I'll take the first shift." Detective Wade hopped behind the steering wheel. It was 7:30 Tuesday morning.

"What's our ETA?"

"Depending on traffic, we should be in beautiful Wilton, Connecticut by 11:30. Of course, driving Scenic Rt I-81, let's make it closer to 12:30. I despise that fucking highway."

Brockington shrugged. "Don't we all? The good news is the Chief gave us an extra day, so we now have two full days."

"What's our game plan for Mr. Palmer?"

"I'm going to ask him if he could spare a few minutes to help us tie up some loose ends on a case we're trying to close, a young female by the name of Peyton Long."

"And if he refuses?"

"There is always the chance he just walks away, refuses to say anything. There's not a damn thing we can do about it. Right now, we have no leverage to compel him to cooperate."

"And if he does that, where do we go?"

"That's when I drop the bombshell that Peyton Long was pregnant at the time of her death. We believe she may have been trying to track down the biological father to give him the good news. The coroner for the city of Syracuse, Thomas

Roberts, is not convinced she fell accidentally and that's why we're here. That should be enough to make him uncomfortable."

Wade turned the white Ford onto I-81 and looked over at his partner. "It's a good plan. Where do think we should meet him? At home or work? They hate it when detectives show up the office."

Brockington was smiling. "You do have a devious mean streak after all. I haven't decided yet."

***

Gwen Cox was in a good but uncomfortable mood. She had waited a few weeks for everything to settle down. The money from Dr. Bob was safely in her bank account in Switzerland, all two million of it. She was worried ever since the transaction was completed, remembering Peyton's warning on the tape. "Nothing happens without Dr. Bob's permission. Nothing. Be careful. I'm not really sure what they're capable of." Dr. Robert Weinstein made her nervous. When meeting him, she was careful not to let it show. In fact, she acted cool and calm to show strength. It seemed to have worked. Not a word from Dr. Bob or anyone in his group. She kept her part of the deal and was ready for the next phase in her life.

Gwen Cox Long put in her two weeks' notice at the accounting firm of Harkness and Way was heading in to work. She felt stiffness in her lower back and soreness in her pelvic region. She attributed it to starting her period. Gwen settled into her cubicle and logged on to her email. She immediately felt nauseous and headed to the ladies' room. *God,* she thought, *I've had some uncomfortable periods before, but nothing like this*. She washed her face and returned to her desk.

"Hey, I hear congratulations are in order."

"Thanks, Steph."

Her colleague, Stephanie Zook, who shared the cubicle next to hers, stopped by her desk. "I just heard the big news. You're moving on?"

"I am."

"And I heard possibly to Zurich?"

"It's all true."

"I am so damn jealous. So tell me all about it."

"I'm single, trying to change. My life's been too stressful. I thought a move at this point would be good for me. It's been very difficult."

"Good for you. So are you staying there permanently?"

"I'm going to see how much I miss the States, but if I find I like it and I can make a living there, then why not."

"When's your last day?"

"This Friday at 5:00 p.m., but who's counting?" They both laughed.

"Gwen, do you feel okay? You don't look well!!"

"Not really. I started my period last night. It has been especially rough. For some reason, I've been nauseous all morning."

"When's your next GYN visit?"

"I couldn't get until the day before I leave."

Steph looked down. "Gwen, your arm is trembling. What—?"

Gwen started to twitch in her chair. "Steph, something is going on with my right eye. It's getting blurry. Oh my God! I can't see. I can't see!"

"Somebody help us!" Steph screamed at the top of her

lungs. Seconds later, the rest of the staff came running.

"What's going on?" Bryan Canter, the manager asked.

"It's Gwen."

Bryan quickly took her hand. "Gwen, are you okay?" Gwen started to convulse. "Call a fucking ambulance now!" Bryan yelled to no one in particular. Steph quickly grabbed her cell. There were four other members of the staff looking on with stunned looks on their faces. Bryan continued to hold her hand and try to converse with her. "Gwen, hang on. Help is on the way." At that second, Gwen's head lurched forward. Her face fell against the keyboard to her computer. Drool started to run down the side of her mouth onto the keys. "Gwen! Gwen, can you hear me? It's Bryan." The other four members of the staff, all females, tried to calm Gwen by talking to her and rubbing her back.

"Bryan, what else can we do?" asked his assistant Susan.

"Get me some moist towels." Susan ran to the ladies' room and returned with some warm, wet washcloths. Bryan took the towels and gently wiped Gwen's mouth and her forehead, all the time saying her name, hoping she would respond. "Where the fuck is the ambulance!" he shouted. It had now been close to fifteen minutes and it seemed liked hours. There was no response from Gwen other than a deep sigh now and then with drool continuing to run down the side of her face. Bryan gently wiped it off.

"Where is she?"

"This way." Steph had waited by the door for the EMTs to arrive. They quickly came bursting down the hallway with their gurney. Bryan stepped aside as the EMTs took over. They quickly moved her onto the stretcher. One started to take her vital signs while the second EMT started an IV to administer fluids.

"Who was with her when this started?" Jeff Stoutland, the head EMT, asked.

"I was," Steph offered.

"Did she say anything? Did she just take any medication that you know of?"

"No, we were just talking and she started to shake. Wait a minute, she did say her period was starting and giving her a difficult time."

Jeff Stoutland had a shoulder mike on, contacting the hospital while still working on Gwen.

"Go ahead, Medic 22. This is Dr. Lewis."

"Yes, I have female, approximate age mid-forties, lapsing in and out of coherence. Her vital signs are irregular, her breathing shallow. We have her on oxygen. She continues to drool, showing possible sign of a stroke. The victim had complained prior that her vision was becoming blurred. She told a co-worker he had just started her period and it had caused her discomfort. I sending her vitals now and you should receive them any minute. Stand by, 22." Seconds ticked by as the staff stood back and watched tears streaming down some of their faces while others just grimaced and quietly prayed to themselves.

"22, this is Dr. Lewis. Continue with OMI patient."

"Vital signs showing possibility of hemorrhagic shock."

"Add 250 ml of lactated Ringers and transport immediately to Mercy General. Have someone there notify the family if possible."

"Copy that. Strap the patient. We're moving within seconds." Gwen was secured to the gurney. "Can someone please notify a family member?" shouted Stoutland as they literally ran through the building with Gwen strapped to the gurney.

"I'll make the phone call," Bryan acknowledged.

"We can take one passenger to ride along and comfort her."

"Steph, you go," yelled Bryan.

They quickly loaded Gwen Long into the ambulance with the sounds of sirens screaming, quickly departing for Mercy General. The staff stood on the street, watching it fade into the distance. Most held hands but didn't say a word, they were to stunned by what had just transpired.

Medic-22 flew into the emergency entrance of Mercy General, where medical personnel were waiting. They quickly removed Gwen from the ambulance and were moving her quickly down the hallway at the same time working on her. Jeff Stoutland turned to Steph. "Wait here. The staff will keep you informed."

"Thank you." Jeff just nodded and followed the gurney down the hall and around a corner, where Dr. Lewis quickly began to assess her.

"She's has a pulse but shallow. Let's go, people! Let's go!" he yelled at the top of his lungs to his staff of nurses and techs. Jeff Stoutland stood back and watched. He had been a paramedic for over ten years and knew a lot of the ER docs. If Gwen Long had a chance at life, she was with the right guy. Dr. Lewis was intense, demanding of his people, and damn good.

"We're looking at toxic shock syndrome. Give me tight glycemic control with a target of <180 mg/dl. I need proper ventilator management with maintenance of plateau pressures of less than 30 cm of water."

"Doc, you want penicillin?"

"No, give me clindamycin."

"Doc, she's going into PVF!"

"Fuck!" Stoutland knew what that meant. Gwen had gone into a potentially fatal arrhythmia. The room was organized chaos. Everyone knew their job. There was some yelling. The hands working feverishly on Gwen Long included two E.R. nurses, Dr. Lewis, and his PA.

Nurse Adrian Russell, who was watching the monitor, screamed, "She's flatlining!"

Dr. Lewis glanced up at the EKG machine. Get me the paddles!" Dr. Lewis quickly grabbed them and placed them on Gwen. "Clear!" There was brief beep on the monitor and flatline again. Again Dr. Lewis screamed and placed the paddles once more. "Clear!" He looked up the monitor. Nothing. Beads of sweat were now pouring off Dr. Lewis' forehead. The nurse wiped his forehead with a damp cloth. They continued to work on Gwen for another forty-five minutes. Totally exhausted, finally sensing there was nothing more he could do, Dr. Lewis pulled down his surgical mask, looking totally despondent. "I'm calling it. Time of death 12:15." The room went eerily silent. Dr. Lewis went over and tossed his mask in the hamper, kicked the ER door open, and left. The nurses quickly disconnected all the machines and covered the body. No one said a word. E.R. personnel pay a heavy price. While the job is tremendously rewarding, it is also both physically and emotionally draining.

Chapter Sixteen

Totally unaware of what had just taken place over 200 miles away at Mercy General, Detectives Laura Brockington and Ed Wade had just arrived in Wilton, Connecticut. They checked into their respective hotel rooms and decided to grab some lunch. “Any suggestions, Ed?”

“Yeah, I Googled restaurants in Wilton and found a place called La Cantina and I love Mexican.”

“That works for me. I love margaritas.”

Ed was surprised. “Detective Brockington drinks while on duty?” he said with a smirk.

“We’re not actually on duty until I check in with the chief and tell him we’re here and that won’t happen until after lunch.”

“Music to my ears, Detective. I love Mexican beer.” They settled in to La Cantina. Detective Brockington went with the taco salad and raspberry margarita. Ed Wade went with beef enchilada with fried rice.

“This is a nice place, Ed. Good choice. I really love the décor.” The restaurant was decorated with Mexican hats, a piñata hanging from the ceiling with Mexican music in the background, vibrant colors everywhere. The waitresses wore the traditional long black dresses and bright red blouses.

"How's the taco salad?"

"Delicious and I'll be back later for another margarita. They are to die for."

"And the enchiladas?"

"Really good and this beer is smooth. So what did you decide for Mr. Palmer?"

"I like your idea. Let's drop in at his place of employment. That should get his attention."

Ed smiled. "I knew it. Under that cool calm demeanor, Detective Laura Brockington could be a real bitch."

"Thank you. I'll take that as a compliment and wear it as a badge of honor."

"Where exactly does our friend work?"

"Roger Palmer is a Research Chemist for Mayfair Biotech."

"Sounds pretty prestigious. Maybe I should put on a nicer tie."

After lunch, the two detectives pulled the white Ford Escape up to the guard shack at Biotech.

"Good afternoon, how can I help you today?"

Detective Wade was driving and flashed his gold shield. "I'm Detective Ed Wade. This is my partner, Detective Brockington. We're here on official business. We need to speak with Mr. Roger Palmer."

The guard, who looked almost to be around seventy-plus, was a heavy-set man with a pleasant personality. He looked at Ed's gold shield. "From Syracuse?"

"Yes, sir. We are."

"Looks pretty official to me. Usually we ask that you be escorted, but I have a feeling you two can find your way around campus. Let me look at my manifest here. Yup, Mr. Palmer can be found in building 700, C corridor."

Ed looked at the guard's name on his shirt. "Thank you, David." The guard smiled and lifted the draw gate. As they drove through, Ed remarked how nice the landscaping was. "This is impressive." There were tennis courts for the employees, a basketball court, even an outside jogging track. "Looks a nice place to work."

Laura nodded her head in agreement. "This is very nice. There it is. 700 building." Ed whipped the SUV into a parking spot. They made their way to the lobby, where they were met by security.

"I assume you're here to meet Roger Palmer?"

"Yes, we are."

"David at the guard house said you were on your way and would be easy to spot. You looked like detectives." He was smiling. Ed thought, *whatever that means*. "Mr. Palmer's office is at the top of the escalator."

"Thank you." They quickly made their way up and came to the receptionist.

"Can I help you?" Her name was Sara Barker, a cute brunette with a great smile.

"I'm Detective Brockington and this is Detective Wade." She flashed her shield. "We would like to see Mr. Roger Palmer."

"Well, I'm his secretary; actually, not just his. I work for all the research personnel. I'm sorry to inform you that Mr. Palmer is out of the country."

"Excuse me, what?" Brockington looked peeved.

"Yes, he is in India until next week on assignment. I'm sorry, is this an emergency? I can contact him."

Brockington, not wanting to raise suspicion until she spoke with him, made it sound routine. "No, it's just we were in the area and wondered if we could have a few minutes with him, but will catch up him in the near future. Just bad timing on our part."

"I'm really sorry. If you like, I can email him. He gets correspondence from us every day."

"No, but thank you. It's really not a big deal." They turned and headed for the escalator.

Ed looked over at Laura on the way down. "What can you do? Just bad timing."

"I know, but if she contacts him, there goes our element of surprise. Damn it to hell."

"Relax, Laura. She may get busy and forget all about us. I thought you played it down well."

Laura shrugged. "I doubt it. How often do two detectives from 300 miles away come by your office? She's probably on her cell as we speak calling him or her co-workers to gossip. Fuck."

Detective Brockington was correct. Receptionist Sara Barker was on her cell, but not calling Roger.

"Hi, Ms. Palmer. This is Sara Barker. I'm Roger's secretary. How are you today?"

"A little sweaty, to tell you the truth, Sara. I just got out of the sauna here at the club and except for this towel on my head, I'm totally naked." She was laughing as she was talking.

"Oh, I'm so sorry to bother you!"

"You're not a bother at all. Besides, I'm the only person in the locker room this afternoon. So let me guess, Roger called from India and he can't find his hotel room." She was laughing as she said it. She could hear Sara laughing on the other end. "I love Roger, but he is at times the absent-minded professor. So what's my hubby done?"

"This afternoon, actually about ten minutes ago, two detectives from Syracuse, New York showed up at my desk wanting to speak with Roger. I informed them he was out of the country until next week."

Lauren Palmer almost dropped her iPhone. She was standing in front of a full-length mirror, the glass half-steamed from the sauna, her friendly disposition immediately gone, replaced with one of anxiety. She could feel her heart racing. But she needed to remain calm. She went over to her locker and put on her white terrycloth robe and took a seat on the wooden bench, catching her breath. She coolly asked Sara, "You said two detectives. Do you recall their names?"

"I do. They were Detectives Brockington and Wade. They were very pleasant, but a long way from home — Syracuse, to be exact."

Thinking fast, Lauren came up with a plausible explanation. "Those two again. Sometimes I swear this will never end. Over four years ago, Roger was a witness to a car accident. A lawsuit filed by one of the persons involved has dragged on since they always want Roger to give another statement. I'm so glad you called me, Sara, instead of Roger. He would have flipped out. Please don't mention it to him. I will tell him when he gets home. He is so tired of dealing with this."

"That must be a headache for him. Trust me, I will not say a word about it, Ms. Palmer, and sorry to bring you bad news."

"That's all right. You did the right thing by calling me. I will break the news to Roger. enjoy the rest of your day, Sara, and we'll talk soon." Lauren sat on the bench taking deep breaths. Two detectives from New York could only mean one thing, but how in the hell had they come up with Roger's name?

Lauren quickly dressed, throwing on her skintight jeans and halter top. She had work to do. Lauren got behind the wheel of her Land Rover put on her Bluetooth headphones, and called Tyler Drake. She was zipping through town.

Tyler answered. "This is a surprise. I don't believe we ever actually talked on the cell. What's up?"

"I don't know, just wondering if you would like to meet later?"

"This is a nice surprise; twice in one week, but no way. I'm working till 6:00 and then make the drive to Turnbull? I'd be exhausted…"

"No need to. You can come to my place. Roger is out of the country till next week."

"Really, your place?"

"It's fine, but don't come till after 11:00."

"I will be there." They talked for a few more minutes before Lauren hung up. She turned up her driveway. *Fuck*, she thought. *Detectives.* She parked the Range Rover and leaned back in the leather seat. She took a long pause and tapped the name on the cell. She waited. Finally, on the fourth ring, he picked up.

"Hi, what's up?"

"Not good news; those detectives from New York were in town today wanting to speak with Roger. They went by his office. Thankfully, he's out of the country."

"That's not good. I thought we were done with them and how in the hell did they come up with his name?"

"I asked myself that exact question. I'm thinking I should

go ahead and start working on the plan I discussed with you some time ago. Roger is not mentally strong enough to handle any type of questioning. Tyler Drake is coming by tonight. I would like to use the information you gave me on his background to try and squeeze him." There was a long pause before she received her answer.

"You realize once we go down that road, there is no turning back?"

"I do. We're running out of options. We can't let anything stop us from our long-term commitment. We have too much invested."

"You need to be right about this. If Tyler doesn't cooperate, we have a real problem."

"I have him under control."

"Keep me informed. We'll meet at our place next Tuesday."

"I'll look forward to it! Bye." Lauren Palmer was what they refer to in the corporate world as a "climber." She was never satisfied. and if someone stood in her way, she had no problem squashing them. She was all about status with a beautiful estate, private clubs, vacations all over the world. Having never worked an actual job in her life and for someone with only a high school education, she led a life most would envy. Two years ago, she decided to make a move she had been planning since the day they were introduced. Lauren Palmer had her sights set on Dr. Robert Weinstein. She would flirt with him whenever Roger or Marie weren't around. Eventually, he called, and they had carried on an affair ever since. So much for that Old Harvard brotherhood. In Dr. Bob, Lauren found someone she considered her equal; not only an attractive man, he was as ruthless as she was. They also shared two common traits: sex and greed; neither one was ever satisfied. As for Marie Weinstein, she was blinded to her husband dalliances. Little did she realize the danger Lauren Palmer presented to her marriage, for being just a girl on the side was not in her DNA. She even convinced Dr. Bob to eventually betray his partners. "Honey," she said, "they're starting to make a lot of mistakes. You need to look out for yourself." She sowed seeds of doubt in his mind and played right into her hands.

Unlike the rest of the wives and unknown to his partners, Lauren Palmer was privy to everything the Crimson was involved in, from Eagle 2 Investments to their bookie operations. Lauren knew all about Roger's fling when they went on their supposed fundraiser weekends. She could have cared less. Frankly, she was surprised he had enough energy to engage in any extracurricular activities. No, she had long-term plans for her and Dr. Robert Weinstein; that was all she was concerned about. A few months earlier, Roger threw a major wrench into her plans, and Lauren Palmer, the attractive blonde everyone assumed was nothing more than eye candy, proved how looks can be deceiving.

Lauren had been relaxing. It was a Saturday afternoon when a green Jeep covered in mud pulled into her driveway. Roger, as luck would have it, was out of town on business. It would be Peyton Long's last trip into Wilton, Connecticut. She quickly made her way out the door. "Excuse me, but whatever you're selling, we're not buying, and if you haven't noticed, you just covered half my driveway with mud."

Peyton slowly put her sunglasses on top of her head. Her driver's side window was down and she looked at the blonde lady with her arms folded standing on the patio. She opened her driver's side door and stepped out, her sandals hitting the pavement at the same time she took her paper coffee cup and tossed it back into the Jeep. In attractiveness, she was Lauren's equal, but that was all they had in common. In her skin-tight jeans and halter top, she stood looking around for a second and then stared Lauren Palmer right in the eye.

"Sorry about the driveway. I didn't realize I was leaving a trail. Actually, not selling anything. I was hoping to speak with Roger Palmer. I believe this is his address."

"It is. I'm his wife. Roger is away for the weekend. How can I help you?"

"I was hoping to speak with him in private."

"Like I said, he is away. How do you know Roger?"

"Can we talk inside?" Lauren was hesitant at first but agreed. They settled into the kitchen, sitting at the breakfast bar.

"Would you like some iced tea?"

"That would be great."

Lauren walked over to the fridge, grabbed two glasses, and poured them each some tea.

Peyton took a drink as Lauren took the stool beside her, taking a deep breath. "I guess you're wondering who I am and what I'm doing here?"

"Well, from those body-fitting jeans and halter top you have on, my first inclination is you're not a Jehovah Witness, so I assume you're here to tell me you're fucking my husband."

Peyton almost choked. "It's not like that at all; this was strictly a business transaction."

"So that's what they're calling it now?" Lauren was almost laughing. "A business transaction?"

"Let me try and explain. This is not coming out the way I intended."

"Relax. I'm not upset. I know all about you and Roger and your weekend getaways. Actually, you were helping me out. I'd rather be out in my garden pulling weeds for all the excitement he provides me in that area."

"So you have an open marriage?"

"No, he just isn't aware that I know of his exploits. So where are you from and how else do you spend your time?"

"I'm a student at Cayuga Community in Syracuse studying to become a dental hygienist."

"You're a long way from home." Lauren couldn't help but crack a smile at the thought of this brilliant Harvard man and the community college coed. "So what brings you to Wilton and to our house?"

Peyton paused. "Not really sure how say this. I've rehearsed it a thousand times. There is no easy way to put this. I'm pregnant and Roger is the father. I may need some financial help." Her voice was cracking, she was so nervous. "I promise this is just a one-time thing. Roger will never hear from me again, but I'm barely getting by. I don't believe in abortion, but with his help, I will find a good home for the baby."

Lauren got up from her barstool and walked across the kitchen floor and opened up the dual wine cellar refrigerator and removed a bottle of Armand de Brignac and grabbed two goblets from the bar. "This calls for a celebration. I'm sure Roger won't mind one bit if we down his most prized possession. After all, we are honoring him. It's not every day one becomes a baby daddy." As Lauren removed the cork and poured the wine, Peyton didn't know what to think or to say.

This was not how she thought it would play out.

Lauren lifted her glass. “Here’s to you, kiddo. You played the game well. I admire that.”

Peyton smiled and they clinked glasses.

“Let me cut up some cheese and crackers. We’ll finish off the wine and see if we can find some common ground that will work for both of us.”

Peyton was so stunned by this turn of events, she was almost speechless. This was beyond her wildest dreams that this could be going so smoothly. She took another drink of wine.

“Thank you for being so understanding I never expected this.”

“Roger, for all his faults, and this is a big one, is still my husband. If he has a problem, then so do I. We need to reach an agreement that works for both of us.” For the next hour, they drank wine and conversed. “I’ll be right back. I need to use the ladies’ room.”

Lauren headed upstairs right for the medicine cabinet, finding Roger’s bottle of Restoril sleeping pills and taking out the last two.

They were on their third glass of wine when Peyton remarked, “I really can’t drink any more. I have to drive. May I have a seat on the sofa?”

“Of course, relax.” Peyton was on the sofa no longer than ten minutes when she passed out from the effects of the wine and sleeping pills that Lauren had crushed up and put in her last drink.

Lauren sat across from Peyton. Finishing her wine, she took the last sip and sat her goblet on the coffee table. She walked over and looked down at the young girl stretched out on her sofa. *Unbelievable nerve*, she thought, *coming to my residence and then basically blackmailing me requesting one hundred thousand dollars for future expenses and you will never hear from me again. I swear, she said! Well, sweetheart, you got the last part right anyway.*

Lauren cautiously lifted Peyton off the sofa and laid her on the hardwood floor. She went upstairs. Returning, she straddled Peyton's body while staring straight down at her. She fluffed the silk-covered pillow with her hands. "Since you shared Roger's bed, I thought you should take part of it with you." She placed the pillow over Peyton's face, pressing down firmly until she drew her last breath.

Lauren then casually went back up to the bedroom and placed Roger's silk-covered pillow on the bed just as she had found it.

Lauren backed the green Jeep into the garage and closed the door. She was hosing off the driveway when her neighbor Annie came by jogging. She took off her headphones and stood at the bottom of the driveway, jogging in place. "Hi, Lauren!"

"Hey, Annie. Out for jog?"

"Yeah, before it gets too hot. What's with all the mud?"

"Idiot delivery man in his van, and to top it off, the package wasn't mine. What can you do? I'll give you a call later."

"Sounds good." Annie went on her way.

Over the next two hours, Lauren removed all of Peyton's clothes, replacing them with a new jogging outfit. When dusk settled over Wilton, she placed her in the Jeep, buckled her, then drove out to Quarry Head State Park. Driving through twice, convinced no one was around, she made her way up

Devils' Path, removed the chain link fence, and pulled alongside the drop-off, looking around once more, then removing the body and laying it prone on the edge, and then with her foot, she pushed it over the edge. It rolled down the embankment, finally coming to a rest some 300 feet below.

Lauren remembered to wear gloves and shoe covers, leaving no trace of her ever being in the Jeep. She parked it at the far corner of the state park and placed the keys in a slit in the carpet she noticed on the floor.

Wearing her own jogging outfit, she made the two-mile run to the park entrance, where she used her cell to call for Uber. The driver was there in ten minutes.

"Hi, I'm Carl with Uber."

"Hi, Carl, thanks for being so prompt. This is so embarrassing. I was out for a run and I started to cramp up."

"Glad to be of service."

Everything went off without a hitch. The only problem was that Lauren could not believe the body was discovered the next day. At the least, she figured a week or more.

It was 11:15 p.m. when the doorbell rang. Lauren had put on a short silk blue negligee. She quickly glanced at herself in the mirror. Tonight was important and she quickly answered the front door. "Well, come in, Mr. Drake." She gave him a deep kiss. He responded by grabbing her and pulling her in. "Slow down, mister. We have all night."

Tyler smiled and released her. "This is some place," he remarked while walking through the living room past the huge stone fireplace, the hardwood floors glistening. "When is Roger due back?"

"Not until the end of the week at the earliest, so you can relax. Would you like a drink?"

"Absolutely."

"Beer or wine?"

"Beer works." She returned with his beer and a glass of wine for herself.

"Roger must do really well as a chemist."

"Yeah, we manage to get by," Lauren said with a grin.

"So am I now a regular?"

"We'll see. You have earned my trust; no easy task. I can be high maintenance and a bitch, to be honest."

Tyler smiled, finished off his beer, and went up behind Lauren, kissing her neck. They moved to the bedroom, where she was more accommodating than usual. Afterward, as they lay under the sheets, he glanced down at Lauren, who was sprawled across his chest. This, he thought, was different. She was not the snuggle type.

"That was exceptional."

She looked up and smiled. "I aim to please." Lauren curled up next to Tyler. "I had you over tonight for more than just this."

"Don't tell me the dishwasher broke."

Lauren laughed. "No, it's a little bigger than that."

"Okay, I'll do what I can."

Lauren sat up in bed as Tyler leaned back against the headboard. "I believe we can help each other out."

Tyler looked confused. "How so?"

"You have some financial issues I can help with." Tyler was totally caught off guard. "Is that right?"

"What the fuck do you know about my finances?" He was pissed.

"I'm aware of your gambling debt. You owe over $150,000 plus interest to people who don't take kindly to unpaid debt, plus all your credit cards are maxed out. The bank holding the mortgage on your townhouse says you're two months behind. Basically, you couldn't get a loan to cover the cost of a postage stamp."

Lauren had moved to the foot of the bed, pulling the sheet up around her, and was facing Tyler, who looked like he could incinerate any second. With a stunned, angry look on his face, he said, "Who the fuck are you? And how the hell do you know about my personal business?"

"Take it easy. Like I said, we can be beneficial to each other. Doesn't matter how I know about your issues. It only matters that I can make it go away."

"Oh, is that right? You're connected, are you?" Tyler got up to get dressed.

"Where are you going?"

"I have no idea who you are, lady, but you know shit that you have no business knowing." Tyler was on the side the of the bed with his boxers on.

Lauren looked at him. "You should hear my offer. At 28 percent interest a week, how much longer can you hold out?"

Tyler was intense, his face beet red. "Go ahead. I'm listening."

"I will take care of your debt, plus give you an extra $75,000 to move away and start over."

"Yeah, right. What do want me to do, kill somebody?"

Lauren bit down on her lower lip for a second. "Actually, I need Roger to succumb to an accident.

Tyler was shocked. "Come again? I'm not sure I heard you correctly."

"No, you heard me correctly."

"You want me to kill your husband?"

"I didn't say that exactly, but accidents happen."

"You're out of your fucking mind."

"Is that right? Where else are you going to turn? You have a serious cash flow problem, which shortly, if not taken care of, will result in a health care problem. This is a chance for a clean start. Move to the west coast, far away from here."

Tyler was biting his nails. "If this is some kind of sick game you're playing, I don't like it."

"I can assure you that is not the case." For the next several minutes, there was total silence.

"I assume you already have a plan?"

"Roger's favorite pastime is parachuting, right?"

Tyler knew instantly what Lauren was hinting at. "You want me to fix it so his chute doesn't open?"

Lauren didn't answer at first, then she replied, "Unfortunately, bad things happen." She got off the bed. Totally nude, she walked over and put on the blue negligee.

Tyler still hadn't moved, trying to absorb what had gone down. Lauren went over to the dresser, took out her hairbrush, and stroked her hair, the whole time watching Tyler's reaction in the mirror. Tyler dressed without saying another word. Lauren reached into the top dresser drawer, removing an envelope containing $25,000 cash. She walked over, put both arms around Tyler, and kissed him, sliding the envelope into his waistband and whispering in his ear. "The rest will be waiting once we conclude our business arrangement; hopefully, within the next few weeks." She kissed him again. Tyler didn't respond; he slipped the envelope into his pants pocket and left without saying another word.

Out in his car, Tyler wondered, *what the fuck have I gotten myself into?* He started to question everything. Did she target him from the get-go? *Lauren Palmer had an attractiveness that drew you in. So do black widow spiders from afar. It's when you get too close, the poison comes out.* Tyler Drake would be the first to tell you he was far from a perfect person; he always had an eye for the ladies, which cost him his only serious relationship. He enjoyed the night life, the bars, but his downfall was gambling. He didn't know when to quit; it had cost him everything, and soon, maybe his life. Lauren was right. He was in debt to individuals who were not into the refinance business; they were into the pay me what you fucking owe me business. Tyler, for all his shortcomings, had for the most part only destroyed his own life. Now he was contemplating murder. He looked down at the money again, rubbing his forehead, turned on the ignition to his black Barracuda, and sped down the darkened driveway pounding his fist on the dashboard, repeating to himself, "You fucking idiot, how much worse can you fuck up your life!"

Chapter Seventeen

Robert Weinstein was pleased. Just over a week ago, he had logged on to the website of the *Syracuse Daily Times* and read the obituary of Gwen Cox Long due to medical complications.

Finally, he thought, *maybe this mess is about finished.* Behind his partners' backs using some creative bookkeeping and Lauren Palmer, he had managed to divert over ten million dollars into an overseas account.

What Dr. Bob didn't realize, he wasn't the only person concerned about Gwen Long's death.

***

Over 250 miles away, Detectives Brockington and Wade had just pulled into the accounting office of Harkness and Way. They had been unaware of this tragic turn of events until yesterday when a routine phone call to Gwen's residence had them hustling to find out exactly what had happened.

"Good morning. Welcome to Harkness and Way. I'm Janet. How can I help you today?"

Both detectives showed their badges. "We need to talk with someone about Gwen Long."

Janet looked upset. "Wait here. I'll get the manager."

Janet returned with a man who looked harried. "Hi. I'm Bryan Canter. Can I help you?"

"Yes. Detective Brockington, Syracuse PD, and my partner Ed Wade. We have a few questions concerning Gwen Long."

"Okay, let's go to my office." Bryan sat behind his desk as the two detectives took chairs across from him.

"Detective Wade will be recording while I ask questions. Is that okay?"

"Fine with me."

"May I call you Bryan?"

"Yes, please."

"Good. Bryan, who was with Gwen when she fell ill?"

"Stephanie Zook. She's an accountant here. She started yelling for help and several of us responded."

"Was she conscious?"

"Partially; not really coherent."

"Did she say anything to Stephanie before falling ill?"

"Just she had started her period the night before and was having a very difficult time. She felt nauseous. Once here at the office, she complained about her vision. Unfortunately, from then on, it went downhill quickly. We called the paramedics. I felt so damn useless; we all did."

"How well did you know her?"

"Not as well as I thought."

"How so?"

"Listen, I don't want to come off sounding like a jerk. This is tragic what happened, especially after just losing her daughter. I started a new girl. She was going through the files and things were not adding up. At first, I figured she's new.

Probably making some mistakes, but being precautious, I brought in an outside auditor who confirmed it. Gwen Long had been embezzling from the firm for the past sixteen months, possibly longer, to the tune of almost $200,000, not a lot for a firm of this size, which is kind of how she was getting away with it. So now here I am, trying to console our employees about the loss of a co-worker, at the same time knowing she was not who she seemed. I did not share that information with them, just the owners of the firm."

"Did you meet any other family members?"

"No, I haven't. We all gathered at the hospital after hearing the news, but I don't recall anyone from her family being there."

"What hospital?"

"Mercy General."

"Wade, anything to add?"

"How long did Gwen work here?"

A little over two years. She had worked at a couple other firms. Came with a clean work history, but if they were to go through their books, I seriously doubt we were the first."

Wade remarked, "So do I."

Brockington asked several more questions before leaving.

Thirty minutes later, the detectives found themselves meeting with Dr. Frank Lewis, head of the ER at Mercy General.

"First off, doctor, thanks for meeting with us. I know you're extremely busy."

"Not a problem. It's not every day detectives come looking for me." Everyone shared a small laugh. "So you had questions regarding the death of Gwen Long?"

"That's correct."

Dr. Lewis leaned back in his leather chair. "Fire away."

Brockington, as usual, did the talking, "I understand cause of death was toxic shock syndrome?"

"That's correct."

"Is that common?"

"Well, you have to understand there are two types of TSS. As it's more commonly known, a serious condition caused by bacterial toxins entering the body, it can rapidly deteriorate your health and threaten your life. That being said, there are two types of bacteria: streptococcal and staphylococcal. The staphylococcal is the milder version and the risk of dying is almost non-existent. The unlucky ones like Gwen Long get struck with streptococcal toxic shock syndrome; almost half die. It's still rare, maybe eight to fifteen cases a year."

"So, you believe she waited too long?"

"Well with proper medical care right away, she probably would have been fine in about two weeks, but toxic shock can be deadly in less than two days. This, of course, if the disease goes unnoticed."

"My understanding is she was trying to see her gynecologist, but couldn't get an appointment."

"Hindsight being 20-20, you go to a walk-in clinic."

"How does this strike such a healthy person?"

"How the bacterium causes the syndrome and the condition the body deteriorates that quickly is unknown. One theory is a tampon left in for excess periods of time, that the old blood attracts the bacteria, which in turns release poisons into the body."

"Doctor, are you positive this caused the death of Gwen Long?"

"Absolutely. By the way you're asking questions, you're

thinking something more sinister at play?"

"We had to make sure. Her daughter, less than three months ago, accidentally fell to her death. The timing seems suspicious."

"That's understandable."

"Did you meet the family?"

"I did not. My understanding is they were able to locate a brother. It took almost two days. Not sure why. If you check with the records department, tell them I sent you. They should be able to fill you in."

They rose to leave. "Doctor, thank you again. If anything changes for any reason, call me directly."

Brockington and Wade made a quick trip to the records department and retrieved a copy of the medical report and the address of Gwen Long's brother. Wade drove back to the station as Brockington scanned the file. "Anything of use?"

"Let's see, her brother Marc lives in Seattle, Washington. That might explain the delay in reaching him. Cause of death natural due to organ failure, then it's just all medical jargon, basically absolutely no use to us. I would like you to call her brother, see if they had been in contact lately. If she had said anything regarding the loss of Peyton."

"Okay. Then what?"

"I need something to show Chief Spence we're not wasting our time. This might just do it."

"Do you think the doc is right? Natural causes?"

"Sounds convincing, but let's be honest. Gwen Long was no angel and nobody's fool. Maybe this time, she got in over her head."

The two detectives sat across from their boss as he read the file and laid it gently on his desk. He took off his glasses and looked straight at Brockington. “I sent you up to Wilton twice. Why would this time be different?”

“I fucked up last time, plain and simple. I should have checked, but Chief, first the daughter accidentally — 300 miles from home — falls down some embankment that even the locals couldn’t find, and now three months later, the mother with a questionable history of being honest ends up dead? It might just be tragically bad timing, but my gut instinct says otherwise.”

“Lucky for you, Detective, your track record speaks for itself. Here’s the deal. You send a certified letter to Mr. Palmer requesting a time and place for an interview.”

“Chief, that gives him ample opportunity to cover his ass.”

“Detective, that’s the deal. Take it or not. I haven’t seen a smidgen of evidence to convince me this is not a waste of time. Only because it’s you I’m giving this opportunity.”

They rose to leave. “Thank you, sir, I will send the letter this afternoon.” Wade sat at his desk when Brockington approached with the letter from the Syracuse PD requesting the interview. “Take this. Make sure you send a private courier. It must be hand delivered, photo ID and signature required. I don’t care about the fucking cost; have it done correctly.”

Wade nodded. “I’m on it.”

***

“How is Dr. Bob these days?”

“Busy. He needs to slow down. I’m trying to talk him into Hawaii.” Marie Weinstein was relaxing in the hot sauna along with her friend Lauren Palmer. “Lauren, I was so glad you called. It seems we can never get together lately. With Bob’s work schedule, if it’s not his devotion to the group’s charity, the Crimson, it’s hard to find free time. This was a great idea.”

Lauren smiled at her friend. Both had white towels around their heads, their bodies dripping, with sweat running down their chests.

“How is Roger these days?”

“Staying busy at work. He was recently in India, not a place I would care to visit.”

“We haven’t taken a vacation in over six months. Damn, we’re spoiled.” They both laughed. “Lauren, can I ask you something private?”

“Of course. It will go no farther. What’s up?”

“Lately, Bob has had very little interest in the physical side of our marriage. You know what I mean?”

“I do. Like you said, he has been working a lot lately; probably just tired.”

“I don’t think that’s it. Sometimes I wonder if he is still attracted to me, you know.”

“Marie, you’re stunning. Men are always checking you out.”

“Thanks, but that’s you, dear, the way men stare. I just hope he’s not fooling around. I mean, if he is, and it’s just some slut for sex, I could care less. We have a great life. I don’t want it fucked up, pardon my French.”

Lauren laughed. “Bob would never cheat on you, Marie. I wouldn’t give it a second thought.”

“How is Roger in the sack, now that you know my problem?”

Lauren smirked. “Using ‘Roger’ and ‘sex’ in the same

sentence. Honestly, I could walk in the living room with nothing on but a towel, drop the towel, and Roger would look up from his laptop and say 'Honey, you should put on a robe; you'll get a chill' and immediately go back to reading."

Marie busted out laughing. "I don't believe that for one minute. Men are always undressing you with their eyes. Hell, I've even caught Bob checking you out."

"What?"

"I don't care. We're friends. Let him have his fantasies about you. Who knows? Maybe it will get his libido going."

Lauren leaned in and gave her friend a hug. "Don't you worry; these things have a way of working out."

***

Roger Palmer ripped into the parking lot of Western State University and made a bee line to the office of friend and confidant Larry Sinclair. He quickly closed the door behind him.

"Damn, this is a surprise. What's up, Roger?"

"This is what's up." He tossed a large manila folder onto Larry's desk. "Go ahead; open it." Roger, clearly agitated, rubbed his head, took off his glasses, and paced the floor.

Larry looked over the document. "When the hell did you get this?"

"This morning. I tried to stay calm. I was at work and got paged to come down to the lobby where the security guard sits and they're waiting. A Connecticut state trooper asked if I was Roger Palmer. Took my driver's license, then made me fucking sign for that. Trust me, he was less than thrilled to be there."

"Damn, Roger, looks like they want have sit-down with you."

"You fucking think, Larry! I don't know what to do."

"You sure it's about Peyton?"

"Of course. What else could it be? They must not believe she died accidentally, but how in the hell did they get my name? Honest to God, I never laid a hand on that girl. I really liked her. How in the hell do I explain this to Lauren?"

"Who else knows about this?"

"Nobody. You imagine if Bob gets wind of this? I'm so fucked."

"Roger, get a grip. First off, go see a lawyer for some legal advice. They might advise you do nothing. It's not a subpoena; it's a request. Tell them you would be glad to meet. Unfortunately, you're tied up for the next two weeks. That buys you some time."

"I like that. You think they will go for it?"

"Why not? What's the worst that can happen?"

"They can show up on my fucking doorstep tomorrow morning, that's what! I don't have a choice. I'll wait two days, then mail back a date two weeks out. Hopefully, by then, I can figure this out. If Lauren gets wind of this, I'm dead. She is not the forgiving type. Larry, this stays between us. Do not tell Bob."

Larry looked at his friend. "Not a word. From me, silence is golden. Did you know that Gwen Long passed away?"

"Oh, shit. When?"

"Not sure of the exact date. Cal told me. Dr. Bob was very pleased the cause of death was listed as natural."

Roger was speechless for a couple of minutes. "Damn, I'm not sure how we got to this point, Larry, but we're treading in some deep water, my friend." Larry just nodded. Roger got up to leave and bear-hugged his closest ally.

Larry then patted him on the back. “We’ll be fine. That’s why we went to Harvard. We’re always a step ahead.”

Wednesday morning, Roger Palmer found himself sitting across from Emit Squires, Attorney at Law. Roger filled him in the best he could without outright lying.

“Roger, if you just want advice, that’s fine. I’ll offer it free. If you want legal representation, the retainer is five thousand, then anything you say is attorney-client privileged information.” Roger wrote out the check. “First off, is there any reason at all they would want to speak with you?” Roger filled in his lawyer on his affair with Peyton Long. “Did you harm her in any way?”

“Never. I hadn’t seen her in over a month when she fell.”

“Why do you think she was in the area?”

“I have no idea. I never even told her I was from Wilton.”

Roger sat for another forty minutes with his lawyer.

“Roger, for now, wait until law enforcement contacts you again. When they call to confirm the interview date, call me.”

“Should I be concerned about this?”

“From what you told me, no. Hell, if they arrested every man in this country who had an affair, half the male population would be doing time. On the other hand, if your memory was clouded and you overlooked something, the best criminal defense team in Connecticut will see that your rights are fully protected.”

As Roger headed for home, he wasn’t quite convinced his lawyer believed in his total innocence. Nonetheless, he hired an excellent legal team, hopefully never to need them. Roger was convinced it was time for a new start somewhere far from Wilton. His partners would be upset. After all, they were lifelong friends, but this thing had started to unravel badly. For now, he wouldn’t tell anyone, especially Lauren, who loved Wilton, but he would make plans to move and soon.

Chapter Eighteen

Detective Brockington walked over to Ed Wade's desk, slamming down a manila envelope. "What's this?"

"Take a look. It seems Mr. Palmer will be glad to meet with us, but the next two weeks are extremely busy for him."

"That SOB is trying to dodge us, hoping we'll go away. So I'm calling his bluff and accepting the third Monday from today at 9:00 a.m. sharp. This should get his attention. Here's my reply." She handed the letter to Detective Wade. "Mr. Palmer, thank you so much for taking time from your hectic schedule. Where is the best place for the interview to happen? We can meet at your home, business office, or elsewhere in Wilton. If transportation is an issue, we will be happy to accommodate you. We can also meet here at the Syracuse NYPD. Headquarters. Regards, Detective Laura Brockington."

Wade was laughing. "You're going to give that poor bastard a heart attack when he reads that."

"What makes you believe that lowlife has a heart!"

***

It was a bright sunny morning. Roger Palmer was feeling relieved. It had been three full days since his meeting with his lawyers and sending his reply to the Syracuse PD about the interview. Not a word. Maybe his lawyer was right; there was a very good chance this whole thing would just blow over. He zipped his white Mustang into the parking lot of the Sikorsky Memorial Airport, grabbed his personal bag, and headed to the hangar.

"Morning, Roger. Jumping today?"

He nodded in the affirmative. "Bill, are you?"

"Not today, my friend. Busy. Enjoy."

"I will."

"Morning, Roger. Beautiful day to jump."

"Morning, Tom. You're right. Gorgeous day to free fall."

Tom Harmon was a seasoned pilot with twenty-plus years' experience flying the Cessna Skyplane the so-called workhorse of the skydiving community.

"Do we have a full jump team this morning?"

"We do. You and three others. They're loading up now. Couple of the regulars, Ben Davis and Shawn, and a new one today: young girl named Susan Patrick."

Roger smiled. "About time we had something to look at around here." Tom barely acknowledged his sexist remark.

It was 11:10 a.m. when the Cessna rolled onto the runway tower.

"This is BlueHawk, waiting for clearance."

There was the usual banter among the four jumpers. Roger introduced himself to Susan Patrick. "Is this your first solo?"

"No, just my first time jumping here. My log book has me presently at seventy-five. How many for you?"

Roger had to think for a minute. "Honestly, mine is at 302

over about an eight-year period. It's my hobby. Nice to see a new face here. Welcome to the team."

"Thanks, I appreciate that."

"BlueHawk, this is tower. You're clear for takeoff off on 12." The small plane taxied onto the runway. They could hear the roar of the engine. In a matter of seconds, they were screaming down the runway. In less than two minutes, they were airborne.

"Good morning, my friends. This is your captain speaking." Everyone laughed because it was such a small aircraft. "We'll be climbing to 12,000 feet this morning. The sun is out, not a cloud in the sky. Sit back and anticipate; I never say 'relax,' because when you're jumping out of a perfectly fine aircraft, just doesn't make much sense." There was more laughter. "I will give a five-minute warning before reaching the jump zone, then one minute before the first jump. Please decide the order now and be safe."

Roger looked at Susan. "I always say ladies first."

"No thanks. You lead the way. Show me how it's done!"

Roger smiled. "Okay!" The order was decided: Roger, Susan Patrick, Ben Davis, and Shawn Cummings last. The group chatted among themselves as the plane climbed farther into the blue sky. They were airborne approximately twenty minutes when Pilot Tom Harmon spoke. "Five minutes to drop zone. Line up."

The group crouched and made their way toward the door opening. "Ready, Number 1," shouted the voice of Tom Harmon. "Spot go!" Roger jumped. Susan made her way to the door "Hold!" came the command. "Spot go!" Susan jumped, followed in order over the next three minutes by Ben Davis and Shawn Cummings.

'Spot' is the correct moment to leave the plane. A good spot allows a jumper to land back in the drop zone.

Tom Harmon headed back to airport. He had another jump crew to take at 2:00 p.m. that day. He was enjoying the tranquility of flying. There was nothing more relaxing to him. When his radio came on, he heard, "BlueHawk, do you read?"

"This is BlueHawk; go ahead."

Dale Stewart, the spotter down at the drop zone, replied, "Didn't you say four jumpers this morning?"

"That's correct."

"Tom, I have my binoculars. I only count three chutes."

"What! Are you sure? Look around and count again. You are mistaken!" There was radio silence for twelve seconds.

"Tom, only counting three. Calling emergency personnel now."

Tom Harmon was shaken to the bone; he was still on the radio. "I had a new jumper today. Young girl, but she had experience. Oh my God, this cannot be happening." Tom Harmon was trying maintain his composure. He felt pressure in his chest as his hands almost broke the pilot's control wheel in half, he was gripping it so intensely. "Control Tower, this is BlueHawk, requesting permission to do a fly back."

"That's a negative, BlueHawk. Return to base." Tom was denied by the tower. They wanted him on the ground as soon as possible for his own safety, not knowing his mental state at that moment in time.

The call came in at 11:40 a.m. "Station 21-4, possible fall victim 815 Limestone Road, Sikorsky Airfield."

Emergency personnel sprang into action, grabbing their gear. Three minutes later, the doors to Station 21-4 flung open, the ambulance with sirens blaring rolling down the driveway.

Dale Stewart watched with anticipation and anxiety as the three parachutists landed near the drop zone, each landing safely, unaware of what was transpiring around them.

"Dale, I spotted him." Bryan Keys was standing up in the back of his Jeep with his binoculars. "Let's go!" Dale jumped in and they were off as the three members of the jump team gathered their equipment, unfazed at first at what was going on around them. As they made their way toward each other, they started to realize what was happening as more emergency vehicles came screaming toward the area, including medical personnel from the airport.

"Oh my God," Susan mouthed to no one in particular. "Where's your friend?" She realized Roger Palmer was not in the drop zone. She started to shake. Shawn Cummings and Ben Davis each put their arms around her as tears rolled down her face. All three looked to be in a state of shock. Ben Davis took a knee. Shawn and Susan joined him, their hands trembling, and prayed.

***

1:15 p.m. at the Ball and Thistle Racquet Club, Lauren Palmer was taking her scheduled tennis lesson. She was working up a good sweat when club manager Trey Capella approached. "Sorry to interrupt, Lauren, can I have a word with you, please?" Lauren looked annoyed but made her way across the court.

"What gives, Trey?"

"I need you to come with me to my office."

"Really? Right now, in the middle of my lesson?"

"I'm sorry. It's very important." Lauren grabbed a towel,

looking pissed, but followed Trey to his office. Inside waiting were two Connecticut state troopers.

"Lauren Palmer, Troopers Harlan and Desabitino. Could you have a seat, please?"

"Why? What's going on here?"

"We're very sorry to inform you there has been an accident involving your husband Roger this morning at Sikorsky Airfield."

"What are you talking about?"

"We don't know all the facts or reason, but his parachute failed to properly deploy. I'm very sorry."

Lauren Palmer was indeed stunned. "This can't be. My husband is an experienced jumper." She was overcome with emotion, tears running down her face. Trooper Harlan kneeled and held her hands. "There must be a mistake!" she screamed. "This cannot be! You're mistaken!" Lauren Palmer's emotions were very real; she had indeed put this in motion, but had no idea when it would take place. She was taken totally off-guard. The reality of what she had done started to set in. She was crying uncontrollably. Trey Capella made some phone calls and Lauren's neighbor was en route to be with her. Trey himself was having a difficult time keeping his own emotions in check. How could you not, watching someone in so much in pain?

***

It was 2:00 p.m. Dr. Robert Weinstein was with a patient when his office manager Sandy popped her head in the office. "Very sorry to interrupt, Doctor. Ms. Weinstein is on the phone. Seems there is an emergency. She needs to speak with you."

"No problem. I'll call her from my office. Could you finish up with Ms. Warren here? It's just paperwork."

"Absolutely."

Dr. Bob closed the door to his office and put his feet up on his desk. Marie's idea of an emergency was she found a good deal on a cruise and wanted to book it, so Bob wasn't alarmed at all about the call.

"Honey, you called?"

"Bob, you need to come home right now. Something terrible has happened."

"Is Matt okay?"

"Yes, I'm sorry. Matt's fine. It's Roger, Bob. He's gone." Marie was sobbing so much, Bob could barely understand her.

"Marie, honey, what do you mean Roger's gone?"

"He was in a parachute accident this morning. Bob, he's gone."

"I'm on my way." Dr. Bob laid down his cell phone. He knew in an instant that Lauren Palmer had indeed followed through on her plan. He reminded himself to step cautiously. They had talked of eventually being together, but patience was not Lauren Palmer's strong point.

***

Nine o'clock Friday morning, Detective Laura Brockington was going through her e-mails when her cell lit up. Not a number she recognized. "Hello?"

"Is this Detective Brockington, Syracuse PD?"

"It is. Who is this?"

"Detective, my name is Emit Squires. I'm an attorney here in Wilton, Connecticut. I'm making this call to you as a professional courtesy. I represent Roger Palmer."

"I see. So Mr. Palmer decided to lawyer up, did he? I'm not surprised."

"Detective, please let me finish."

"Sorry. Please go ahead."

"The reason for this call is to inform you that Mr. Palmer fell to his death yesterday morning during a parachute exercise. I thought you should know."

Laura Brockington was speechless for a minute. "You're fucking kidding me, right?"

"I wish I were, Detective."

"Skydiving accident?"

"Correct. My understanding is parachute malfunction, but it's still early for a final determination. The possibility remains he may have suffered a coronary or had another medical condition. We'll have to wait for the coroner's report. May I speak off the record, Detective?"

"Of course."

"I'm not sure what allegations you were looking into regarding Mr. Palmer. I only spent a few hours with him legally. I knew him slightly before he came to my office, just small talk at the some of the same clubs we were both members of. I found him the morning we talked agitated, even a bit unnerved. My suggestion, Detective, is you may want to excavate a little more, but you didn't hear that from me."

"Thank you, Mr. Squires, for the call, and I sincerely apologize for my attitude earlier. You are a true professional. I will take your advice in total confidence."

"You're welcome, Detective, and good luck. You will need it. Wilton's a very close-knit community. They like to protect their own, so to speak."

Laura Brockington was at a loss for words. In less than four months, three deaths, all accidental or natural causes, the latest Gwen Long and Roger Palmer, the two people most connected to Peyton Long, who had recently come under suspicion from the Syracuse PD. Now both were gone. Laura Brockington stared straight ahead at her computer, in deep thought. The fact that a prominent attorney basically told her to watch her step spoke volumes. Detective Brockington's presence in Wilton had made someone uncomfortable, but enough to commit homicide? If she was right, there was a lot more going on in Wilton than just Roger Palmer with some young coed. She grabbed the case file and made her way to Chief Spence's office. They needed to talk.

Chapter Nineteen

Eight days later

It was a sunny but brisk Wednesday morning as the mourners filed into the beautiful old chapel off Salem Lane in Wilton. Like the town itself, the church was immaculate with landscaping to make any gardener envious. Ivy adorned the south side of the red brick church, flowers in full bloom. Bright orange marigolds ran along the sidewalk leading to the entrance where Father William waited to greet them, but there was no pleasure to take from all the beauty this morning. They had come to say good-bye to a good friend, colleague, and husband. Hopefully, kind words of inspiration would lift some spirits.

Lauren Palmer sat up front, looking withdrawn. Her closest friend Irene held her hand as Marie Weinstein put her arm around her back to comfort her. Marie herself was having a difficult time accepting what had happened.

Cal Estrada and Larry Sinclair, with their wives, sat in the second pew along with immediate family members. Both struggled to maintain their composure. One member of the Crimson was gone. They all were invited to speak, but were too emotional, so Dr. Bob would give the eulogy.

The choir sang several hymns as everyone was seated and Father William gave the opening. “We cannot understand today what has caused us so much heartache, but take comfort in knowing that Roger is among many who love him and have welcomed him into the Kingdom of Heaven.” The sermon was quite stirring and helped lift spirits among the grieving. Several friends spoke, and finally, Robert Weinstein took the podium.

“It is with tremendous sadness that we are here today. Roger was a good husband, son, and lifelong friend to many. A man of virtue, he had a great sense of humor and was not beyond pulling off a prank for a good laugh. His charitable work with the Crimson foundation has benefited the local police, little league, fire department, and scores of others for no other reason than to help out. I’ve known Roger since our days at Harvard University as members of the rowing team. He always stood head and shoulders above everyone else, not only because of his height, but also because of the content of his character. His devoted wife Lauren we consider family and we ask in the coming weeks and months to keep her in your thoughts and prayers.” Dr. Bob spoke for almost twenty-five minutes. When he finished, there was not a dry eye to be found.

For those who did not know the whole truth, one assumed that Dr. Bob and Lauren Palmer had lost a dear friend and wonderful husband. Not everyone who attended was sold.

The mourners retuned to Dr. Weinstein’s residence for a nice catered lunch and to comfort each other. As the others chatted among themselves, Cal Estrada and Larry Sinclair walked the estate, totally torn over the loss of their friend.

"I have to tell you, Cal, he came to my office last week. He was a wreck. The Syracuse PD wanted to interview him."

"What?"

"Yes, about Peyton Long. He was in a panic and made me promise not to tell Bob. He was afraid he would go off on him again."

"Did you?"

"No, not a word to anyone until now."

"Damn, Larry, how did we get into this fucking mess? The Syracuse PD. Bob will flip out when he gets wind of this. How did they tie Peyton and Roger together?"

"Roger wondered the same thing. Now this happening. You know they will be back asking questions. That means Lauren is going to find out about Peyton Long and Roger."

Cal paused. "Damn, not only did she lose her husband, now she's going to find out he was a sugar daddy to some young chick. I feel really bad for her. Larry, you realize once the wives find out, they'll be questioning us about our road trips. This is just fucking great."

The two walked among the hedges making small talk and reminiscing about Roger, the geek with the great sense of humor. With the fountains running, it was a beautiful estate. Finally, Cal turned to Larry. "Do you think Roger had anything to do with Peyton's death?"

"No way. He liked Peyton way too much. Besides, Roger couldn't step on an ant. Who knows? Maybe she was screwing someone else in Wilton besides him."

"Cal, you ever just think fuck this is, move out of Wilton and not look back?"

"No, not really. I mean, we have a lot going on. I guess you have?"

"Yes, but Susan would never agree. She loves it here and it's not like I can explain to her why I want out."

"After Roger's passing, I can only imagine Bob's response to you leaving."

"Honestly, Cal, I wouldn't say squat to him until the Atlas van was loaded and pulling out my driveway. The last sixteen months has changed him, he's not the same guy we knew from college or even two years ago. I've seen a side to him I didn't know existed."

"I guess we should go back. I wonder what the hell Lauren does now with that big house and just her?"

"I assume eventually she will sell and move away. We'll never see her again."

Cal shrugged his shoulders and grimaced. "Yup, life sucks." The two friends hugged and walked back to the house. They both hugged Lauren, who was in the kitchen talking with friends. She was fairly composed for all she had been through.

***

Nine o'clock a.m., central command office of the Syracuse Police Department. There were four chairs, all occupied. Chief Gary Spence was convinced beyond a reasonable doubt that the deaths of first Peyton Long and then her mother and now a possible suspect who had come under suspicion, all accidental, didn't, as they say, pass the smell test, but they needed evidence.

Chief Spence stood. "Good morning. You will notice a new face in the crowd. I would like to introduce Detective Clayton Fisher. Clayton, to your right, the lead detective on this case, Laura Brockington, her partner, Detective Ed

Wade." They all shook hands. "Clayton comes to us from the white-collar division of New York State Police. We're very fortunate to have him join us on a temporary basis. I had to beg, so make use of his time. Clayton, Detective Brockington will bring you up to speed on the case, but I can give you a very brief summation. We have three deaths all centered on a very wealthy close-knit community. The deaths have led us to believe someone with a financial interest may be trying to hide how they procured some of that wealth. Seems they're willing to do whatever it takes to keep it that way at this point. It's only a theory we're working on. We need proof. We're hoping you can help since you specialize in white collar. Brockington, anything to add?"

"Detective Fisher, glad you're here." She looked at the forty-five-year-old man with the athletic build, short brown hair, and brown eyes. He seemed much younger than his age. "This case is tough. The town is very wealthy. The police department was less than thrilled we were snooping around, so we won't get much help there. We need something solid to go on. We need a break."

Clayton spoke. "I can tell you from experience if its money laundering, it will take some time. I will need information such as the victim's home address, places of work, previous address — anything and everything. I just need one opening; you would be surprised when someone is facing twenty years for income tax evasion or wire fraud how quickly they remember things." Everyone smiled at that.

Chief Spence looked at Brockington. "What's next?"

"While Clayton works from here, Ed and I are going to Wilton to speak with Ms. Palmer. We met once before briefly. She was less than thrilled. The timing is not the best with

Roger's death ten days ago, but she needs to know about his past. Maybe she can provide us with the names of Roger's associates. I have a copy of Roger Palmer's obituary on my laptop. Not much in there beneficial to us. I can pass it around. Feel free to read it."

Detective Wade scanned the obituary quickly before passing the laptop. "Laura, can I see that again?"

Laura handed him back the laptop. "I know that face."

Laura looked at him. "What?"

"Remember I told you he looked familiar from the driver's license we had?"

"Yeah."

"Now I know where I saw his picture. When we were in the Wilton Police Department, I was looking at all the photos on the wall while you were talking, I remember asking Chief Pain in the Ass there about them. He started bragging those were taken at one of many events. That group of men has raised funds for the police department. I know that face. Roger Palmer was in those photographs. I thought they were cool because they were all done in black and white. I dabble in photography as a hobby."

Detective Clayton Fisher cracked a big smile. "You two need to visit the Wilton Police Department and get a copy of that photograph."

Wade spoke up. "That might be easier said than done. They didn't exactly roll out the welcome mat for us last time. Hell, if they find out we're looking at their financial benefactors too hard, they might not help us or bury any information they have."

"I hate to break this up, gentlemen and Brockington. I'm sure you will come up with something. I have a meeting to attend. From here on out, you no longer need permission to go back and forth to Wilton, but keep me up to date. I need to see some progress not possibilities."

"Thanks, Chief." He nodded and left the room.

"Ed, show Clayton his new desk and introduce him around. I need to make a few calls."

***

Two days after the funeral.

Lauren Palmer was stretched out on the sofa going over Roger's will while sipping a martini. She texted Dr. Bob. *Can you talk?*

In my office. Call me.

Lauren quickly called his cell. "Good morning. Nice to see the doctor is in."

"I'm surprised to hear from you."

"Why is that?"

"Are you not the grieving widow?"

"You're an asshole." They both laughed. "Honestly, how do you think I did?"

"I was impressed. An Oscar-winning performance. You looked the part."

"Well, sir, you as well. That eulogy was one for the ages. So when can we get together? It's been over three weeks. I need male companionship."

"Have a pen handy?"

"Hold on. Okay."

"Write this address down. 13 Sparrows Lane Weston, Connecticut. Just plug it in your GPS. It's fifty-five miles from Wilton. I'll meet you there Tuesday at 6:00."

“What is it? Some hotel?”

“No, it’s actually a townhouse. I’ll explain when we meet. If you have any problems finding it, just text me. I hate to rush, but I have a patient waiting. Before I forget, any issues with Tyler?”

“No, that particular day, he worked his regular shift. Had already put in his notice two weeks prior as not to raise suspicion. Told them he was leaving for a better offer on the west coast. Tyler has already left town.”

***

Tyler Drake had indeed moved to the west coast after paying off his gambling debts. He was asked a few questions by the Federal Aviation Authority about his procedures that day, specifically the packing of Roger Palmer’s parachute. He had a simple explanation. He hadn’t packed it on that fateful day. Roger himself was an experienced packer and did his own parachute. This, of course, was an outright lie, but only two people knew and one was no longer talking. They assumed Roger an experienced jumper, then in full panic mode, was in bad body position on deployment and was unable to activate the reserve. In the official report, aviation officials listed the cause of death, as accidental. The immediate family had accepted this. No further inquiry would be needed. The aviation industry’s main job, like all businesses, is to protect the image; the less press coverage of an accident the better. After all, it’s hard to recruit new people to the industry if people are dying. In its undisclosed report, the Aviation Authority determined that Roger Palmer’s accidental death was due to carelessness and bad body position combined with improper packing of his parachute.

Chapter Twenty

Tuesday evening at 6:00 p.m., Lauren Palmer pulled her blue Land Rover into the parking area at 13 Sparrows Lane. There were only three townhouses in a very secluded area back off the road. She noticed a silver Mercedes that looked like Bob's. The black auto tag PAINKILLER didn't look familiar.

"So you coming up or what?" came the voice.

Lauren looked up on the balcony. Looking down was Dr. Bob. Lauren looked up and smiled as she exited the Land Rover. "I recognized the car, but the tag threw me off."

"It was a gift from my son. He thought it was cool."

"Your son has good taste!" Lauren made her way up the steps greeting Dr. Bob with a kiss. "So tell me about this."

"Come in. I'll give you the ten-cent tour and explain."

Lauren looked around. It was very nice townhouse with hard wood floors, a newly remodeled kitchen with oak cabinets and emerald-colored counter tops. *Very unique*, she thought. Dr. Bob showed her through. It had high ceiling and wood floors throughout, a large master bedroom with a built-in mirror on the headboard. She grasped his hand tightly. "Can we try it out?" she said with a wicked grin.

"Shortly, my dear. Let's finish the tour and I'll explain

everything." Dr. Bob opened up a second bedroom. "This room is to stay exactly like this at all times." Lauren looked around. It had a single bed and small nightstand. The room was painted a nice shade of green. There was a reading lamp on the nightstand that looked to be twenty years old, a bookcase that one might one find in bedroom of a young boy, loaded with Disney books. The curtains contained images of trains, the bed sheets and pillow covered a western theme.

Lauren was baffled. She turned to Bob. "I don't understand."

Bob grabbed her hand. "For right now, you don't need to. I will fill you in when the time comes, but it's very important nothing in this room is to be moved. The rest of the place, feel free to do whatever. Let me show you the outside deck."

"This is nice, Bob." The deck was on the second story with a patio table and chairs, and an umbrella to ward off the afternoon sun overlooking the nearby woods.

"What's over there?" Lauren was pointing to a track.

"That's St. Vincent High School off to the left. The high school track runs behind our place and I have permission. We can use it anytime. Of course I made a small donation to the athletic department." He grabbed Lauren's hand and they walked back inside. "Have a seat. I'll get some iced tea and explain."

"You have any alcohol?"

"Of course, I'll grab some wine." Bob returned shortly with a bottle of red wine and two glasses. He poured them and took a seat on the burgundy leather sofa next to Lauren. "To us." They clinked glasses.

"So did you buy this little hideaway for us?"

"In a way, yes. We need to stay discreet." Bob put his

glass down and turned serious. "You realize until now this has been a lot of fun, but things have changed. Those detectives who came to visit Roger will return."

"Because he's dead?"

"Exactly. I've done some research on this Detective Brockington. She is extremely bright. She won't buy this accident thing without proof, so you need to be prepared if she shows up in your driveway asking questions."

"Fuck," Lauren replied and downed her wine.

"That's just what you cannot do. You must remain calm. Remember, you're a grieving widow. Look upset when they say his name. They're going to tell you about Roger and Peyton Long. Act like you knew, that it pissed you off at the time, but Roger promised to break it off, that you still loved him and forgave him."

Lauren was visibly upset. "Get me more wine." Bob obliged by refilling her glass.

"What else should I do?"

"Have pictures of you and Roger on the mantel, boxes of tissue on the coffee table, and use them, often. I need you over the next few weeks to start bringing some clothes here. No one is to know about this place. Then quietly pass the word among some friends that you're considering moving. There's too many memories for you to remain at the house Roger and you shared as a couple."

Lauren sat patiently as Dr. Bob continued to give her advice. Lauren finished her second glass of wine. She had never seen him so intense. Finally, she took his hand and broke in, "You have given this a lot of thought and I thank you, but I'll be fine." Dr. Bob gently but firmly put his right hand on the back of her neck and looked into her deep blue eyes.

Lauren felt the roughness of it and it unnerved her.

"Lauren, up until now, my dear, this thing of ours has been nothing but fun and games, but with the death of Roger, this just got real. Any mistakes from here on and we'll both be spending the rest of our lives looking out through iron bars. Do you understand that?"

"Of course. There will be no mistakes on my end. I just want us together, no matter the cost."

Dr. Bob smiled. "Good. That's all I needed to hear."

"So why did you purchase the townhouse? For us, I hope?"

"That's part of it. We can't take even the slightest chance of anyone knowing about us. This place is totally secluded. In a few months, it's going to serve a much larger purpose, but for now, we can meet here."

Lauren smiled. "I like that, although I don't know how I'll handle it without a gear shift banging against my ass while we're making love."

Bob laughed. "What, you don't like enjoy the challenge of auto sex?"

Lauren stood up and unbuttoned her white blouse, the opening partially showing her exposed breasts. "Now that I don't have to rush, the possibilities are endless." She placed her finger in her mouth, licked the tip, and put it in Dr. Bob's mouth. Bob got up from the sofa. Lauren quickly undid his tie and tossed it on the floor. Bob gently slid the blouse off her shoulders and let it fall to the floor, then quickly undid the clasp of her bra. He then moved in closer. Lauren smiled and dodged his kiss, backing away. Bob looked confused. "What gives?"

"Bring the wine. I believe we have a new bed to break in."

She slowly licked her red lips and walked away.

***

Detectives Brockington and Wade were on their way to Wilton. They planned on paying a visit to Lauren Palmer. They needed to inform her of Roger's involvement with Peyton Long. This would be a delicate matter under the best of conditions, but the death of her husband would make it more so. Nonetheless, it was vital to the investigation.

Detective Clayton Fisher had been working on the case for three days, barely leaving his desk going over the files of Peyton Long and her mother Gwen, scouring bank records, tax returns — anything that would raise a red flag to him. This was his bread and butter. He was not a typical detective in the mold of Brockington or Wade, but he could be just as effective and had put many men who were accustomed to tailored suits into orange one pieces.

Clayton was going over the life insurance policy owned by Gwen Long. The payout was a typical $80,000-dollar policy payable upon death to her beneficiary, her brother Marc.

There was nothing unusual about that. After all, he was her only surviving family member, but Clayton knew where to go with that. Using his contacts, he pulled up the financial history of Marc Long.

Marc Long was a school teacher and his wife Ann a legal secretary. Standard middle-class couple. Looking over their financial history brought a smile to Clayton's face. Just three months prior to his sister's death, Marc Long carried a mortgage of $245,000, drove a six-year-old car, still owing

$1,800 on it. His wife's car was four years old, still owing $4,200. They carried a second mortgage totaling $18,000 and credit card debt of almost $14,000. Basically, they were working like most Americans to keep their heads above water.

The thing that caught Clayton's eye was a little after six weeks since Gwen's death, Marc and Ann had purchased a $35,000 new SUV for her, a $42,000 truck for him, had new kitchen counters and appliances totaling over $25,000 installed, and had bought themselves a new camper for $61,000.

The math didn't add up for two people struggling to stay afloat. They were now living a very upscale lifestyle, not the kind one enjoys with $80,000 from a life insurance payoff that alone wouldn't have paid off their bills. No, it seemed the couple had come into a large sum of money. The question now was how and from whom? Clayton Fisher would be on the morning flight to Seattle Washington.

While Clayton Fisher looked into the financial aspects of the case, Detectives Brockington and Wade had checked back into their hotel in Wilton with no check-out date. They wanted to accomplish a few things. The first on the agenda was meeting with the medical examiner who performed the autopsy on Roger Palmer.

Chief Medical Examiner for City of Wilton was Gus Bryant, a balding sixty-something, wire glasses, and very thin. He sat behind his desk with his lab coat on and pulled out the file on Roger Palmer.

"I must be honest, Detectives, this is new to me. The only police I see, it's usually about an auto accident. It's a long way from Syracuse. Why the interest?"

Brockington smiled. "We're just tying up some loose

ends, Doc."

"I understand. Well, here are the photographs and my notes. Obviously, he died from numerous injuries to the body. I listed the cause as head trauma. It very well could have been internal bleeding. No way to precisely determine."

Brockington held up the black and white photos of Roger Palmer lying on the examiner's table. The body was badly bruised. "A lot of bruises, Doc."

"That's to be expected. Try falling about 12,000 feet into hard ground."

Wade winced at the idea. "Doc, what are these? They look like small holes. One in his ankle, one under the armpit, one through the rib cage?"

"Yes, those. Well, it seems when Mr. Palmer's parachute failed to deploy, he fell outside the drop zone into a freshly cut cornfield. Those small holes would be where the corn stalks went through his suit and penetrated the body. It's amazing the impact when you're descending downward at that speed. Generally speaking, once you exit the plane, you're traveling forward, but that speed quickly bleeds off as your body picks up vertical speed and slows its forward speed due to drag. Once you've reached terminal velocity, you're traveling about 120 mph in the neutral position. At that speed, slamming into big hunk of granite we call earth's protective clothing is pretty much useless." Both Brockington and Wade looked at him, slightly shocked and speechless.

"Excuse me." Detective Wade got up and left the room, feeling nauseous.

"I apologize. In my line of work, I've seen it all, but I forget sometimes not to be so descriptive. My wife is often reprimanding me for that."

Brockington smiled. "Don't worry, Doc. Wade will be fine. I guess my main reason for being here, Doctor, were there any signs of narcotics in the body, anything that would have impaired Mr. Palmer?"

"Nothing. I checked his bloodwork. Totally clean. I understand the questioning. From my understanding, he was a very good jumper, but no nothing out of the normal. Sorry, Detective, I believe this was just an unfortunate accident."

"Strange you should mention that, Doc. Seems to be the number one cause of death in Wilton. Thanks for your time."

"You're welcome. If I can be of further assistance, don't hesitate to call."

Brockington looked at Wade. "You okay to drive?"

"Yeah, I'm fine. Hell, I've seen mangled bodies from auto accidents, shootings, people being slashed with razor knives. Just that picture in my mind of Roger hurtling toward earth got to me."

Detectives Wade and Brockington made their way to the Town of Wilton police barracks. They knew Chief Snow would be less than pleased they were back in his territory asking questions. Their goal was simple: while Brockington made small talk and took verbal abuse, Detective Wade was to use his iPhone and snap pictures as quickly as possible, and what did they want pictures of? The very ones that Chief Snow had hanging in the lobby with Roger Palmer and friends taken during a fundraising event.

Chief Snow of the Wilton Police Department was less than thrilled that his out-of-town guests from the Syracuse PD were once again sitting in his office. "Don't misunderstand me, Detective Brockington, I appreciate the professional courtesy call by you letting me know you're back in town, but

I have to ask why?"

"I'm here strictly to tie some loose ends, Chief. Close the books, as they say."

"I assume you're here once again about the young girl who accidentally fell to her death a few months back?"

"Correct."

"Where is your sidekick?"

"Detective Wade is using the men's room. He's fascinated by all the black and white photography in your lobby. I noticed they're similar to the ones in your office."

"You're very observant. Yes, the same group of individuals. They have raised a lot of funds for us over the years. Interesting group. They attended Harvard together and settled here in Wilton as neighbors, then started a charity called the Crimson in honor of their old alma mater and have raised money not only for us, but this community."

"That's great."

"Detective, I hope for whatever reason you're in town, you can quickly finish your business. Like I said before, not a lot of criminal activity here. Since you're from New York, we have an unfortunate number of car thefts when our citizens spend time in the city, so if you could help us with that."

"I would be glad to, Chief. Unfortunately, I no longer work in Manhattan. I would recommend they take public transportation."

"That's funny, Detective, a resident of Wilton riding a bus. Now they may own the bus company, but rest assured they have never ridden on one."

Detective Wade made his way into the office, making sure to shake Chief Snow's hand. After a little more conversation, they got up to leave. Brockington looked at her partner. "Can you think of anything else?"

"No, I believe we're good."

Chief Snow showed them to the front door. "I assume crime is way down in Syracuse if they can afford to have two detectives spending time in Wilton. Have a safe drive back."

Brockington just nodded, got into the white Ford Escape, and drove off. "What an asshole!"

Wade laughed. "It was worth it. I got the photos."

Brockington smiled. "Good Chief Douchebag just helped us out. He told me those pictures are of Roger and his friends from college. I recall Peyton's roommate Joy telling us that when Amber, the young girl Peyton befriended in Miami, said she couldn't recall the names of Roger's friends at the hotel in Miami that night, only Roger was definitely Peyton's date for the evening and the main guy was someone called Doc. Let's see if there's a doctor in that photo. Once we're back at the hotel, get those photos off to the lab and have them blown up."

"Okay then, what if it's still just a photo?"

"Then, my friend, we pull some strings and have the Connecticut State Police help us do a DMV search of doctors in Wilton. With a population of 25,000, difficult but doable. Before the hotel, it's time we revisit 114 Heritage Court."

Wade grimaced. "Who gets to break the news to Ms. Palmer?"

"I will."

The white Ford Escape turned up the long black paved driveway. It was quite a view. The lawn was manicured, beautiful white and pink dogwoods out in bloom. The detectives took it all in, very impressed.

Lauren Palmer was in her upstairs bedroom and saw the white Ford Escape coming up her driveway. She knew the vehicle from before. Dr. Bob said they would be back. He was right and she was well prepared.

Lauren sat in front of her mirror, grabbed her make-up brush, and in a matter of moments, her eyes looked as if she hadn't slept in days, darkened and red from eye drops she added. She glanced at herself in the mirror then quickly threw off her silk pajamas and slipped on a weathered robe with old slippers. She waited for the second doorbell to ring. "Coming, be right there!"

Brockington heard the reply and smiled. "At least she's home." The door opened slowly with Lauren Palmer looking around the corner like an older person would do.

"You two look familiar."

"We're Detectives Brockington and Wade. We met very briefly a few weeks back."

"Now I remember."

"May we come in?"

"Of course."

Brockington noticed right away this was not the vivacious five-foot-three-inch blonde model she met last time. Lauren Palmer looked tired. They made their way into the living room, where Lauren treated them to coffee. She was friendly compared to their previous encounter.

"Detectives? You're from Syracuse?"

"That's correct."

"I assume this has something to do with Roger?"

"Yes. I feel badly having to intrude. You have our condolences. We just need to clear up a few items and we'll be on our way."

Lauren drew a deep breath. "I will answer for you what I can, but bear with me. This has been a very traumatic experience. I'm coping the best I can."

Brockington smiled. "I understand this is difficult, but I have information you need to be made aware of. There is no easy way to say this. We are investigating the death of a young girl, Peyton Long."

Lauren took a tissue from the table and looked at five feet, eleven inches tall Brockington, her long blonde hair pulled back, her detectives gold shield pinned to her belt.

"I know that name and it's very hurtful to me."

Detective Brockington glanced over at Wade. "How so?"

"First off, let me say I'm very sorry that young girl accidentally fell to her death. Very tragic. I know that she and Roger were having an affair." Lauren looked over to the mantel, where a wedding-day picture of her and Roger was placed.

"You know it was more than just an affair?"

"Of course, he confessed to everything."

"When did you find out?"

"I knew about three months prior to confronting him. I was hoping it was just a one-night stand. Of course, it wasn't. He apologized, cried, begged me to give our marriage one more chance. I threatened to leave him, but I still loved him, so I stayed. After I forgave him, he became a lot more attentive. This goes to show you, life has no guarantees."

"How did you become aware of his affair?"

"There are always signs. Less contact in our bedroom, last-minute meetings out of town; men are so obvious and believe they're not." Lauren Palmer grabbed more tissues and started sobbing. "This is very painful, Detective. I'm trying to remember all the good times we had. Bringing this up hurts badly."

"Sorry, just a few more questions and we'll be on our way. How well do you know Roger's friends?"

"We have a couple of mutual friends. Mainly, I have my own. Quite frankly, I found his friends boring. I wouldn't know them if they were standing here."

Chapter Twenty-One

Wilton Police Chief Snow was having his morning coffee with a fresh bagel when he turned the corner onto Heritage Court. He enjoyed riding through the neighborhoods; it was good PR. People liked seeing police presence. When he looked up the driveway at 114, he almost spilled his coffee. *What the fuck!* He tossed his bagel on the dash and sped up the long and winding driveway. He knew the owner and recognized the white Ford Escape.

Lauren Palmer was answering each question quietly and with a lot of emotion when the doorbell rang.

"Excuse me, I'll be right back. Hello. It's a pleasure to see you."

Wade heard a man's voice but not the question.

"Yes, they are here. Come in." Lauren returned with Wilton Police Chief Snow right behind her. "Chief Snow says that you have met?"

Brockington rose to shake his hand. "Yes, we have on few occasions. How are you, Chief?"

"Surprised, I guess would be the word. I didn't realize you would be visiting with Ms. Palmer today."

"Yes, we just finished up. We had a very nice

conversation under some very unfortunate circumstances. Can you think of anything else, Ed?"

"I think we have everything we came for."

"Thank you again Ms. Palmer. Again, our deepest condolences."

"I will walk them out, Ms. Palmer."

"Thank you, Chief." Lauren grabbed another tissue from the box.

The trio exited the house and closed the door behind them. Chief Snow waited until Detective Wade was behind the steering wheel and Brockington was fastening her seat belt when he leaned into the car. With his hands on the side of driver's side door, his Tennessee drawl coming out, he looked at Brockington. "I guess I shouldn't expect anything less, you two being from the city, but my God, you can't even leave a grieving widow to some privacy. I mean, she just lost her husband. What is wrong with you people? Have you no moral decency and what on this God's earth could she have helped you with?"

Brockington looked at him from the passenger seat. "I hate to burst your bubble about the little town of Wilton, Chief, but it seems that young girl who fell to her death, Peyton Long, was pregnant at the time, possibly by her sugar daddy, none other than Mr. Roger Palmer. Chief, our question all along has been did Peyton fall or was she pushed? If she was, who had reason to do so? Seems to us the rich have secrets and vices just like regular people. You have a pleasant day now." The look on his face was priceless; red as a beet, he didn't say a word as Detective Wade lifted the chief's hands off his window, smiled, and slowly backed down the driveway. Chief Snow just stared.

Wade looked at his partner. "Well, I hope you realize any chance we had of him treating us to dinner just went to shit."

Brockington cracked a smile. "Can't help myself. I just have a knack for making people happy."

"What did you think of Lauren Palmer?"

Brockington thought for a moment. "Honestly, just not sure. I feel bad for her. There is something I can't put my finger on. I don't mean to sound like a bitch, but they just don't seem like a match, that's all. Who knows? People marry for all kinds of reasons."

"Let's get back to the hotel. We can also see if we can persuade the Connecticut DMV to help us out with those photos."

"Forget that. I have a better idea that will take a few days if we're lucky."

"Why didn't you push Lauren harder about Roger's friends?"

"I'm not sure what she knows or who and I wasn't about to tip our hand."

Lauren Palmer watched from her upstairs bedroom. Finally, Chief Snow left the driveway. She immediately took off the old robe and slippers, slid on her silk bikini bottoms with blue shorts and skintight sports bra, washed her face, put on pink lipstick, licked her pearly white teeth, checked herself in the mirror, smiled, and grabbed her purse. She had a massage appointment in twenty minutes and didn't want to be late. She texted Dr. Bob on her way for a massage. *Call me ASAP*. She was halfway to her appointment when Bob called her.

"What's up?"

"Can you talk?"

"Yes, I'm in my office at work."

"You were correct; those detectives from Syracuse came by today. I was well prepared thanks to you. Everything went off without a hitch. I was the depressed widow; they even felt sympathy for me. To make it better, Chief Snow saw their car in the driveway and stopped in. He was none too pleased that one of his constituents was being harassed. I truly believe they bought it."

"Your knight in shining armor, Chief Horny Snow, came to defend your honor, so he's still hoping to get some action, I suppose. How long has he been chasing you now?" They both laughed.

"Is that a note of jealousy I detect from Mr. Self-assured himself?"

"You know as well as I do he's been hitting on you since the day he laid eyes on you and of course you led him to believe he had a chance."

"I feel obligated to help mankind; it's my calling."

"You're too kind. I thank you for the good news about those detectives."

"Maybe now they can move on to something else far from here. They can't have much to go on."

"I have a question. Where did you say that Tyler Drake moved to?"

"West. Last we spoke, he settled in Sacramento. Get this, he's working for a casino as a dealer. Told me it helps him stay clean. Why?"

"We need to make sure there are no mistakes. I assume you used a burner phone with him?"

"Of course, trashed it right after our last conversation. There is no record of Tyler Drake and me having ever met or spoken, nothing to worry about. Listen, I'm at the racquet club and scheduled a massage for this morning."

"Alright. Let's meet again at the townhouse on Tuesday about 6:00?"

"Sounds good; see you there." Dr. Bob took out his iPhone. In his notes, he texted, *Tyler Drake Sacramento?*

***

Detective Clayton Fisher was thankful his rental came with GPS. This was his first trip to Seattle, Washington. He was fascinated by its sheer beauty; no doubt, under better circumstances, he would be making a return visit. The GPS took him onto Alaskan Highway past Seattle's beautiful waterfront. He put down his car window to take in the fresh salt air, the scent of seafood past the merchant ships unloading their freight on the docks onto what is known as Olympic Sculpture Park. The sun was out and so were the tourists. *Damn,* he thought, *if only I had a few free hours to burn, this would be great*. He continued along the waterfront past Safeco Field. "Turn right," came the voice from his GPS. "Now turn left onto Occidental Drive. 312 Occidental Drive is on your right. You have arrived at your destination."

Detective Fisher pulled into the driveway. A nice two-story red brick on the front with white shutters, a newly paved driveway. There a were a couple of young boys playing basketball. They glanced at him for just a second then went back to their game.

Clayton was getting ready to exit the car when a tall man who looked forty-plus, with a lean build, a small beard, and thinning brown hair walked toward his car.

"Can I help you?"

"I hope so." Clayton exited the car. "My name is Clayton Fisher. I'm a Detective with the Syracuse, NY Police Department. Looking for Marc Long."

"That would be me. I'm not sure why you bothered to come all this way. I already told some female detective several weeks ago we don't have a lot to say about my sister's death other than it was painful, so if you don't mind, Detective, I have things to get done." He turned and started to walk away.

"Mr. Long, I can assure you I didn't fly over 3,000 miles without a very good reason. I'm very sorry for the loss of your sister, but I feel it may be in your and Ann's best interest to answer a few of my questions."

"Why? I have nothing to tell you."

"Mr. Long, I know all about the large purchases you have recently made: motor homes, new cars; by my last count, over $250,000 since the death of your sister. That 85,000-dollar life insurance she left you didn't buy all that. Matter of fact, it wouldn't have paid off your debts. Were you aware that income tax evasion and wire fraud can carry up to twenty years in prison?" Marc Long stopped dead in his tracks, sizing up the detective with his eyes. "I honestly don't care a rat's ass about the money or how you spend it, but you are going tell me where you have it and how you got it or I'm going to see that you spend the next fifteen years in state prison. Now that I have your attention, where can we talk?"

Marc's face turned ashen. He looked shaken. "Follow me. We can talk in the den." They entered through the living room, which was very nice with a brick fireplace with a large mantel, large flat screen TV. Just then, an attractive brunette of medium height with a pleasant smile walked in. "This is my wife, Ann."

"Pleasure to meet you. I'm Detective Clayton Fisher." They shook hands.

"Marc, what's going on?"

"Detective Fisher is here about Gwen. He would like to ask some questions. Ann, can you join us?" Marc motioned her to.

"Of course." They settled in to the den. Ann was wearing jeans and an old tee shirt. She sat on the sofa next to Marc while Detective Fisher sat across from them in a high-back wooden chair.

"Ann, I was discussing with Marc your financial situation. It seems to have dramatically improved of late."

Ann looked at him combatively. "We work diligently for all we have. Detective. I'm sure in your position, you can appreciate that."

"I do."

"Ann, Detective Fisher is aware of our recent purchases and would like to know all about our financial windfall."

Ann stared directly at him. "Why are our finances of importance to the Syracuse NYPD?"

"Because of how you may come about receiving some of the money. It may help us untangle a case we're pursuing. We have reason to believe your niece Peyton may not have accidentally fallen to her death. She was pregnant at the time. Very few people were aware of that. Peyton may have approached the biological father for financial support. The possibility exists Gwen became aware of this and may have intervened on Peyton's behalf, not aware of the danger that existed, so we're also looking into Gwen's death."

Marc spoke up angrily. "That's impossible. Gwen died of

toxic shock syndrome. If she thought someone harmed Peyton intentionally, she would have gone straight to the police."

"Were you aware that Gwen had been embezzling funds from her employer?"

"What?"

"Unfortunately, it's true. She also told one of her co-workers she planned on moving out of the country. Did she inform you?" Marc shook his head no. "Let's talk about how seemingly overnight you came into a lot of money."

Ann glared at her husband. "We should contact an attorney first?"

Detective Fisher replied, "That is certainly your prerogative. If you choose to, you will leave me no choice but to get the Feds involved."

Marc spoke up. "Let me get the letter." Ann didn't say another word. Marc returned shortly with an envelope, handing it to Detective Fisher. "This arrived about seven days after Gwen passed. It came certified. I had to go down to the post office and show proof of who I was to receive it. Honestly, I thought it was a mistake, a registered letter from the Bank of Zurich."

"May I open it?"

"Yes."

There was a smaller letter attached to the outside of the envelope. It read: *Mr. Marc Long, as required by law, this official notice upon the death of Gwen Long is being sent to you, having been named beneficiary of the following account# 20005450023. You are required to contact our home office immediately to receive the entitled benefits. Failure to do so within 30 days of receipt will require legal action on our part.* It was signed Luca Altherr, CFO, National Bank of Zurich.

Detective Fisher opened the envelope. It was a handwritten letter addressed to Marc. It read: *Brother, I know we have not always been close; however, I do care about you and always have. If you're reading this, I have departed this earth. Such is life. Hopefully, I have done enough good things over the years to leave a positive memory. I will be the first to admit I was no saint. I've made mistakes, but I was a survivor. I leaned very early in the game of life the playing field is not level, so I learned to adapt. I've been fortunate over the years to save and invest wisely. Enclosed you will find a bank book with an account number drawn on the National Bank of Zurich. You will need both to access the account. Your first question, of course, why an overseas account? This was a personal choice. I planned to live there in the near future. Obviously, if you're reading this is wasn't meant to be. Please use the money wisely. In regard to the tax situation, common sense prevails here, so use yours (I know, the first time is always the hardest. LOL!!). I have never been one for long goodbyes, so until we meet again, go forward and enjoy life. XX Gwen. P.S. Now might be a good time to buy that Corvette you always wanted. Personally, I always preferred the Mustang!!!* Detective Fisher could not help but notice that Gwen never mentioned Ann in her final thoughts. He laid the letter down on the table in front of them. "I assume from your recent purchases that you have accessed the account?

Marc nodded they had. "I was surprised by the fact that Gwen had a Swiss bank account. I could not figure why it was only a few years ago I was sending her money on occasion to help her pay rent and utilities before she became a CPA."

Ann quickly injected, "Yes, but she never offered to reimburse us once she landed on her feet."

Marc just glanced at his wife; his facial expression said it all.

"How much was in the account?"

Marc hesitated, finally quietly saying, "Two million plus interest. I was positive they had made a mistake, thinking they meant $20,000. I checked four times. The bank started getting irritated with me, frankly telling me the Swiss, unlike the Americans, do not make mistakes in banking, so I asked myself where did the money come from? I finally accepted I would never know. Are we in legal trouble?"

"Give me your full cooperation and I'll work with you."

The couple quickly agreed. "Tell us what to do."

"I need you to contact the bank. I need the dates of all transactions, including deposits and withdrawals."

"I'm sure they were made electronically."

"Doesn't matter."

"Detective, I'll do my best, but the Swiss have very stringent privacy laws. They divulge nothing. I thought I would have to give a blood sample to prove I was Gwen's brother."

"If you need to personally go there for this information, I suggest you make flight arrangements quickly." Detective Fisher was in no mood to bargain. "Did Gwen have a regular boyfriend?"

"Not that I knew of."

"Any close female friends she may have confided in?"

"Detective, we lived 2500 miles apart. I have no idea what my sister did or whom she did it with. We didn't have that type of relationship." Detective Fisher sat for close to two hours with Marc and Ann, finding out everything he possibly could about Gwen Long. He felt that he had made a major break in the case and was leaving nothing to chance. Finally, at 4:15 p.m., they wrapped up. The Longs looked exhausted but relieved. They had cooperated completely.

Detective Fisher packed up to leave. “I will be in touch and I will need that bank information within one week. Any issues, you call me immediately. Understood?”

They both replied yes. “Detective Fisher I realize this isn’t your problem. Do you think I should contact a lawyer about the money and possible tax implications? I don’t want any more legal problems.”

Detective Fisher looked at Marc for a moment. He obviously was not a criminal. “My best advice: the Swiss could care less about US taxes and whether you pay them. You shouldn’t call so much attention to yourself spending money like you won the fucking lottery. For all you know, one of your neighbors works for the IRS. I would return the RV for starters. I mean, I flagged you and I don’t know shit about taxes.”

Marc shook Detective Fisher’s hand. “Thanks for the advice and giving us a chance to make this right.”

“Don’t thank me just yet. Trust me, I don’t get that bank information, our next conversation won’t be as cordial.” Detective Clayton Fisher was excited. This was no doubt a major break in the case. Now he had to find out how Gwen Long had come into two million dollars. Who paid her? And the big question: why? What did she know, and more importantly, who was willing to pay for her silence?

Clayton Fisher was waiting at Seattle-Tacoma International Airport when he texted Detective Laura Brockington with the following message: *Leaving Seattle. Will be back in Syracuse tomorrow morning. Very successful trip!!*

Will know more within the week. Following the money as they say.

The wait for a response was short, less than five minutes: *Cannot wait to hear all about your trip. Staying in Wilton two more days. Things are starting to break!*

Detective Ed Wade was driving when his partner Detective Brockington said, "Yes! Damn straight. About time."

"What's up?"

"Our new man Clayton for some reason is in Seattle and says it was a very good trip. Sounds like he has a good lead."

"That sounds encouraging. Why the fuck is he in Seattle?"

Laura thought for a minute. "I know Gwen had a brother living there. I tried to contact him after learning he claimed her body. Wouldn't give me the time of day."

"Sounds like Clayton has a way of making friends."

Laura smiled. "Seems that way. Tell me about this plan of yours with the picture?"

"We're going old school." He pulled into the Wilton Public Library, made a quick stop at the front desk, showed his detective's gold shield and headed straight to the private computer room. "Pull up a chair, Detective, and watch the master at work."

Laura sat next to Ed. First he searched online for newspaper periodicals in Wilton, Connecticut for news about charitable events there. He found four such events in the last three years, including donors and awards. Detective Wade was scanning all the articles when his eyes lit up. "Will you look at this in the *Wilton Bulletin*, a story about a group, the Crimson, that had raised money for the New Police Athletic Center along with a picture of them handing over a check to Chief

Snow." They had no idea who the other three were, but there was no mistaking Roger Palmer.

Detective Brockington grabbed Wade by the shoulder. "I could kiss you right now."

"I'm game." He clenched his fist. "This has to be them and I'm betting one of those assholes is the good doctor."

They both kept reading the article. It talked about how the town always pulled together, everyone pitched in when called on, how this community took tremendous pride in its appearance. *The Wilton Police and Fire Departments want to send a special thanks to the Crimson Charity headed by Dr. Robert (Bob) Weinstein, Roger Palmer, Cal Estrada, and Lawrence Sinclair, once again going up and beyond. We are truly blessed to have such a fine organization here in Wilton.*

"Yes!" Brockington and Wade were ecstatic. Finally, they had names; only names at this point, but the pieces were starting to fit.

"We have names; where do we go?"

Brockington thought for a moment. "These are some very wealthy and powerful people. Let's go back to Syracuse see what Clayton has for us from Seattle. We have some research work to do. Who are these guys really? How does the Crimson charity raise money? Who founded it? Who else is a member beside these four? Where does the name come from?"

"Those are all good questions, Laura, but it's going to take time to find the answers."

"We have time."

"I hope you're right about that. Seems to me every time we get close, someone succumbs to a fatal accident."

Chapter Twenty-Two

Over two months had passed since Tyler Drake had made the move to the west coast. Sacramento, California seemed to be working for him. For the first time in years, he was no longer looking over his shoulder to whom he owed money. He landed a position at the Landmark Casino. It was the perfect answer for his addiction. Just like many a reformed alcoholic became bartenders, his counselor recommended he work in the casino industry, telling him it's not the money you're after; you need to be around the action, as they called it, Tyler at first seemed reluctant. It was like asking an arsonist to play with matches, but it worked. The counselor was correct; his new job allowed him to be a part of it without risking everything. Tyler still attended Gamblers Anonymous every Monday, taking no chances of falling back into his old habits. His pit boss at the casino liked his work habits; he was always willing to work an extra shift or a weekend on short notice, telling him he had a real future at Landmark. Presently working the roulette wheel, Tyler was training to become a blackjack dealer. Finally, he thought his life had turned a corner.

Antonio Ricci had been working the casino for over five years; he was also a small-time hood peddling Oxycodone, pills, and when called upon, roughing some people up. Tyler Drake knew none of this when Antonio befriended him a few weeks earlier, thinking he was just another casino employee. They were approximately the same age with the same vices: alcohol and attractive women. Tyler and Antonio, as was their custom when working the midnight shift, stopped for a drink at the Alamo Bar, a popular night spot. The pair had their usual, Tyler a gin and tonic and Antonio rum and coke. It was 1:30 a.m. when they made their way to the El. The train was consistently on time. The train station this time of the morning was deserted, not even a security guard as they stood making small talk in a darkened corner of station waiting for their stop. Another train whizzed by. Antonio took one last look around, reached into his pants pocket, pulled out his hand now wearing a set of brass knuckles, slamming them into in unsuspecting Tyler's midsection. He immediately crumpled to the ground, trying to catch his breath while bleeding internally and gagging on his own blood. He got to his knees, blood slowly drooling out the side of his mouth, totally confused why this was happening. Still unable to catch his breath, his eyes glazed over. The last thing Tyler Drake felt on this earth was not the warm touch of a loved one, but a foot on his backside, pushing him onto the southbound lane of Track 2.

Eight days later.

Lititz, Pennsylvania was a small town with a population of 9,000 set in the middle of Amish country. The tall green stalks of corn stretched across the farmlands as far as the eye could see, a quaint community where you raised your kids without fear, the neighbors always waved, the grass always cut. The small white church sat on the top a of hill overlooking some of lushest farmland on the east coast. This was where

Tyler Drake spent his youth riding his bike through our neighborhoods. The minister said, "Life, as we know, changes us from children to adults. We lose our innocence no matter how far we travel away, home is where the heart is. So we bring Tyler home now to once again be among those who always cared for him, who never judged him. Who amongst us is a perfect person? I daresay no one I have ever met in my lifetime. Tyler, like all men, had demons he battled throughout his adult life. Gambling, like all addictions, is hidden from the outside world, but tears at the soul of men and women it ensnares. Tyler seemed to have a handle on his addiction, had moved to new location and started fresh. We don't know the inner torment of what this young man was going through. We assume that possibly he felt himself once again succumbing to the urges of his addiction and decided that he could no longer put himself or those who loved him through this pain again. We ask ourselves why does one decide to take God's greatest gift the gift of life and bring it to a close? Do not judge Tyler Drake by the closing of his life, for unless one walks in one's shoes, you cannot fathom the pain they may be enduring." The minister spoke for another twenty minutes about Tyler Drake's life.

His mother Liz was fifty-seven years of age. Along with his sister Shelly, they could not understand why Tyler decided to take his own life. Tyler, it seemed to them, had finally found some peace in his life. He even spoke of having Shelly visit him on the west coast.

Some 400 miles north of Lititz, Pennsylvania, Dr. Robert Weinstein knew exactly why Tyler Drake had ended up on track 2 of the southbound lane. Loose ends could be an opening to problems down the road, so he had it closed.

***

Laura Brockington, Ed Wade, and Clayton Fisher were comparing notes on what had transpired over two weeks ago, looking for something they might have missed that would help with their case. The National Bank of Switzerland was not cooperating with Marc Long. He went there personally at the insistence of Detective Fisher. It made no difference; they would not give out any personal information made from foreign deposits other than the account number. There are no names on Swiss accounts. This was standard protocol for the Swiss and that was why people had accounts. Their privacy came first. Detective Fisher spoke. "We must have the person's name who transferred money to that account; just the bank routing number does nothing for us. I assure you The National Bank of Switzerland has that information. Whoever deposited two million into Gwen Long's Swiss account paid her for what she knew and I strongly believe they had no intention of paying her another dime. We find out who made that deposit, we can tie the money right to them."

"We know who these guys are now: Dr. Bob, Larry Sinclair, Cal Estrada. I know this money is coming from them. I fucking know it." Brockington stared at her boss. "Chief, any suggestions?"

"I do. Detective Fisher, you're the white-collar guru. Suppose we send you to Switzerland to meet with their bank officials and kindly explain to them the deposit information they refuse to divulge may be covering up a possible homicide here in the US. We would hate for it to make the papers that the world respected National Bank of Switzerland was not cooperating. This might bring extra scrutiny to deposits being made there by our law-abiding citizens, possibly an IRS investigation, but with their help, we may be able to keep the matter below the radar, so to speak."

Clayton smiled. "Chief, that just might get it done. They don't care for any publicity."

"That settles it. I will pull some strings with the powers that be. It's going to take a few days. This is not something we do every day. I hope to God you're right about this or I will have a lot to answer for."

"Chief, I've done this type of work my whole career. That bank account is crucial to us solving this case."

"Brockington, you're leading this case. What's next on the agenda?"

"Chief, why does Clayton get to spend time in Switzerland?" She stuck out her tongue and they all laughed. "I think we have enough circumstantial evidence to pay a visit to the good doctor and his friends and see if they're willing to answer a few questions."

"You don't really expect to get any answers, do you?"

"No, but I know it will put them on alert we're on their asses, and sometimes, that's all it takes for one person looking to save themselves and start talking."

"Laura, I need a favor."

"You're going to fucking Switzerland, Clayton. What else can I do? Buy you dinner before you leave?" Everyone laughed.

Clayton was grinning. "In all seriousness, you cannot bring up anything about the Crimson charity when talking to those guys. I don't want them knowing we're looking into it. That would make it way too easy for them to start burying the evidence."

"Fuck! I understand, but that kind of ties my hands."

"Give me a couple of weeks. I told you when I came on board that paper trails take time."

Brockington reluctantly agreed she would hold off on any interviews until they had the bank information.

***

Hamilton's Steak House was one of the best around for those who paid no attention to the bill. It was a Saturday evening. The group had not been together to talk business or down a few beers since the death of their friend and former partner Roger Palmer. The Crimson group dined on the finest cuts of filet mignon with grilled parmesan broccoli. Dr. Bob looked at his friends. "I propose a toast. He was one of kind and will always be a part of our group. To Roger!"

"To Roger!" they all shouted and clinked glasses. They were on their fourth round of beer.

"Gentlemen, I guess we have business to discuss." Bob looked at Cal Estrada. "Our point man at Eagle 2 Investments, how we doing?"

"We are printing fucking money. I need help with the bookkeeping. Roger was my backup, and with football season almost here, the action is only going to double. People love to wager and I love watching them lose." They all busted up laughing. "Seriously, I could use some help."

"Cal, we can't. There is no one we can trust with our business. Too much of a risk to bring in an outsider."

"Larry, you're an economics professor. I could show you how we cook the books, so to speak. I cannot do this alone.

Too time consuming for one person; hell, sometimes for two."

"Listen I don't know shit about it, but I'm willing to learn do my share. Somebody has to take up the slack."

"Great, we have that settled. Gentlemen, and I use that term loosely with this group, on a serious note, I have a suggestion and I want your honest opinions on this. We all feel awful about the accident, losing Roger. There is nothing we can do to change that. Marie has told me Lauren is taking this extremely hard, even considering selling the house and moving, which I understand needing a fresh start. I was wondering how we could help her. My thought was Roger was our friend and partner. I was considering taking a large share of his money, which is now ours, of course, and giving it to Lauren and helping her out financially. I mean, she is a beautiful woman but has no real formal education to fall back on. Roger was her income, so to speak."

"Bob, I think that is a great idea and very thoughtful."

"Thanks, Cal."

Larry concurred. "Let's do it."

"I knew I could count on you guys. I'm sure this will help her emotionally, not having to worry about finances. She has no idea about Roger's financials with us. Cal, what would Roger share be for this year, rough estimate?"

"Looking at six million easy. She would be set for life."

"Okay, so it's settled. We'll have to set up some kind of wire transfer, maybe an overseas account she could access. Could you do that, Cal?"

"Easy, give me a week." They hoisted another beer to Roger. They were all in a good mood and getting rowdy.

Bob looked at Cal. "I have to ask. Did you ever get it on with Lauren?"

"What are you, fucking crazy? Roger was a friend, but she is one hot lady. How about you, Bob?"

"Marie would kill me, but I swear she always wore the tightest fucking jeans. She had to be poured into those damn things. Look at Larry, all calm and grinning his ass off, not saying a word. Probably been sneaking over to her house at night."

"Yeah, right." They were all laughing. "She wouldn't give my fat ass the time of day. Good thing she's a looker; Lauren Palmer has the IQ of a fucking houseplant." Everyone busted up laughing.

"We're all going to hell. That being said, I hope she meets someone special when she's ready. Very deserving."

"Bob, speaking of moving money, and I could care less; we have more than we can ever spend. I have to ask to make it look good on the books. Over the last few months, you moved a lot of money."

"Yes, all electronically. I didn't tell you guys because I felt the less you knew the better off you were. The passing of Gwen Long was a financial obligation we had to meet, as they say. If you want a professional job, you must be willing to pay a professional price."

Cal interrupted, "Stop! I don't need to hear anything else."

Dr. Bob smiled. "Good.

"Bob, since we're on the subject of moving money around, it's becoming difficult to launder all our income in the rental properties and the one car wash. Our bottom line is growing."

"Cal, I assume you have an idea?"

"I do, gentlemen. The car wash business is great cover, mainly a cash business. We can even print 5,000 coupons for $5.00 off and burn them. Who the hell knows? That money goes right on the books. There just happens to be one for sale just south of Wilton. The sale price 1.5 million. We can make that back in ninety days. Bob, your thoughts?"

"Let's make an offer sounds like a good deal. If he hesitates, just pay full price."

"What are we calling this one?"

"Same as the other. Blue Horizons. It's easier to balance the books."

"Gentlemen, another round of drinks?" the waitress interrupted, casually grazing her hand on Dr. Bob's shoulder.

Bob smiled. "Yes. Thank you, Sasha."

The tall blonde smiled. "I'll be right back." Dr. Bob gave her the once over.

"Damn, Bob, I think Sasha might need a ride home after work." They all laughed.

"Yeah, right, only thing she wants from me is a big tip, but you know the old saying: money makes women horny. Next subject before I get into trouble," he said, grinning.

"Bob, any word from our good friends the Syracuse PD?"

"Not a word. I understand they visited Lauren once then left town. I have every reason to believe we have seen the last of them with the passing of Roger. They know nothing about us; he was their interest."

Cal sighed. "That's a big relief. I bet they fucking told Lauren about Peyton Long and Roger, so now she has that shit to deal with, knowing Roger had some action on the side."

Dr. Bob shrugged his shoulders. "Hopefully not." He quickly changed the conversation to the group's next vacation together, a cruise to Aruba next spring.

They had last call around 11:00 and said their goodbyes. Dr. Bob was heading home to Marie, but texted Lauren first. *Congratulations. As the grieving widow, you just inherited six million! Looking forward to helping you spend it. Meet me next*

Friday at the townhouse. xx.

It didn't take long for Lauren to answer back by text: *You rock! Six million holy shit! That might even keep me happy. No easy fucking task! On Friday, I will reward you for a job well done so rest up! XX Loz!*

Chapter Twenty-Three

Detective Clayton Fisher had arrived in Switzerland only twenty-four hours earlier and slept like a rock, the long flight having taken its toll. Trustees of the National Bank of Switzerland had agreed to meet with him but promised nothing. The large glass structure was impressive, the lobby vast with comfortable seating and a coffee bar with a large screen TV; not your average bank. Clayton was inside no more than two minutes when he was politely approached.

"Hello, I'm Luca. How can I assist you today?"

"Hello." Clayton gave him his papers.

"Welcome to Switzerland, Mr. Fisher. Hopefully, your flight was comfortable." He quickly pulled out his small iPad. "You are scheduled to meet with Mr. Julian. Follow me, sir." Up the escalator they went. It was quite impressive: a huge fountain in the middle of the lobby, a large crystal chandelier hanging from the ceiling, polished oak railing and chrome. It reminded one more of a four-star hotel than a bank lobby. He soon found himself sitting across from Mr. Julian Arnet, mid-forties with a neatly trimmed beard wore a sport coat and a dark blue turtle neck no tie, which Clayton liked. He was pleasant and cordial as they sat across from each other, the large oak desk separating them, with the Swiss Flag displayed proudly on the corner.

"Mr. Fisher, I understand your position completely. No one wants to see justice unfulfilled, especially in your situation, a possible homicide. I ask that you look at our position. Our whole business is anchored by one premise: total anonymity. We don't have any names for that reason; only account numbers. Did you know that with a population of 8.4 million residents, there are exactly five individuals that have the information you request? We take confidentiality to extremes. That being said, the US friendship to our country is vital. As your letter said, we are not looking to invite any unnecessary investigations. How can I be sure no one from the bank will call to verify the information you request in a court of law? If our bank officials or the bank's name is used publicly in court, can you imagine what our depositors will think? That their privacy could be violated. This we cannot have under any circumstances."

"Mr. Arnet, I will guarantee you in writing if necessary any privileged information given to us will remain totally confidential and will never be made public." The two men spent the next three hours over the wording of the legal document that Mr. Arnet would present to the board of Trustees of The National Bank of Switzerland asking to release all information regarding bank #20005450023.

"I will do my best at the next board meeting when the trustees meet to convince them of your integrity and honesty. That is all I can do. It will not be, as you say in America, a slam dunk. They may very well not even consider it."

Clayton Fisher thanked Mr. Arnet for his time and effort. Hopefully, it was enough. Back at the hotel, he called

Detective Brockington and the others. They had been waiting patiently all day for his call. They sat around the table at police headquarters listening by speaker phone as Clayton filled them in. Chief Spence listened carefully; after all, he had a lot riding on this. "Tell me, Clayton, what's your gut feeling?"

"Chief, it's a crap shoot. Mr. Arnet was honest; it may not go our way. He has no way of knowing."

"When will we get the word?"

"That's another bit of bad news. The five trustees who make the decisions on these matters meet quarterly. The next meeting is four weeks out. And there is nothing we can do to speed that up."

"Good job, Clayton. Come on home." He hung up. Chief Spence looked at the face of a disappointed Detective Brockington. "So, we wait four weeks. It's not an eternity."

Brockington ran her fingers through her long blonde hair. "Damn. Four more weeks. I just hope it's worth it."

***

Lauren Palmer, recently widowed, sped along the freeway with the radio blaring, her hair blowing in the wind. The sun was still out, the gauge on the speedometer now topping 90 mph, and she could have cared less. She got a rush driving the pearl white Mustang that had been Roger's pride and joy. The way she looked at it, he no longer had a need for it. She might as well enjoy it.

She had a date with Dr. Bob at their new place. She loved the idea of them having a place they could call their own. This would do for now; she was biding her time, her plans centered on them being together permanently with a much larger estate.

The time was 8:00 p.m. when she zipped the Mustang into the townhouse right next to Dr. Bob's Mercedes. She always laughed to herself when she saw the new license tag PAINKILLER. How appropriate, she thought.

Lauren quickly hit the button to automatically put up the top on the Mustang. After all, she wouldn't be returning home this evening.

She checked herself in the mirror and quickly ran a brush through her windblown hair. Next she put on glossy pink lipstick. All the men she knew had sexual turn-ons. This was one of Dr. Bob's. It always got him aroused. She was feeling rather sensual herself. They hadn't been physical in over two weeks. For Lauren, that was about eleven days too many. She undid the top two buttons on her white blouse and made her way up the outside stairs.

The front door was open. She stuck her head inside. "Hello, anyone home?"

"I'm down the hall in the spare bedroom."

Lauren quickly threw off her shoes and made her down the hall to the spare bedroom. She looked in. There was Dr. Bob sitting at a desk made for a seventh-grader. She was laughing. "What in the world are you doing at that desk?" He turned and smiled and was eating cereal out of a small cup but didn't say a word, just stared at her. "Bob, is everything okay? You're starting to freak me out a little bit here." Bob still said nothing, just smiled. "Bob, fucking talk to me. This is not funny. Matter of fact, it's weird." Right then, from behind her, came a "Boo!"

Lauren almost jumped out of her pants. "What the fuck?" she screamed. Turning, she saw Dr. Bob. "What is this? I don't get it. What the hell is going on?"

"Relax, Lauren."

"Relax? I'm seeing two of you. What's going on?"

"Lauren, I would like to introduce you to my brother Samuel. I've always called him Sam."

Lauren was stunned and still taking it all in. "A brother? You never mentioned having a brother."

"No, I didn't and I apologize for that. I had reasons."

"I can't wait to fucking hear them. He looks exactly like you."

"Yes, that's why they refer to it as 'identical twins.'"

"Fuck you, Bob. This isn't funny. I'm very upset here. How could you not have told me? So are you going to introduce me or what?"

"Of course. Samuel, this is Lauren, a very special friend of mine." Sam just smiled and went back to reading his book and eating his dry cereal.

"I don't understand all this."

"Samuel is a very special person and is challenged in life. He has spent the last twenty-plus years in a very nice group home. Matter of fact, his room there looked exactly like this, down to the books on the shelf. That is why it is of the utmost importance that we maintain things precisely as they are."

Lauren looked over toward Samuel. "Very nice to meet you. Does he communicate?"

"Let's talk in the living room and I will fill you in all about Samuel." Dr. Bob poured himself and Lauren a glass of wine and settled onto the sofa. Bob told her about his parents, how they took care of Sam for as long as they could and then placed him in Meadowood. "A Godsend, such caring people. Of course, you have to be able to afford it. You were asking me does Sam talk? Rarely, the nurses at the home say. On occasion, he will say a couple of words. His books are his world. He considers the characters part of his family. Of course, Samuel is very docile, mild."

Lauren took another sip of her wine. "He sounds so sweet. Do you know the cause and at what level he functions, just so I have an understanding when I talk to him?"

"The cause we don't know. We just know he is very happy in his life. He functions very well within his world and that is why it is vital we maintain the lifestyle he knows. His room must never change, his books exactly the order he leaves them, breakfast a bowl of his favorite cereal Charms, with one piece of toast and orange juice, his daily routine. He bathes himself, lays out his own clothes, neatly of course: sox, underwear, shirts all in separate drawers every day. This is how he functions at 11:00 a.m. and 4 p.m. He walks the track every day exactly three times around Every time. Rain, sleet, snow; doesn't matter. That's the routine. That's why I bought this townhouse backing up to the high school track."

"Bob, honey, that's wonderful, but who is going to be here every day at those hours to walk with him?"

Bob smiled. "It's all arranged. The high school track coach and the school principal understand the situation and have provided me with members of the track team who have already met Sam and they love him. Of course, I also pay them nicely, but they genuinely like doing this with him. He gets the biggest smile walking the track with his new friends. Last week, the school gave him a team jacket to wear, so all that has been taken care of. As for his daily needs, I do have some connections in the medical field, so it was fairly easy to find some nurses' aides who were more than willing to work for cash, and since I know who recommended them, no need on my part for an extensive background check."

Lauren smiled. "You just think of everything, don't you?"

"I try. I'm going to need your help twice a week, Mondays and Wednesdays. Those two days I cannot be here. Marie and I have a standing date at the club every Monday evening. I don't want to raise any suspicions as to why I cannot make it and Wednesdays are always my long days at the office."

"Bob, honey, I will do my best, but I do have tennis lessons, hair dresser appointments, salon treatments, plus I have social obligations."

Dr. Bob took the glass of wine from Lauren's hand and sat it on the coffee table. Now holding her hand, with the other hand running slowly through her hair, Bob looked her in the eyes. "Lauren, this will be painful and hard for you to understand. For the first time in your life, you're going to have to think of someone other than yourself."

Lauren pushed his hand away. "Even if it's true, you're a real dick for saying that."

"Like it or not, Lauren, we're all in now. There is no turning back. I'm taking every precaution, leaving nothing to chance."

"Bob, why is Samuel here? Doesn't that make our situation more tenuous?"

"Samuel is part of my long-term plan, so to speak. For now, that's all you need to know."

"Long-term plan, Bob?"

"Yes, Lauren, intelligent people always plan for the unexpected. The best of plans can go awry quickly. I cannot explain now, but Samuel can be of a great benefit to us if the need ever arises, so you will be here to check on Sam's well-being Mondays and Wednesdays?"

“Of course.” Lauren would never tell Bob, but the thought of having his brother around long term was not the future she envisioned with him. She had no choice for now than to go along with it. “What exactly am I to do when I’m here with Sam?”

“Basically, just make sure the aides stop in that day, did they get his lunch and dinner? Do the laundry? I mean, you can come and put on music or whatever. There is a four-hour period between the aides’ shifts when Sam is here alone. Trust me, you won’t even know he’s here. If anything, he might walk out and get a glass of milk and some cookies, then he just goes back to his room and his books. What time do you have?”

Lauren looked at her watch. “Nine fifteen, why?”

“Come with me.” Lauren followed Bob down the hall. He slowly opened the door to Samuel’s room. “Take a look.” Lauren peeked inside. There was Samuel, sound asleep, covered by a cowboy blanket. “See how regimented? Sam is always lights out at 9:00 p.m. sharp.” They returned to the living room and finished their third glass of wine. Dr. Bob went over and turned on some music. His favorite, of course: soft jazz. “I love the sound of the sax, so relaxing,” he remarked. Lauren walked over and dimmed the lights, walking ever so slowly back toward Bob. She stood over him then undid the buttons on her white blouse. Bob stood up and slowly slid the blouse off and let it drop to the floor, kissing her neck. He removed her bra, her breasts now fully exposed. He whispered in her ear, “I love the pink lip gloss.”

Lauren ran her tongue across her lips. “I know that.” She slowly undid his belt and went to her knees.

***

Lauren rolled over and looked at the alarm clock. Eight o'clock a.m. "Who gets up at this hour?" She threw on her robe and slippers, making her way to the kitchen. There were Dr. Bob and Samuel having breakfast.

"Nice of you to join us."

Sam just smiled then went back to eating his Charms cereal and one piece of toast with jelly, no butter.

Dr. Bob poured Lauren a cup of coffee. "Would you like eggs and bacon?"

"Sure."

"Coming right up."

"I assume this is part of Sam's routine?" Bob grabbed the counter stool next to Lauren.

"Yes, it is. He does, however, have two cereal choices: he likes, besides Charms, Chocolate Puffs and one piece of toast only."

Lauren was enjoying her eggs and bacon. "This is nice. I could get used to a man cooking for me." She grinned.

"You're in luck. I happen to be a pretty good cook."

"That's good, because I pretty much suck at it. I'm the reason take-out was created." They both laughed.

"Is Samuel always up at 8:00?"

"Actually, 7:45 on the dot." Bob had a mischievous smile. "You realize in the working world, that's actually a routine start time for most people?"

Lauren squeezed his leg under the table. "I've heard that rumor. I never took it seriously nor do I plan on trying it anytime soon."

Bob laughed. "Listen, the morning aide will be here around 10:00 if you would like to hang out for a while."

"Thanks, but I have an appointment to keep at 12:30."

"Don't tell me. Having your nails done, correct?"

"Very funny, Bob. You have no clue. I always have my nails done at 10:00 so they have time to dry before lunch. I do have a dentist appointment, having my pearly whites polished. They seem to go well with the pink lip gloss, wouldn't you say?" Bob smiled.

Lauren finished her breakfast, quickly showered, and made her way to the car. Bob gave her a kiss good-bye. "Text me when you're home."

"Okay."

"We probably can't see each other again until the end of the week."

Lauren shrugged. "That works. Just curious, where did you tell Marie you were last night?"

"I didn't have to tell her anything. She's out of town until tonight visiting her sister. You will be here Wednesday, right?"

"I will be here as promised. Maybe I'll bring a few more items from the house."

"Sounds good. We'll talk soon."

Lauren Palmer was miffed at Bob. How was this going to work out if their relationship wasn't difficult enough with Marie still in the picture? Now his brother. She sped down the highway, totally pissed at him. Keeping a secret like that; what else didn't she know about him? She was in love in him, but he scared her.

Chapter Twenty-Four

It had been three weeks since Detective Clayton Fisher's trip to Switzerland. Still no word. Detective Brockington was getting antsy. Sitting back had never been her forte. She was working other cases, but the ongoing Long case was her priority. She was busy going through her e-mails when her partner Detective Wade dropped by her desk. "Have a minute?"

"Always for you, Wade. What gives?"

"Remember you had us check the backgrounds of these guys, but we didn't find anything that stood out? Just the usual college bullshit we all did?"

"Yup."

"I was bored, so I dug a little further, all the way back to Dr. Robert Weinstein's high school days."

"Don't tell me he played hooky from school and went to the beach? That's cute."

"No, it seems that our esteemed doctor had an encounter with law enforcement his senior year."

Brockington's ears perked up. "Really? Tell me more."

"Yeah, well, here's when it gets interesting. I looked for open cases from the Wilton Police Department. Seems that a young Bob Weinstein was questioned about someone named Ann Tasker. The case was quietly dismissed, but since it was never adjudicated, it was still in the files. I found an Ann Tasker. Her name now is Ann Howser. That was the only Tasker last name within thirty miles of Wilton, so I assume that's our girl."

Brockington sighed. "That was a long time ago. What was it about?"

"You will love this. Sit back and relax. I'll fill you in."

Brockington listened intently until Wade finished then smiled at her. "So can we pay her a visit? She's now living in Brick, NJ, nearly 300 miles away, practically our backyard," he said with a laugh.

"We can do it, but before we drive almost 300 miles, make sure that's our girl and that she will talk about what happened all those years ago."

Thursday morning found Detectives Brockington and Wade at the residence of Ann Howser. Extremely attractive for the age of forty-six, she stood about five feet six inches tall with long brown hair, an athletic build, and green eyes. They sat in her living room drinking iced tea. She was very pleasant. "So you asked me about Dr. Robert Weinstein on the phone. When I knew him, it was Bobby and he was no doctor." They all laughed.

Detective Brockington asked the questions. "So how did you two meet?"

"Are you ready for this? I was working at a place called Kelton's Pharmacy, a family-owned business. I was working the register when Bobby and some friends came in, bought some sodas. He started hitting on me and he was cute. We couldn't have been more different."

"How so?"

"Let me count the ways. Detective, I lived in a mobile home park and Bobby was from Wilton. Ever see those commercials? People make fun of mobile homes; you know gnomes in the yard, plastic flowers — that was us. Here was this high school kid driving his own brand-new car — I couldn't believe it — hitting on me. Make a long story short, he asked me out. I'll tell you, the first time I visited his place, I couldn't believe people lived liked that. I mean, their living room was bigger than my mobile home and they had an inground pool. I was speechless. I met his parents once briefly. I don't think I was what they had in mind for their son. We went on three dates. He came to my place once to meet my mom. He was pleasant enough; no warning signs, just another high school kid."

"So what went wrong?"

"This is off the record, correct?"

"You have my word. We're just trying to get a feel for the real Robert Weinstein."

"He asked me to his high school prom. I was in heaven. I wanted to go so bad. My parents, God bless them, were the salt of the earth, but that kind of money for a dance was not in the cards. My dad was an auto mechanic, my mom a nurse's aide, but she saw the look on my face. She was going to make it happen. She and her sister sold all kinds of stuff at yard sales to get my prom dress. I will never forget the look on Mom's face. My dad's eyes just lit up that night when I came out with that long blue dress holding a white purse and white heels. Mom had tears, she was so proud. I think my dad took a hundred pictures that night. I was their only child. They doted on me, Detective, not with the latest video games or outfits —

they didn't have money for those things — but with more love and kindness anyone ever received and you can't buy that.

"But that night changed everything for us. The prom was held at some upscale hotel and it was amazing. Those kids from Berkshire all had money, or at least their parents did. Hell, in the ladies' room, the girls were doing lines of coke. I felt stupid, not even knowing why the hell they were putting a dollar bill up their noses.

"Yes, I tried it. I was young and stupid and wanted to fit in that night.

"Later that evening, there were eight of us back at some hotel room they had rented for the night. They had beer and wine, smoking cigarettes, smoking pot. I had to be home by 3:00 a.m., but after the last drink, Bobby gave me, I felt really dizzy and I couldn't even walk. The next thing I remember was Bobby laying me down on the bed, closing the door behind us. I kind of sat up; there he was, taking off all his clothes. He kissed me then pushed me back on the bed. I was trying to push him off, telling him I was not ready for sex. I was having trouble fending him off. I know now he spiked my drink. My head was spinning. Then the boy I dated who was so polite changed in an instant. He forcefully stuck his tongue down my throat, pinning my shoulders down until banging his knees against my thighs, talking rough. 'Get used to this, bitch,' he said, then he actually flipped me on my stomach, almost tearing my dress off and ripping off my underwear and bra. I was crying. He had his hands all over my body, everywhere, rubbing his penis everywhere. Finally, I guess he was too excited and had an orgasm all over my stomach. I'll never forget what he said. 'Damn, was that intense or what?' Like I actually enjoyed it.

"The next day, I was still in shock over what happened. My mom kept asking me if I had a good time.

"That night, I took my mom back in the bedroom and told her everything. I showed her the bruises on my shoulder, the inside of my thighs from his knees, totally black and blue. This was when I learned there are two sets of law for people in this country: those with money and those without.

"I didn't want her to; I just wanted to move on forget it ever happened. My mom was so upset, she called the Wilton Police Department. That was a mistake. We didn't know we should have called the state police. The Chief of Police for Wilton at that time was Ben Swain, who has since passed away. I knew right away this was not what my mom or I expected. We were sitting in a private room with him at the police station. He started asking me about that night. I will never forget. Was I drinking? Did I go to the hotel voluntarily? What was I wearing? Had I been intimate with Bobby Weinstein before that night? How much did I drink? He never asked to see my bruises until my mom insisted he look. Then he said, 'Ms. Tasker, young people and alcohol; all those hormones.' He didn't even offer to have a medical doctor examine me. My mom insisted we were pressing charges regardless and we left. The next day, Chief Swain came to our mobile home, but not alone. He had with him a lawyer representing the Weinsteins. No doubt the chief called and informed them of what was going on. We all sat around the kitchen table, including my father. We went over everything again. Their lawyer, Mr. Hogan, asked that we understand the gravity of the situation we were creating for all parties involved. Yes, he was sorry for what happened, but he was hoping we could reach a settlement where I wouldn't press charges.

"'He has been accepted to Harvard University next fall. All that is off the table if you file these charges, which I guarantee you will not hold up in a court of law. The Weinsteins are well-respected members of this community. They will spare no expense to exonerate their son. I agree none of this should have happened, but young people checking into a hotel with alcohol involved — any jury will look at that with doubts about what really happened.'

"My mom interrupted. 'And what will the jury say, Mr. Hogan, when we show them the bruises on my daughter's legs and arms and her torn dress?' Detective, you could have heard a pin drop in that room. I mean, there was silence. After a couple of minutes, Mr. Hogan asked to meet with my parents alone. Of course they made an offer. $100,000 to drop all charges. You have to understand, to my parents, that was like ten million and I don't blame them one bit for taking it, but they asked me first and I agreed on one other condition, that Bobby Weinstein write me a letter of apology. We got the money. I'm still waiting on the letter."

"I'm so sorry. That's terrible. Hopefully, twenty-five years later, something like that can't happen today."

"Not your fault, Detective. You know, my parents took that money and we moved into a nice small rancher, but a year later, my father was gone. The coroner said he died from a heart attack. I don't buy it. Bobby Weinstein killed my father just like he assaulted me. Taking that money hurt my father bad, the one time in his life he couldn't take care of his little girl. My father didn't die from a heart attack, Detective. He died from a broken heart and I will go to my grave believing that."

Detectives Brockington and Wade spent the next two hours looking at photos of a young Ann Tasker and her family. She was beautiful girl in high school, no doubt about it. They laughed about the bell bottoms the boys wore and the hairstyles. Her parents had raised her well. She was a genuinely nice person. Detective Brockington got up to leave and gave Ann a hug. "I'm not sure what Bob Weinstein did, Detective, but I wish you luck in finding out. Maybe there is some justice in the world after all."

As they headed for the long drive back to Syracuse, Wade was incensed. "I hope we get that bastard, but it won't be easy."

Brockington agreed. "Nothing worthwhile ever is. Wouldn't it be ironic that Dr. Bob helped convict himself for something he did twenty-five years ago?"

"I couldn't figure out why that file was still in the system."

"I don't follow?"

"The only reason that file wasn't tossed decades ago was they couldn't close it. Part of the legal settlement was the apology letter Bobby Weinstein never wrote. His lawyer would have had to file a copy to show both parties complied with the agreement."

***

Two days later.

"Chief, have a minute?" Sergeant Roy Davis walked into his boss's office. Chief Snow looked up from his desk.

"What's up?"

"I just wanted to make you aware of something. You know how we share files with other law enforcements agencies? If they request a copy, we forward one and vice versa?"

"Yeah, somebody need something?"

"They actually already have it. When someone takes a copy of the file from our system, we get a notification of who took it and when. It seems that a file on Bobby Weinstein was requested from the Syracuse Police Department."

"What? Let me see that." Sergeant Davis handed his boss the very slim folder, basically three pages containing information about a case settled before charges were brought. "You realize this damn thing's over twenty-five years old? How in the hell is it still on record? Those pricks from Syracuse just won't let this thing go. You know this is about Dr. Bob Weinstein when he was in high school, for crying out loud."

"Yeah, I took a peek at it. Ridiculous. I have no idea why it's still in the system. That should have been tossed when the charges were dropped." Chief Snow grabbed the folder and left. Ten minutes later, he was in the waiting room of Dr. Robert Weinstein's office, flirting with his twenty-two-year-old secretary Sandy.

"Give me one minute, Chief. I believe he just finished with his last patient." Sandy returned, promptly followed by Dr. Bob.

"Now this is a surprise I don't get every day. Is everything okay, Chief?"

"Yeah, Doc. Can we speak in private?"

"Absolutely. Let's go to my office. Sandy, give me ten minutes before my next appointment."

"Not a problem. Nice seeing you again, Chief," Sandy said with a nice smile.

Dr. Bob closed the door behind him and took a seat behind his desk. "Have a seat, Chief. How can I help you today? If you want some male stimulants, I have a couple of new products the pharmacy rep just dropped off. I can hook you up."

They both laughed. "Listen, Doc, the reason I dropped by, and I'm sure it's nothing, but your group is so good to our department. I just thought I would give you the courtesy of knowing the Syracuse Police Department requested an old file on you. Seems from back when you were a senior in high school. Does that ring a bell?"

Dr. Bob started laughing. "They kept that on file? What did it say?"

"Nothing really. Just you were questioned about a female and no charges were brought."

Dr. Bob smiled. "Man, does that take me back to some good memories. I took this girl, Chief, to the school prom, and I mean, man, she was a looker. Anyway, teenagers and hormones being what they are, we're at this hotel after the prom drinking, doing things teens do. Next thing you know, she strips down in the bedroom, so I quickly join in on the fun. The truth be told, we were both so inebriated, I don't know if we had intercourse or not. The only telltale sign was all over her stomach when we woke up around four o'clock in the morning, both of us naked lying across the bed. She gets in a panic. 'Did you get me pregnant?' I was trying to stay calm and be nice to her and she starts throwing pillows at me and demands I take her right home and accuses me of tearing her dress. It's early a.m. I drop her off at her mobile home and tried to tell her I had a wonderful evening. She gets out and slams my car door shut and bolts for her front door. Chief, next thing I know, she accusing me of assault, but her family may be willing to have her drop the charges if we can reach a settlement. I was one hundred percent against it. This was nothing but pure blackmail. My parents insisted on paying. I was going to Harvard in the fall. They didn't want anything to mess that up. That was the last I ever heard of it until now."

"Damn, Doc. That's not right, but I'm glad you weren't charged. So even in high school, you were chasing the pretty ones." They both laughed. "Alright, well, I have to get back to the station."

"Chief, thank you for taking the time to come down here for that nonsense. I do have a question. You said the Syracuse Police Department requested it. I don't understand?"

"Don't worry about it, Doc. Doesn't really concern you at all. Not even sure how they got your name, to be honest with you." Chief Snow left, convinced the Syracuse PD was way off track with his good friend Dr. Bob.

Dr. Robert Weinstein was surprisingly caught off guard, a first for him. How did they get his name and why were they digging into his background? He had carefully covered all his tracks and was confident in his own ability to outwit law enforcement. The key, of course, was always be one step ahead, and he was.

Dr. Bob grabbed his iPhone and started to text: *Can you talk?* His cell rang almost immediately.

"What's up?"

"Here's what I need you to do." Bob detailed his plan.

"Are you sure?"

"Trust me." The conversation was short. Dr. Bob calmly returned to the front desk. "Sandy, I'm ready for my next patient."

Chapter Twenty-Five

Cal Estrada was at his office Briarcliff Realty-Investments looking at his computer when he was startled by the voice. "Cal, are you busy?" There in his doorway stood Lauren Palmer.

"Oh my gosh, Lauren." He quickly went over and they hugged. "How are you?"

"I'm hanging in there."

"Here, have a seat." Lauren took a seat on the leather sofa. Cal sat next to her. "I must tell you, this is a pleasant surprise. I really wanted to come by and visit with you, but I kept putting it off. I just didn't know what to say."

"Cal, it's fine. People have been great. It's not easy for anyone. You guys were all like brothers. I understand. I really do."

"How are things? Any better?"

"I'm just taking one day at time. It's a huge adjustment. I mean, all the plans for the future have changed. I have to adjust, you know, try to put my life back on track."

"Is there anything I can do?"

"Actually, that's why I'm here."

"I would love to help. What can I do?"

"I've decided to move, so I will need to put my house on the market. There is no one else I would trust that to."

"Lauren, I would be honored to do that. Thank you so much. You don't mind me asking, where to?"

"To Texas temporarily. I have a close friend there. It will give me a chance to figure things out long term."

"I'm humbled that you came to me. It means a lot. I will accept under one condition. I will take no commission."

"Cal, I can't ask you to do that."

"You're not asking. I'm insisting. We will get your house sold and help you move."

Lauren wiped a tear from her face. "You guys were such good friends and this is why it's so hard to start again." She gave Cal a hug.

"Listen, I will draw up all the paperwork. When it's ready, I'll come by. We'll dot all the I's and cross all the T's and get this thing moving."

"Hopefully, this will give me a chance to reflect before making any hard decisions. I just need to move. Too many memories here."

"I understand, but we will miss you. The door is always open." They talked at length about all the good times spent together as couples.

"Cal, I need to be going." She stood up and they embraced. "We'll talk soon." Cal nodded. He was still deeply troubled by the loss of his friend.

Cal sat behind his desk, turned on his computer, and pulled up the property at 114 Heritage Court, the last selling price 1.2 million to Roger and Lauren Palmer. While going over the estate, he pulled out his iPhone and placed a call.

"Hello there, stranger," came the answer on the other end.

"To what do I owe this?"

"Bob, do you have a minute?"

"Always for you, Cal. No patients for the moment. What's up?"

"You won't believe who just left my office."

"Who?"

"Lauren Palmer. She has decided to move and asked me to list her home."

"Really? Lauren is moving?"

"Yes. I felt bad for her. Said she's moving to Texas temporarily until she decides what her future holds. Seems she has a friend living there."

"I'm sorry to hear that, but it may be for the best. She can go there try and figure out what's next. She has no kids. I mean, Roger was her life. It must be very painful for her. So when is it going on the market?"

"I'll have the paperwork ready by tomorrow, then I just need her to sign off on it."

"I'll get the word out. It's a beautiful home. I can't imagine it will be on the market long. What's the asking price?"

"Roger bought it for 1.2 million. That would be a steal today. It will easily command 1.9 or more. I'm not sure what they owe on it, if anything, but she should do fine on the sale. I told Lauren under no circumstances was I taking any commission. It's the least I can do."

"That's nice. Roger would have appreciated that."

"Hopefully, in time, she lands on her feet and enjoys life again."

"I'm sure she will. Thanks for the info. I'll let Marie know. Maybe she and Diane can stop by and help her out with some of the packing."

"Bob, when was the last time you saw Lauren?"

"I have to think. I'm ashamed to admit it, but not since the funeral."

"Now I don't feel quite so bad."

"Same here. I kept putting it off not knowing what to say, but that's a piss poor excuse. Don't beat yourself up too much, Cal. She knows how much we care about her. Marie calls her almost every day. We all wanted to do more; just didn't know how."

"I guess you're right. Listen, I have a couple of calls to make. Talk to you soon."

"Okay, pal, hang in there." Dr. Bob was pleased with Lauren's house now going on the market. He could move quickly if need be. There were still issues that needed attending to, but making everything seem natural would be the key to his long term plans.

***

It was Wednesday morning. Detective Clayton Fisher was having coffee at his desk when he was approached by desk Sergeant Brenda Crews. "Sorry to interrupt your busy morning, Detective, but I have a Fed-Ex driver at my desk requires your signature on a delivery."

"I didn't order anything, but if you say so, Sergeant, lead the way." Detective Fisher signed for the envelope then quickly noticed it was sent over-night express and the address First National Bank of Switzerland, Zurich. He practically ran down the hall, almost choking on the doughnut he had in his mouth, fearing bad news. He said nothing, quickly returning to his desk. He inhaled deeply then tore the strip off the cardboard back and removed the letter inside.

To: Detective Clayton Fisher,

Sir, we have received your request regarding information about one of our depositors.

As you may understand, we take the privacy and trust of our customers extremely seriously. After all, that is how we built the foundation of our business.

Your request, then, represents to us a moral dilemma. We, of course, have many depositors and associates from the United States. We consider it an honor, the trust they show in our institution.

That being said, we also cannot turn our back if a serious crime may have been committed and that we may have unknowingly contributed to the cover-up of a criminal act. Therefore, if you can meet our requirements, we will forward the information you have requested. The conditions are not negotiable.

1. All information received from the National Bank of Switzerland is for informational purposes only and will not be offered as evidence in a court of law. (We must remain neutral on this.)

2. All paperwork will be shredded at the conclusion of your need.

3. No one's personal name from the National Bank of Switzerland will appear on any court documents nor will any individuals be asked to testify to the authenticity of such documents.

Detective Clayton Fisher, you will have five business days to accept this offer. You may reply by signing the enclosed legal document. We await your decision.

Sincerely,

Mr. Liam Oberly

Board of Trustees National Bank of Switzerland.

"Hell yes!" Clayton Fisher's voice could be heard down the hall. He gathered the paperwork and quickly hustled around corner to the desks of Detective Brockington and Wade. Both were busy. He casually pulled up a chair. "I know how busy you two are. Do you have a few minutes?"

Laura Brockington smiled. "For you, Clayton, always."

"I was wondering, could you take a look at this paperwork? I'm not sure its correct."

Laura shrugged. "Sure, why not?" and grabbed the paperwork. In two minutes, she looked up. "Is this legit?"

"Hell, yes. It came this morning."

Detective Wade quickly made his way over to check it out. "Damn, alright!" he screamed and quickly was fist bumping with Detective Fisher.

Brockington made her away around the desk, hugging Clayton. "You are amazing. I didn't think you had a chance in hell of pulling this off. What's the next step?"

"I'll show this to Chief Spence and get the okay to sign off on the agreement and send this express overnight. Hopefully, in a couple of days, we'll have a name."

Brockington, smiling, spoke up. "Then get moving, Detective. Time's wasting."

"On my way."

Chief Spence was impressed by Clayton Fisher's good work. "Thank you, sir. May I sign off?"

"Absolutely, Clayton. You have my word we will not break our promise. The information you receive will stay confidential."

Detective Fisher returned to his desk, signed off on the paperwork, and headed to the nearest Fed-Ex office. He was taking no chances. He would personally see that envelope mailed. Returning to police headquarters, he made sure to inform all front desk personnel any mail arriving by courier for him to track him down immediately and not let them leave the building with that package.

Desk Sergeant Brenda Crews, seeing his seriousness, thought she would have a little fun. "Detective Fisher, suppose you're in the john. What should I do?"

All the police officers in the area cracked up. Without so much as batting an eye or laughing, Detective Fisher replied, "Sergeant Crews, in that instance, please come into the men's restroom and knock on the stall door. I will cut it off and finish later."

Sergeant Crews stuck her tongue out. "Touché, Detective, I will do just that."

Detective Fisher didn't have to wait long. Less than seventy-two hours after mailing the reply to the National Bank of Switzerland, they had received the confirmation and reply. Now sitting in the conference room with Detectives Brockington, Wade, and Chief Spence, they waited impatiently as Clayton Fisher removed the strip from the back of package and removed the contents. Twenty-five pages in all mostly legal paperwork that protected the bank. Brockington looked on in her white blouse and blue trousers, her gold shield attached to her belt clip, Detective Wade with his standard white shirt with blue and gold tie with black slacks. Chief Spence was seated at his customary spot at the end of the conference table with his white shirt, black tie, and black slacks; always dressed dapper, his shoes reclining on the end of the table. Detective Fisher would read one page, then pass it on around the oval table. They finally came to page 15, what they had all been anticipating. Detective Fisher looked up. "I have it."

There was silence, all eyes focused on Detective Fisher. "Read it out loud, Detective. Let's go," came the command from the end of the table. "At precisely 10:45 eastern standard time by wire, the amount of two million American dollars was transferred from Bank Account #36789-0000-22. The name on the Corporate Account, Eagle 2 Investments, Wilton, Connecticut." There was more legal paperwork to read, but they had what they wanted. Chief Spence stood up. There was sense of relief the last four weeks had not been a waste of time. "People, this is a big step. Now the question is who the hell is running Eagle 2 Investments and what exactly are they investing in?"

Wade chimed in, "My money is on our good friend Dr. Bob somehow being involved, but if its privately owned, how do we know?"

"Good question. Clayton, you're our white collar specialist. How do we?"

"Not easy. There are difficulties in searching for private company information. It can be done. We just have to be creative. Start with directories. The most common one is Dunn and Bradstreet. We need to send someone to the Wilton library. Many local library systems subscribe to databases for citizens running a local business so individuals can research it. There are also firms that conduct backgrounds on privately run enterprises. My favorite is Prince Corp. They have information on over one million privately owned companies. Of course, it costs to access their information, but it may be worth it. Last but not least, if we strike out with those efforts, Chief, do you have any political clout?"

"Depends on who I need to talk to. Why?"

"Companies are required to file with the Secretary of State of which they are established, so whoever that individual is for Connecticut will have every listing. We could find out real quick the CEO of Eagle 2 Investments."

"The way you calmly said that, Clayton, I assume most states don't share that information willingly?"

"No. They want a court order and a good reason." Everyone laughed.

"Fuck," said Brockington. "I guess a couple homicides might be a good reason."

"Alright, let's work the other sources first. In the meantime, I will try and schmooze some people just in case we need to go that route."

"Chief, I have a concern involving Clayton."

"What?"

"He needs more of a social life. No man walks around with that much boring information he can recite off the top of his head." Everyone laughed.

"I will have you know, Detective Brockington, when I'm at home with my lovely wife, sometimes on the weekends, we're up until 11:00 p.m. drinking wine and reading *Southern Living*." Everyone laughed, including Clayton. The one thing they all knew about their new colleague, when it came to white collar crime, Detective Clayton Fisher was indeed one of the best.

***

Susan Sinclair, the five-foot-two-inch brunette, and Diane Estrada, her long auburn hair held back by the white sweatband, were having drinks on the terrace at the Blackstone Tennis Club, having just finished playing. The outdoor bar was busy with patrons from sipping wine and dinning on fresh seafood.

Susan and Diane took a table overlooking the gardens that were in full bloom under a beautiful afternoon sun.

"Diane, I was so glad you called to get out here again playing, socializing, to just relax. The last couple of months have just drained me mentally."

"Trust me, you're not the only one. Cal is really having a tough go of it since Roger's passing. He's just not himself. It's going to take time. I try and comfort him, but mentally, it's been so hard on him. How is Larry coping with it?"

"The same. Good days when he's back to normal, then sullen, quiet, moody even."

"So what did you think of the big news of Lauren selling the house?"

"Not too surprised. Cal was pleased she asked him to be the realtor. Makes him feel good helping out a friend. I mean, this isn't the best town to be single in. Everybody's married. She's still young, not to mention the fact that she's eye candy to every guy in town." They both laughed.

"Diane, don't think bad of me for saying this, but I just never saw the connection between her and Roger. He was like this bookworm who would talk physics while Lauren was discussing the latest color in lip gloss."

"Trust me, you think Cal and I haven't said the same thing, but they made it work."

"Yes, they did. She's moving to Texas once the house is

sold. Marie's been visiting with her, calling her. Diane, do you and Cal ever discuss the business part of these guys' relationship?"

"You mean the Crimson charity?"

"Yes, I mean, it's been very successful. They have raised a lot of money for some good causes. Why?"

"Larry never really lets me see any of the financial aspects of our marriage. I understand. After all, he does teach economics at the University. I've never even seen our tax returns. It's all so secretive."

"Is that a problem? I mean, you're obviously doing very well."

"Diane, the math just doesn't add up. I mean, a professor's salary at the University is public record. He does well, but not for the way we live. I'm not complaining. We have everything. I guess what made me question it was two weeks ago, I was going through his closet. I noticed a small brown duffel bag in the corner. I go to put it up on the shelf. It was heavy. I'm thinking, great month-old dirty laundry. I open it up. $10,000 in cash. I was stunned."

"Really?"

"Yes, I know men keep mad money from their wives, but it's usually like a hundred bucks, not ten grand."

"Did you ask him about it?"

"No, I waited for a week and checked back. The bag was empty."

"I'm sure there's a logical explanation."

"Just seems odd to have that kind of cash stuffed in the closet, don't you think?"

"Who knows with men? They all have quirks. I mean, when you look at it logically, Larry teaches economics. He's probably doing some investing and figures you wouldn't agree with the risk. Men are always pulling that shit."

Susan laughed. "You're probably right. Larry doesn't exactly come across as the mobster type. I feel better now. Had all these crazy thoughts running through my head, like maybe another female. I quickly extinguished that idea. I mean, we're talking Larry here. Mr. Physique he is not." They both laughed.

"Speaking of that, I stopped by Marie's last week. Susan, guess what our discussion was about?"

"No idea, what?"

"Okay, but this stays between us."

"For sure, not a word."

"We're having coffee. She confides in me she feels Dr. Bob is having an affair."

"Whoa, what?"

"That's what she said, so I asked with who? She's not positive, but all the signs point to him screwing around. Coming home late from the office, last-minute appointments out of town, lack of being physical with her. So I said hire someone to find out instead making yourself crazy.

Marie said she's not doing that. She then said that over the course of their marriage, Bob had these stretches where she was suspicious he was seeing someone, but she didn't care; he always returned home to her, and eventually, everything returned to normal. She said they have a great life and she didn't wanna rock the boat. She said likes being Ms. Robert Weinstein. She said this time just feels different. He's been very preoccupied. She's hoping it's just work, but she has her doubts."

"Wow, that is a surprise. I couldn't live like that if Larry was having an affair. I would send his ass packing tomorrow."

"Would you really, Susan? We all say that, but give up the big estate, the new cars, the travel for some bitch? Excuse my French. I wouldn't. Now I might fucking run her over with my BMW, but I'm not letting her enjoy the fruits of my labor, not without a fight."

Susan was laughing. "I never thought of it that way. You're right. It wouldn't be an easy decision, but I feel pretty safe in that department. Larry's a dork, but I know he loves me."

"Same with Cal. I never worried about that. I totally trust him."

"I'm glad I told you about the money. I feel better now. These guys with their Harvard education. I guess they have interests we wouldn't understand or find boring."

Right then, a young male waiter walked by. "Excuse me. Could we have another round of drinks?"

He was tall and tan, maybe twenty-three, with blonde wavy hair. "It would be my pleasure. I will be right back with your drinks."

Susan smiled as he went for the drinks. "I didn't really want another one, but why should the men have all the fun looking. Damn, to be twenty-three again for one night."

Diane was laughing. "You are incorrigible."

"Don't I know it."

Chapter Twenty-Six

Two weeks had passed since receiving the information regarding Eagle 2 Investments from the National Bank of Switzerland. Detectives Brockington, Wade, and Fisher had scoured records from every source they could: the Wilton Library, Dunn and Bradstreet, etc. all were fruitless. None listed any information on the investment firm of Eagle 2. It was as if it never existed. Whoever was in charge made sure the brokerage firm avoided the limelight. The investigation had come to a standstill.

Syracuse Police Chief Gary Spence found himself sitting in the office for the Assistant District Attorney for the State of New York. He found the Assistant D.A. Gina Davis engaging. She was tall with short brown hair and blue eyes, wearing a navy-blue dress and sport coat. She was soft spoken, but make no mistake; she was a tough prosecutor.

"Chief, the way I understand the problem, you're having a difficult time getting the Secretary of State for Connecticut to release this information you requested regarding Eagle 2 Investments."

"That's correct. We were rebuffed for privacy issues."

"I read the case file. It's quite extensive. Seems you have

spent a lot of time pursuing this. Obviously, it's something you feel strongly about."

"I've lost track; at least six months, probably longer. We have been everywhere from Seattle to Switzerland and our detectives have spent countless manhours, many on their own time."

"I am looking through the file. You believe this may involve everything from blackmail to money laundering?"

"Yes, possibly more, but for now, we want to pursue the financial aspect. We feel that's our strongest case at this point."

"Chief, give me three days. If necessary, I will make a trip to Connecticut and visit the State Secretary myself. We can help each other with this case."

"How?"

"I will get you the names of those controlling Eagle 2 Investments. In return, I want to prosecute the case myself here in Manhattan, not Syracuse."

"Why Manhattan?"

"If I'm being brutally honest, this case has all the making of garnering a lot of attention.

Harvard Graduates from one of the wealthiest communities in the Unites States running an ongoing criminal enterprise. Yes, it would help my career. Also consider they will have the best legal team that money can buy. I have under me here in Manhattan over two hundred lawyers and other legal personnel at my disposal to help prepare the case for prosecution. I would doubt the city of Syracuse has that."

Chief Spence was laughing. "I appreciate your candor. You're right. We may have fifteen lawyers in our legal department. As for who prosecutes the case, I could care less, just get the conviction or the headlines for doing so."

"Good. I would like to meet soon as possible with the lead detective. Bring me up to date on everything that has transpired recently."

"That will not be a problem. She knows her way around Manhattan, trust me." They shook hands. Chief Spence was pleased. The case had almost been derailed by what he referred to as authoritative bullshit. Finally, someone who could cut through all the bureaucratic red tape.

***

Tuesday afternoon, Dr. Robert Weinstein was relaxing at home for a few hours before heading to his office, when his cell phone lit up. Usually, with a number he didn't recognize, normally, he would just disregard it, let it go to voicemail. This time, he did answer, "Hello?"

"Is this Dr. Robert Weinstein from Wilton?"

"Could be. If you're selling something, I'm very busy at the moment."

"No, sir, I'm not. I'm actually making this call as a courtesy to you. My name Daryl Newport. I'm the Secretary of State for Connecticut. Your donations over the years to our party have not gone unnoticed, so I wanted to pass along some privileged information that recently came to my attention."

Dr. Bob took a seat in his recliner. "Well, you have my attention."

"First off, Doctor, I must ask that information I'm passing along to you is strictly confidential and may not be shared with anyone. You have been a good benefactor, so I felt you should be made aware of this."

"Thank you. Whatever you share will stay between us."

"Good. Recently, actually, yesterday, I had a visit from the District Attorney for Manhattan. She was requesting information on a privately held investment firm called Eagle 2 Investments."

Dr. Bob sat up in his recliner, no longer relaxed, and listening intently.

"This was not the first inquiry made for this information. I had rebuffed previous efforts from the Syracuse Police Department. After all, businesses that wish to keep a low profile, in my opinion, should be able to. This was different; she was not taking no for an answer, threatening possible litigation against our department if cooperation was not forthcoming, so I had no choice. Hopefully, this will not taint your future donations to our cause."

"No, not at all. I appreciate the call. Tell me, was there anything the D.A. was especially interested in?"

"Yes, the names of the trustees of the firm was foremost on her list, followed by all financials investments your firm was involved in. The D.A. made copies of all the files we have of your company. I tried to make light chatter with her. That woman has all the charm of a rattlesnake." They both laughed. "Her name, in case you're interested, is Gina Davis, Assistant D.A. for New York City. I hope, Doctor, this isn't a great cause for concern."

"No, not at all. I'm sure it has something to do with a tax shelter my accountant put me in. That's why I stay out of all the financial stuff. I just try and take care of my patients. I couldn't even tell you what Eagle 2 invests in. I'm a trustee in name only for tax purposes. I do know we incorporate in New York, probably looking for more revenue. We probably shorted them fifty bucks." Daryl Newport and the doctor laughed and then talked a little politics for twenty minutes and hung up.

Dr. Bob leaned back in his leather recliner, contemplating the conversation that had just taken place.

The Manhattan District Attorney, he thought. This was a new twist. How were they able to track down Eagle 2 Investments? At least for once being a political donor had benefitted him. He would have been totally blindsided without the tipoff they were examining the group's financial holdings.

The right thing to do, of course, would be to share the information with Cal and Larry. After all, they were business partners and lifelong friends, but this, he thought was well beyond their bonds. This was literally their freedom possibly at stake. For now, he thought it best to keep the information to himself in case someone had to take the fall. Maybe this could be to his advantage.

Bob walked to his patio doors, looking out over his luscious green lawn meticulously maintained almost like a golf course. He was proud of his estate; everything always maintained and pristine. Then he thought to himself, This Detective Brockington was going to be an issue. He walked across the room to his mini-bar. Reaching below, he poured himself a shot of Remy Martin, his favorite brandy. He sipped on it while thinking, then went over to his aquarium, one of his favorite hobbies, observing the exotic fish, among them a bright yellow swordtail angelfish; over one hundred different species in all moving about in the 300-gallon tank. He finished the brandy and laid the glass on the mantel behind the aquarium.

He gazed incessantly at the fish moving about. He took

his small net and scooped out the bright yellow swordtail, which squirmed about in the net. Bob was thinking about Detective Brockington when he grasped the fish with his bare hand, squeezing it tightly until its eyes literally popped out, then walked into the bathroom, dropped the dead fish into the toilet, and flushed.

Bob then calmly walked over to the sink and washed his hands. Looking in the mirror, he straightened his tie then combed his hair. He returned to the den, gently laid his suit coat over his arm, and headed out the front door. He had a patient to see in thirty minutes.

***

Friday morning at 10:00 a.m., Syracuse Police Chief Gary Spence sat at the head of the conference table. Joining him were Detectives Brockington, Wade, Fisher, and Manhattan D.A. Gina Davis. Chief Spence turned to the D.A. "I believe this is your show, so I will turn this over to you."

"Thank you, Chief. First off, I want to compliment all of you on the work you have done on this case. As the District Attorney, I'm totally impressed by the professionalism you have followed, every lead, even to Zurich. Nice work if you can get it." Everyone laughed. "This is, of course, a serious case. I have managed to acquire the names of the trustees for Eagle 2 Investments. You will notice each of you has a folder in front of you containing that information. It goes without saying no one outside of this room sees that folder. The number one thing we have working in our favor moving forward on this, the people listed in that folder are unaware of we are looking into all aspects of their business and how they make their money. This is a substantial advantage. People who are actively committing criminal acts will continue to operate as always. They have been doing it safely for so long. You may open the folder. You will notice the trustees of Eagle 2 Investments consist of Dr. Robert Weinstein, who runs a private practice, Lawrence Sinclair Professor of Economics, Cal Estrada owner of Briarcliff Realty and Investments. Until recently, Roger Palmer was also a trustee. Unfortunately, he met an untimely death. Of course, we're all aware of those circumstances. We'll discuss those situations in a minute.

"Please turn to page 65. This lists all of the group's assets. Three car washes, several rental properties as their primary sources of income. I had to curry some favors. I was able to get the personal income taxes filed by these individuals last year. They all did well. They are professional people, nothing out of the ordinary.

"Their charity work, the Crimson Group, donated $125,000 last year to police and fire departments. Very nice gesture. It's also good business to keep local law enforcement on your side. Smart PR on their part.

"Now turn to page 188. All the way at the bottom, net income from their business over 22 million last year alone. One of their scams I already have evidence of is medical insurance fraud. Seems our esteemed medical doctor Robert Weinstein likes to refer all his patients for physical therapy.

"Seems like a caring doctor until you discover his group runs the clinics he recommends, then bills the insurance company. Amazingly, his patients are fully recovered once the insurance is used up. Of course, his name is not listed anywhere on the clinic's directory. To me, this is just the tip of the iceberg. To be bringing in this type of cash flow on a yearly basis is more than cooking the books on their car washes and rental properties. This is either drugs or gambling. I don't believe these men are the drug-dealing types. More white collar; you know the type. 'I'm smarter than you.'

"Moving forward with that in mind, I would like to proceed building this case, using the RICOH statute, running an ongoing criminal enterprise."

"I'm not thrilled with that plan."

"Why not, Detective Brockington?"

"You're letting these guys off easy. They may have committed murder."

"I understand where you're coming from, and believe me, I wish we could bring capital charges, but, Detective, we have only a strong belief, no proof. The coroner already said Gwen Long died from toxic shock. Roger Palmer's death, the FAA ruled it accidental.

"Yes, I believe someone may have caused the death of Peyton Long. We have nothing to go on. I don't believe for a minute she ended up on some remote trail and fell to her death, but with the present evidence, I couldn't even get an indictment. With the RICOH statute, we're looking at numerous charges facing these men. I can make a strong case a jury will understand. That's important. Not all juries are manned by brilliant people.

"In an odd way, Detective, this may be more appropriate. They will lose everything financially and imagine going from their present lifestyle to three hot meals and a cot for the next thirty to forty years."

"I hear what you're saying. I just feel once again because of who they are, these so-called pillars of the community are getting a break."

"Detective, I won't dispute that the reality of the situation is if we seek a capital case and we cannot get one of them to take a plea bargain and talk, don't forget we only have two choices, Larry or Cal, because Dr. Bob is the kingfish we're after. I guarantee you, with the legal team they will have in place, all three may walk."

The room was silent. Chief Spence gazed at his detectives. They had put countless hours into this. More importantly, he knew they felt an obligation to Peyton Long. They wanted to see justice done for her.

The tension in the room was combustible. Finally, Detective Brockington stood up and faced the D.A. "I want Robert Weinstein to rot in prison. Do not underestimate him."

"Detective Brockington, you have my word this case will take precedent in my office."

There was a sigh of relief. They had come too far to let personal feelings get in the way of what needed to be done. They had to work as a team.

"Alright, Ms. District Attorney. What's next?"

"Thank you, Detective. Next, we start going over all the tax records of these individuals, then we start looking under every rock of Eagle 2 Investments business filing, unusual business transactions, money transfers to foreign banks, wire transfers. We will go through everything and will dig deep. My office has the skilled people to do this. Detective Fisher will move to Manhattan temporarily to help since he's well-versed not only on this case, but in white collar crime. We will gather all the evidence then have the grand jury subpoena Eagle 2 Investments records that will inform them that a criminal law enforcement agency has initiated an investigation before a grand jury to determine if certain individuals should be indicted for criminal activity.

"This will allow us to obtain even more evidence because corporations have no Fifth Amendment privilege, and therefore, a corporation may not refuse to produce its corporate books, so wherever else they may be laundering money, foreign banks, etc., we will obtain that information. That will add the charge of income tax evasion."

The detectives were impressed. D.A. Gina Davis had done her homework. The group spent the next three hours poring over their investigation files.

The case was now out of the hands of the detectives. All they could do was wait. Detective Clayton Fisher would keep the group up-to-date on a weekly basis and promised to let them know the minute the grand jury issued the subpoena to Eagle 2 Investments, at the minimum, six weeks.

Chapter Twenty-Seven

Four weeks had passed since hearing from the Secretary for the State of Connecticut. Dr. Robert Weinstein, if he was concerned about their discussion outwardly, it didn't show. He went about his business as always. Saturday night was a big event for Dr. and Mrs. Robert Weinstein, the annual Medical Professionals awards, a black-tie affair, this year being held at the prestigious Belmont Hotel.

Dr. Weinstein was getting dressed. Marie walked in wearing a beautiful blue one-piece sequin gown with white pearls. "My dear, you look fabulous in that dress."

"Thank you. You're looking quite dashing yourself. I thought these might add a little sparkle to your wardrobe."

"What, pray tell, is this?"

"Open it."

Bob lifted the lid on a small mahogany box. "Oh! My, Marie, they're magnificent." Inside were two gold cuff links with the initials RW encrusted in small diamonds. "You shouldn't have."

"I know, but I did it anyway. I would like to see them on," she said with a smile.

Bob put the cuff links through his white pleated shirt. The

RW in diamonds glistened. “They’re wonderful.” He gave Marie a kiss. Dr. Bob put on his black tux and fixed his tie while facing the full-length mirror. Marie looked on admiringly. She truly loved her husband.

The Belmont was everything as advertised. Huge chandeliers hanging from the ballroom ceiling, the music provided by an eight-piece band that included a sax player that Bob raved about. The food outstanding: shrimp cocktails, crab imperial, beef Wellington — no expense was spared.

Marie slow danced with her husband along with other men who asked. Bob did likewise. After all, they knew practically everyone. The guest list easily passed two hundred. The alcohol was flowing freely. Bob was seen at the bar most of the night, making his rounds with drink in hand talking to old friends. Marie had settled in at their table talking with the other wives. She turned to Jan Whitman, the wife of Dr. John Whitman. “Honestly, Jan, I didn’t know doctors could talk so much bullshit.”

She laughed. “Isn’t that the truth? I think they get it from lying to their patients all the time.” They laughed.

“How is John doing? We haven’t seen you guys in at least six months.”

“He fine when he’s not fucking his secretary.”

“What?”

“Sorry about that, Marie, must have been that last bottle of champagne I just finished off. Sometimes it just feels good to tell the truth.”

“Jan, I’m so sorry. I had no idea.”

“That’s okay. Trust me, I’m not going away. It just galls me that he comes across to everyone as this Mr. Nice Guy All-American. I already laid down the law. Finish it up with this twenty-eight-year-old twerp or I spill the beans to our teenage daughter who thinks her dad walks on water. After that, I will take the house and the car."

"What did he say?"

"For the first time in his life, the asshole was speechless, but last week, the secretary was no longer employed, so I believe he got the message." Jan turned up her glass of champagne. "So how is Dr. Bob these days?"

"Good. We're doing fine. His medical practice is growing and we're planning a cruise in the spring."

"I'm happy for you, Marie. Glad to hear there's still a few good men around." The drinks and music lasted long into the night. They gave out numerous awards. No one really seemed to care who got them; this was just to socialize, eat, and drink.

It was after midnight when Dr. Bob came over sit with his wife. "Marie, dear, I have a favor to ask."

"What?"

"Dr. Reese has invited me and a couple others back to his place to play pool and tell more lies. Would you mind?"

"Not at all. Enjoy yourself. I can ride home with Dr. Lewis and Diana. They go right through our neighborhood. Gives me a chance with to catch up with Diana. We can talk on the way home. Honestly, I'm boned tired. You go. Drive safely."

Dr. Bob gave his wife a kiss. "I will see you in the morning. I promise to be quiet coming in."

The party broke up around 12:30. Dr. Bob climbed into his silver Mercedes. He had plans for the evening, but playing pool was not among them. He was headed to the townhouse some thirty-five miles away. He sped out of the parking lot, arriving at the townhouse 1:15 in the morning.

Sequoia Hills is known for two things: breathtaking views

overlooking the countryside and hairpin turns. There are numerous signs posted "20 mph; sharp turn ahead." There are wide pull off areas for visitors to pull off and park their cars while taking pictures or just admire the foliage. At 2:25 in the morning, there is nothing to see but total darkness or the occasional beam of headlights from a passing motorist.

Lee and Bridget McIntyre had a beautiful home for over twenty years at the corner of Hilltop Drive and Sequoia Parkway. The area was so quiet at night, if you listened closely enough, you could hear the owl off in the distance. They were sound asleep when they heard a thunderous bang. Both sprang up in bed, both were startled. "What the hell was that?"

Lee looked at his wife. She shrugged. I have no idea. Sounded like a crash of some sort." Lee quickly threw on his jeans and sneakers and grabbed a sweat shirt. "Where's the flashlight?"

"On the kitchen counter. Be careful; take your phone." Lee grabbed the flashlight and headed down the driveway. Bridget put on the porch light. In a matter of minutes, it was so dark, Lee was out of sight. Lee quickly headed down Sequoia Drive. Around the first sharp turn, he saw lights across the road. Running over, he looked down *Oh shit!* At least 200 feet down the hillside, a car had slammed head first into a tree. The headlights still worked and the brake lights flickered. Lee quickly reached for his cell.

"This is 911 emergency. How can I help you?"

"My name is Lee McIntyre. I need to report an accident."

"Are you okay, sir?"

"It's not me. There is an automobile at the bottom of a ravine. I heard the crash and came running."

"Sir, are there injuries?"

"I have no idea. I can't reach the car from where I'm at. It's at the bottom of the hill."

"Sir, can you give me the closest address?"

"Yes." Lee gave his home address. "I will be out in the road with a flashlight."

"Sir, I have dispatched emergency personnel. Remain calm. They are en route as we speak. Are you in a safe area off the road?"

"Yes."

"Okay. Keep yourself safe; they will arrive shortly. Do not put yourself in any danger."

"Thank you." Lee was pacing frantically, feeling helpless to do anything but wait. The rock face made getting down to the car without climbing gear impossible. Bridget made her way to the scene.

"What's going on?" Lee indicated the wreckage over the embankment. "Oh God, I hope they're okay."

"Yeah, me too. The rescue unit is on the way. I feel useless." Finally, the roar of sirens could be heard off in the distance. In a matter of minutes, lights flashing and sirens blaring shattered the quietness of the countryside. Lee stood out in the road waving his flashlight so they knew where to stop, first the ambulance, then a paramedic crew with rescue gear right behind them. The chief was first out already with his gear on.

"Where's the wreckage?" Lee showed him then got out of the way. Lee and Bridget stood back holding hands as emergency personnel swung into action. In a matter of minutes, the whole hillside was bright as day from floodlights. Lee could make out a silver car but little else. They tried to watch without interfering. In less than ten minutes, two men had reached the car. One had his shoulder mic and was talking to his commander. "We have a white male, approximately age fifty. Air bag was deployed. Victim shows signs of a possible internal injuries from impact. Vital signs very weak. Lacerations on the face. Bleeding from the left ear. Request immediate air lift. Roger that. Stand by. Will confirm ETA for air lift." Less than twenty minutes later, an air emergency helicopter was hovering overhead. Lee and Bridget watched as the helicopter air lifted the victim then waited as a tow truck arrived and cabled the car to bring it up the hillside.

After close to an hour, the car was up on the road from the ravine and loaded on a flatbed. Lee looked at Bridget. "That's a nice car; silver Mercedes, well-made and safe. Hopefully, the guy is all right. That's an interesting license plate. PAINKILLER."

Bridget agreed. "Wonder what it refers to?"

***

Wilton Police Chief Erik Snow was a very light sleeper. When his cell phone lit up, he picked it up immediately. "Hello?"

"Is this Chief Erik Snow of the Wilton Police Department?"

"Yes, it is. Who is this?"

"Chief, sorry to disturb you at this hour of the morning. My name is Sergeant Wes Spielman of the Branford Police Department. Early this morning at approximately 2:15, we recovered a wreckage. The driver of that vehicle has been identified as Robert Weinstein of 4 Cherry Blossom Lane, Wilton. Are you familiar with him?"

"Yes, I've known Dr. Bob for years. Is he okay?"

"I'm very sorry. He succumbed to his injuries early this morning."

"What? Are you absolutely certain?"

"Yes, we have his wallet containing his driver's license, which matches him along with the car registration belonging to him for a 2015 silver Mercedes. Chief, you still there?"

"Yes, just stunned. I was just visiting with him last week. I can't believe it."

"Chief, we need to inform the family. I can send a patrolman if you like. We are about forty miles away."

"No, but thank you. I should go myself."

"We will need a positive ID from the family. I'm sure they will want to see him. Mr. Weinstein's body is presently at our coroner's office. I will text you all the information. I've spoken to the coroner. His office will remain open until six this evening. I'm sorry to be the bearer of bad news."

"Sergeant, are you absolutely certain about the victim?"

"Yes, sir, I confirmed with the coroner before calling you. I would not risk taking any chances with something of this magnitude."

"Thank you, Sergeant, I will notify the next of kin."

Chief Snow sat on the edge of his bed, still slightly in shock. He decided make a pot of coffee and wait until daybreak before breaking the news to Marie. At 7:40 a.m., Chief Snow pulled into 4 Cherry Blossom Lane, took a deep breath to compose himself, then made his way to the front door. Marie Weinstein had been up since 6:00 a.m. When she woke to find Bob had not returned home, she called Dr. Reese. Yes, he had invited Bob and a few others over for pool and drinks, but Bob had declined. Marie was incensed. All kinds of thoughts raced through her mind, mainly her suspicion of

Bob having an affair. She was on her third cup of coffee when the doorbell rang. Chief Snow entered the foyer a few minutes later. The sounds of a ceramic coffee cup hitting the tile floor could be heard along with the aching pain in Marie Weinstein's voice.

The steady stream of cars out of 4 Cherry Blossom Lane continued all day. Finally, at 2 p.m., Marie had composed herself enough to make the drive north to see her husband's body. Her brother-in-law Wayne drove while she was comforted by her sister. Their son Matt sat up front, keeping Wayne company. It was a very depressing drive; a lot of tears with a few jokes about Bob to lighten the moment. Marie's world had been turned completely upside down.

The scene at the coroner's office was a tortuous affair. She kissed her husband and spent some alone time with him, telling him no matter the circumstance, she would always love him. Before leaving, she received all his personal items, among them his wallet, Rolex watch, gold wedding band, and of course, the diamond cuff links with RW shining brightly she had just given him the previous evening. It was the last gift she had purchased for her husband. Marie was overcome with grief. Little did she know, another bombshell was about to land.

Chapter Twenty-Eight

One week after the confirmed death of Dr. Robert Weinstein, Detectives Laura Brockington, Ed Wade, and Clayton Fisher sat around the office desk of D.A. Gina Davis, who wore a burgundy blouse with a dark blazer. Her blue eyes seemed to be able to penetrate when she looked at you. All were at a loss. They had wanted to see Robert Weinstein indicted and tried, now this. Gina Davis spoke first. "I know how disappointed you are. No one, of course, could have predicted this. I guess you could say Robert Weinstein escaped justice. I'm not sure. The grand jury, I've been informed, has issued subpoenas for Cal Estrada and Lawrence Sinclair. They will be required to appear and answer questions on the fifth, three weeks from today. I've been informed they will be receiving their summons to appear on Friday, the day after Dr. Robert Weinstein's funeral. That was not intentional; the court sets the docket. They will be indicted; the evidence is overwhelming. You name it, these individuals were involved in it: wire fraud, bookmaking, income tax evasion, medical fraud, offshore money laundering. They're facing over one hundred charges. They will die in prison. I wanted everyone here today so you're aware of our plans going forward once a trial date has been set. I've gone over this case. I've decided to move forward by first offering a plea bargain to both Cal Estrada and Lawrence Sinclair in exchange for everything they were involved in along with Robert Weinstein. If they accept eighteen years without parole plus forfeiture of all illegal gains, they will be financially wiped out, everything gone: the mansions, cars, Rolexes, the club memberships. My main reason for making the offer is we may not be able to try Robert Weinstein in a courtroom, but we can in a court of public opinion. This case will garner a lot of publicity. His true identity will be known. I will try, but I don't expect cooperation on the fate of Peyton Long."

There was a long, tenuous discussion. The detectives finally agreed this was probably the best case moving forward. Detective Brockington had one request. She asked D.A. Gina Davis could she and Detective Wade have the pleasure of serving the court summons to Cal Estrada and Lawrence Sinclair. The D.A. smiled. "I believe that can be arranged."

The District Attorney made good on her offer to have Detectives Brockington and Wade deliver the court summons. She also allowed them to delay delivering them until the following Monday after Dr. Robert Weinstein's funeral. There was the possibility of family members visiting; they didn't want to create a scene or have any distractions.

The two detectives stopped for coffee and breakfast one last time in Wilton. They asked themselves again, when you literally have everything in life this good, why? At 9:55 a.m., the white Ford Escape pulled into 105 Lantana Drive, a beautiful two-story brick colonial with a winding brick sidewalk nicely landscaped with hedges along the walk with a large white lamppost at the corner of the walk.

Cal Estrada was at home when his doorbell rang. It had been a dreadful week with the funeral of his friend and business partner. His wife Diane was beside herself. Two close friends lost in the last few months. The last thing he wanted to do was deal with some salesman. He was in his robe and slippers even at 10:00 a.m. He opened the door. There stood two serious-looking individuals. "May I help you?"

"Yes, are you Cal Estrada?"

"I am."

Brockington studied the man in front of her for a minute. She had waited a long time for this moment. She pulled the blue summons from her vest pocket. "Consider yourself served." She slapped it in his hand.

"Summons for what?"

"It's all inside, sir. Time and date to appear before the grand jury." With that, they turned and left. The same scenario played out at the home of Lawrence Sinclair. Both men knew they were facing serious legal consequences.

Across town, Marie Weinstein was trying to make sense of everything. How could she go on? All their plans for the future were gone. Matt would be going off to college soon. She would be all alone in this huge estate. She had taken some solace. Her good friend Lauren Palmer who had gone through the same situation had temporarily moved in with her to keep her company, having recently placed her house for sale. They sat at kitchen counter having coffee and Danish. Marie asked, "I would like to know what was Bob doing that night, Lauren, so far from home?"

"I don't know. An old friend, maybe?"

"You're too kind. I just have this feeling and it's not a good one. Maybe he was seeing someone then tried to make it home, was tired, and fell asleep at the wheel."

Lauren put her arm around Marie. "Don't let such thoughts in. If Bob was here, I'm sure he would tell you he had a good reason for being where he was. I know how you feel. When I lost Roger, I thought how, will I ever get through another day? It's hard, Marie, but I promise you it will get easier. Don't believe the lie time heals all wounds. It doesn't, but it makes it bearable. You're a bright, vibrant woman with a great life in front of you. It will get better."

Marie hugged Lauren. "I'm grateful you're here."

Lauren smiled. "Look at us, two widows. Who would have thought? I should tell you I have a buyer for my house."

"Lauren, that's wonderful. So you will be moving to Texas?"

"I will, but I plan on staying here with you for a couple more weeks if you'll have me."

Marie was crying. "It's not necessary."

"I want to be here for you. Now get dressed. I believe we need to take a ride in the country and I'm bringing wine!"

Marie embraced her friend, her eyes still weepy. "Bring the biggest damn bottle you can find."

On the morning of September 8 at 9:00, Cal Estrada and Lawrence Sinclair both appeared before the grand jury in Manhattan, New York. Try as they might, the probing questions surrounding the financial aspects of Eagle 2 Investments had them both backtracking on their answers. The outcome was never in doubt. They were indicted and charged under the RICOH statute, running an ongoing criminal enterprise. Both were facing sixty years in prison if found guilty on all counts, meaning they would die as inmates in the New York State prison system. Three days after being indicted, they found themselves, along with their lawyers, sitting in the office of District Attorney Gina Davis. Hers was a onetime offer with no negation with full cooperation expected. The D.A. demanded full admittance of guilt on all charges from money laundering, medical insurance fraud, income tax evasion, illegal gambling enterprise. She wanted the full extent of Robert Weinstein's involvement along with all bank accounts, foreign and domestic, going back the last ten years. The discussion would take over three hours. Cal Estrada and Lawrence Sinclair only spoke through their lawyers. Herbert Benson, who represented Cal, asked the D.A. if would she ask the court to consider the possibility of early parole with good behavior.

"Yes, but I cannot guarantee the court will listen." At 4:00 p.m. the meeting was adjourned. The two men were given seventy-two hours to accept the plea. Afterward, it would be withdrawn and a court date would be set. On the way out, Lawrence Sinclair stopped in the men's room to relieve himself and started crying. How could he face his wife and tell her they were about to lose everything? Just the thought of prison terrified him. From Harvard University and a well-respected professor to wearing an orange jumpsuit. Less than forty-eight hours later, Cal Estrada and Lawrence Sinclair, on the advice of their lawyers, accepted the plea. They really had no choice; without accepting the plea, they surely would die in prison. Sentencing was set for October 30. They had fifty-two days of freedom left.

Diane Estrada and Susan Sinclair had spent the last few weeks totally shocked. How could their husbands have kept so much from them, literally leading a double life? Everything they had cared about was over. They commiserated together every day since their husbands came clean. Both decided to stand behind their spouses no matter the outcome. It was not an easy decision. They would be in the courtroom on October 30. Both wives understood a few years from now they might feel differently.

Cal and Larry set up a meeting with Marie Weinstein and Lauren Palmer to tell them everything. After all, their deceased husbands' reputations were about to be destroyed. The gossip and news coverage would be rampant. They needed to prepare themselves. To say Marie Weinstein was shocked and devastated would be putting it mildly, at first refusing to believe what Cal and Lawrence told her about Dr. Bob's involvement, to blaming them, finally admitting, "I knew he was into something, but I never would have guessed this in a hundred years. Maybe," she told Cal, "he knew the end was near and decided to purposely drive off that cliff. I guess we'll never know for sure, will we?" She looked at Cal, his head down. "Why? Not one of you needed to be involved in anything like this."

Cal, his voice barely audible, replied, "I don't have a good answer right now. I'm sorry for all the pain you're going through. You deserved better."

Lauren Palmer was more understanding, telling both Cal and Larry, "This is bullshit. You guys never hurt anyone. So what? Who doesn't gamble and avoid paying taxes? Look at all the money the Crimson raised for charity. That should count for something." She hugged them both and promised to stay in touch with Diane and Susan.

Two weeks later before sentencing, Lauren Palmer, her estate settled, stood in the driveway with Marie Weinstein. She hugged her good friend while whispering in her ear, "I know you will find your way." Lauren placed her suitcases in the blue Land Rover then slowly backed down the winding driveway. Marie stood at the top waving goodbye, tears running down her cheek. Of the four wives, Lauren, of course, was the only one now with no financial problems. Besides all the money she and Bob had transferred overseas, Lauren also moved all the money given to her by the group for being the heart-broken widow. Lauren Palmer was heading to Texas, never to set foot in Wilton, Connecticut again.

Attorney Herbert Benson called Cal. The D.A. had one last offer on the table to help reduce his sentence. Larry was offered the same deal. "What?" Cal yelled. "Just name it." Tell them everything he knew about the death of Peyton Long. "Sorry, Herb, no can do. I honestly know nothing about her other than she was seeing Roger. I can assure you he never harmed that girl. For all I know, her death was an accident." After speaking with his lawyer, Cal thought it ironic the D.A. never asked about the death of Gwen Long, something he knew all about, but of course implicating oneself in a murder-for-hire plot would probably not be good for his long-term outlook.

The autumn leaves were turning a vibrant yellow and gold, the sun shining normally on a typical Wednesday morning at 123 Hoyt Street, U.S. District Court of New York. There was the usual bustle of lawyers milling about the courthouse steps having coffee and conversation, this morning was vastly different. Several news crews had already set up out front. A crowd had gathered, hoping to get a seat in courtroom 7. For the past few weeks, they had been astounded by what they read and heard as the top story on the evening news. The internet updated it hourly. Four Harvard University graduates, highly respected in their community, had for years been running an ongoing gambling enterprise right in the middle of one of the wealthiest communities in the country. There were internet rumors of a call girl who had died under mysterious circumstances. The group, led by a highly respected doctor, now deceased, who might have taken his own life with law enforcement closing in. The story line had all the makings of a future movie. The courtroom was packed, standing room only. There was the usual small talk and a sense of anticipation when the court was called to order.

"All rise. The honorable Judge Madeline Urbine presiding."

The judge took her seat and looked out over the packed courtroom. "Please be seated. I would like to remind everyone this is a court of law. Please no talking during the proceedings or photographs. Counsel, are you prepared?"

Attorney Herbert Benson rose from his seat. "We are, your Honor."

"D.A. Davis, are you prepared?"

She rose. "We are, your Honor."

Judge Urbine looked down at her notes and then to D.A. Davis. "I believe the state has reached a plea bargain with the defendant. Is that correct?"

"We have, your Honor."

"Fine, you may be seated. Mr. Benson, please have your client rise." Cal Estrada rose nervously with his hands folded in front of him, wearing a blue suit white shirt and tie. He glanced back to see his wife Diane seated in the first row holding hands with Susan Sinclair. Lawrence was to be sentenced later in the day. Who he didn't see in the back of the courtroom, the people responsible for him being here today,

Detective Laura Brockington and her partner Detective Ed Wade, had come to watch the proceedings. "Mr. Estrada, I'm going to ask you series of questions you will need to answer." Cal nodded he understood. "Mr. Cal Estrada, do you enter this plea willfully without any coercion?"

"I do."

"Do you understand that a jury of your peers may find you not guilty of these charges?"

"I do."

"You understand by taking this plea, you waive all your rights for a future appeal of your sentence?"

"I do."

"Do you understand you're waiving your right to testify in your own defense?"

"I do."

"And the right to have the prosecutor prove the charges beyond a reasonable doubt?"

"I do."

"Lastly, do you fully understand that by accepting this plea, you will be committed to the state prison system, although you may be eligible for an early parole. That is entirely up to the court."

"I do."

"Very well then. Before I pass sentence, I have to ask. Someone of your background, a Harvard graduate, by all accounts very successful before falling into this other life, I know the public is curious and you're not obligated to answer, but why?"

Cal was silent for a minute then spoke quietly. "Your Honor, over the past eight weeks, I've asked myself that a million times. I guess the simple answer is greed, but it was more than that. I belonged to group of guys who were family to me. We liked the excitement, the adrenaline rush. Being truthful, we never thought about being apprehended. Our egos convinced us we were untouchable. After sometime, the money was just the end result, not the reason. People will scoff, but we did enjoy raising money for different causes. We got caught up in our own self-importance, thought we were smarter than everybody else."

The judge looked down at him. "Thank you for answering. Mr. Estrada, is there anything you would like to say before sentencing is passed?"

"First off, I'm grateful my parents are not alive to witness how I disgraced them. I was not raised this way. I want to apologize to my wife. She is an innocent bystander in all of this who is paying a very steep price for my greed and selfishness. I'm truly sorry." There was silence in the courtroom as Cal stood with his head bowed, Diane seated behind him, crying for them both. Cal's attorney grasped him by the by the arm, sensing he might collapse, his body wobbling.

"Very well then, Cal Estrada, having pled guilty to the following charges: running an ongoing criminal enterprise, including but not limited to illegal gambling, money laundering, income tax evasion, and medical fraud, the court sentences you to be remanded to the state prison system for a period of no less than eighteen years, eligible for parole at the discretion of the court. May I advise you to use this time constructively to reassess the important things in life so when you return to society, you learn to give more than you take." The judge nodded to the bailiff, who was already standing behind Cal. "Please take Mr. Estrada into custody." In a matter of seconds, Cal's hands were behind him and he was being handcuffed. A large sob could be heard coming from Diane. Cal felt his knees buckle. He was so scared. Cal was led from the courtroom and placed in a temporary holding cell in the lower level of the courthouse, pending transport to the state prison, his new home for the next decade plus.

His blue suit was quickly replaced with an orange jumpsuit. He paced in his 8x12 cell. Diane would be allowed one fifteen-minute visit. The bailiff approached. "Mr. Estrada, a Detective Laura Brockington from the Syracuse Police Department would like to have a word with you with your permission."

Cal was surprised. "Yes of course." The bailiff nodded in the affirmative.

A few minutes later, escorted by the bailiff, Detective Brockington appeared, her gold shield displayed on her belt. She turned to the bailiff. "Thank you. We'll be fine." The bailiff turned and left, closing the door behind him. "Mr. Estrada, thanks for seeing me. I wasn't sure you would."

"At this point, Detective, why not? We haven't really ever spoken. That's not to say I haven't heard your name mentioned more than once sometimes with a few adjectives."

Laura smiled. "I understand. I won't take it personally. So how are you holding up?"

"On the outside, fine. On the inside, nervous, scared. Being honest, I never saw my life going this route. No one to blame but myself. I assume that you made the case against us?"

"I had a lot of help, but it was originally assigned to me."

"I have to ask, what was the tipoff? We had been running the same operation for years."

"A coroner never believed Peyton Long accidentally fell to her death. From there, it kind of spiraled."

"Men and pretty women; we never learn. You may not believe this, Detective, Roger Palmer never harmed that girl. I honestly don't know who did."

"I believe you, but her death was no accident."

"Sorry to hear that. I thought she was a nice girl, kind of quiet. Dr. Bob would never speak to her. He didn't like the idea of Roger seeing the same girl more than once. That was our unwritten code. He would say, trust me, it will bite us in the ass. I guess he was right."

"How was your relationship with the good doctor?"

"From college to neighbors and business partners over twenty years, just great. The last twelve months, I saw a side to him I never knew existed. Bob put a pool stick across Roger's throat. Damnedest thing I ever saw: four well-educated men acting like white trash."

"I can tell you from my law experience, the people you least expect sometimes have a dark side. In a way, Mr. Estrada, I feel bad for you and Mr. Sinclair taking the fall alone for this. I was hoping Dr. Weinstein would have been joining you. I guess dying the way he did, some would say he paid the price."

Cal put his hands on the cell bars and made a slight smile. "Ah, the morality-destroying vortex of Dr. Bob. Didn't anyone ever tell you, Detective? Evil never dies; it just moves to another town."

Chapter Twenty-Nine

Six Months Later

The Maldives is a tropical nation located in the Indian Ocean composed of twenty-six ring-shaped atolls that are made up of more than one thousand coral islands. It's known for its beaches, blue lagoons, extensive reefs, and for being a vacation mecca for the well-to-do. The capital is Male (pronounced "malee") with a busy fish market, shops, and restaurants. The population is approx. 450,000, where the locals always greet you with a smile. The weather is a dream: periodic rain complements the sun-draped white beaches, where you can walk out a quarter-mile into the aqua blue ocean while the fish all shapes and colors swim nearby. With one thousand islands all at your beck and call, the unchartered sandbanks provide plenty of opportunities to go island hopping. After sunbathing and snorkeling, eating is a must. The cuisine is excellent: fish and coconuts, which are plentiful, fixed in a variety of ways by the locals, is always a treat. With so much to offer, the affluent often find vacationing second to none. Some like it so much, they attain citizenship status. Attracting foreign capital had always been a major objective in the country, economic strategy as a way to encourage foreign investors. One way is to offer permanent residence to those who would like to make the Maldives home. The fee is a minimum of five hundred thousand in US currency. How many Americans have residency is not known. Their privacy is considered privileged information.

The American couple was stretched out in their cabana overlooking the ocean. She wore a native floral dress and sandals. She looked stunning with her blonde hair and deep brown tan. He was in a neatly ironed short sleeve white button-down shirt with a gold chain and tan khakis with sandals and a white panama hat to block the sun's rays. He remarked to his companion, "Looks like they're setting up for a wedding."

One of the unique aspects of beach weddings in the Maldives, locals and anyone walking the sands are encouraged to attend. The ceremony is considered a sign of good fortune to the couple. A rope is put around the perimeter for spectators to enjoy the moment.

There was a gathering of around twenty when soft calypso music started to play. An elderly cleric carrying a hymnal started walking toward the rope. The gentleman looked over to the lady stretched out on the cabana. "I believe they're ready for us."

She smiled back at him. "So they are!" She stood up and took his hand, walking across the white sand. They made their way to the small wedding ceremony area. Everyone smiled at them as they entered walking now arm in arm down a thin, rolled-out mat.

The elderly cleric dressed in a long white shirt that went to his knees and sandals, his bronze skin showing the years of age and wisdom that came with it. His smile made everyone feel warm and comfortable.

"Welcome. What a beautiful day. We have been blessed with once again, here on the most beautiful place on earth. It is always wonderful when two people decide to commit their lives to one another. What a special gift saying to someone 'here take my hand; we will walk together forever.' Today, we have such a couple not only joining us in matrimony but as permanent citizens of our islands. Please hold hands and repeat after me. I, Samuel Bennett, take you, Lauren Palmer, from this day forth and forever more to be my wife, to walk beside me in good times and bad. We will navigate through life together as one. He repeated the lines and then Lauren Palmer repeated the same lines. "Samuel, you have a gift to show your love for Lauren?"

"I do." Samuel removed a beautiful solid gold band ring from a box.

"Please place it on her finger."

"Lauren, have you a gift of love for Samuel?"

"I do." She also had a gold band and did likewise. They faced each other holding hands. The ceremony, like many there, was short and sweet. As the calypso music started playing softly, the priest, with a big smile, announced loudly:

"It is with great joy and promise of a new life together that I introduce you for the first time as man and wife, Samuel and Lauren Bennett. Please kiss your new bride!"

As they kissed, the spectators clapped and cheered. As the newlyweds exited, the couple shook hands and received hugs from people they had never met. The Maldives' charm was captivating.

Samuel Bennett and his blushing new bride strolled across the beautiful white sands hand in hand, finally making their way to the marina, where waiting for them was the new Sunseeker 60 Express yacht Samuel had recently purchased. Known as the sports car of yachts for its sleek look with an enclosed deck, it slept six below, the back part still open to enjoy sunbathing complete with outdoor bar and built-in lounges.

They boarded the new elegant white and blue beauty, the flag of the Maldives flying high. Samuel kissed his new bride Lauren. "You look radiant."

"Thank you. She kissed him again. "You look rather dashing yourself."

Samuel laughed. Before we embark on our honeymoon, we still have to christen our new vessel." He pulled out a large bottle of champagne. "You may have the privilege."

Lauren was beaming. "Really?"

"Of course. We're partners now." They walked toward the bow of the yacht.

"This is going to sound stupid, but how do I do this?"

Samuel smiled at his new bride. "It's simple." Samuel placed the bottle of champagne in a small see-through net, then, taking a thin piece of yellow rope, tied a knot around the top of the bottle. "Lauren, just take hold of this end of the rope then toss the bottle overboard, letting it hit the side of the yacht, breaking open the champagne and letting it run into the ocean. This will appease Neptune, the god of the sea."

"Oh! I love this; it's so exciting." Lauren took the rope. She kissed Samuel once more. Here goes nothing! With this, I declare our new yacht '*SECRETS*!'"

Lauren heaved the bottle of champagne over the side. It smashed against the hull, breaking open and spilling into the ocean.

They held hands for several minutes without saying a word, just looking out over the vast ocean. Samuel looked at his bride. “I believe it’s time we set sail.”

Lauren smiled, licking her lips. “You start the engine. I will make the first round of margaritas.”

Within minutes, the new watercraft and newlyweds were out to sea.